Books by Anina Collins

The Eleventh Hour (Poppy McGuire Mysteries #1)
After Hours (Poppy McGuire Mysteries #2)
Top of the Hour (Poppy McGuire Mysteries #3)
The Darkest Hour (Poppy McGuire Mysteries #4)
Happy Hour (Poppy McGuire Mysteries #5)

HAPPY HOUR

ANINA COLLINS

2016 Eight Feathers Press, LLC

Published in the United States
ISBN: 978-0-9972153-8-0

Book Cover design by Natasha Snow Designs
www.natashasnowdesigns.com

Happy Hour

Poppy and Alex are back in Happy Hour!

Springtime brings warm weather and murder to Sunset Ridge, and for Poppy, this particular case strikes close to home.

Antiques dealer Marcus Tyne is found dead in the front seat of his friend's car outside of McGuire's after a Cinco de Mayo celebration, but at first glance, there's no reason why he's dead.

Until the coroner finds out he's been poisoned.

When a second man is poisoned, Poppy and Alex are thrust into a mystery that threatens to tear them apart. While they struggle to solve the case as their differences become more apparent, a murderer walks free in Sunset Ridge and may have another victim in their sights.

Chapter One

THE CHILL OF the early May evening hit me as soon as I opened my front door, so I grabbed my favorite black sweater and headed out on my way to McGuire's hoping to catch some part of my father's first annual Cinco de Mayo celebration at the bar. Always interested in finding ways to make the business more successful, he decided that a promotion of the Mexican Independence Day would be a great way to liven up Sunset Ridge in the slow period before the Founders' Day events and summer took over the town.

That Sunset Ridge had not even one citizen of Mexican descent hadn't dissuaded my father from his plans, even though I'd mentioned to him more than once that our incredibly homogenous town had never celebrated the fifth of May for a reason. Forever hopeful, he'd answered me every time with his same explanation of how this country had been founded by immigrants and bringing a little of the outside world to Sunset Ridge couldn't hurt.

I didn't think it would hurt as much as not work. Our small town wasn't so much insolated as just somewhat backward. The old guard who had ruled the town for what seemed like forever ensured that things rarely changed. That said, Sunset Ridge residents were good-hearted people at their cores, so I hoped his customers would join in the Cinco de Mayo celebration.

He'd asked me to man the bar for a few hours just in case the crowd became too much, but I'd begged off after a particularly long day at *The Eagle*. My boss, the indefatigable Howard Fleming, had hovered over me all day, trying his damnedest to find a way to make the police blotter article I wrote each week more exciting. My refusal to include salacious details of crimes and facts the Sunset Ridge police department preferred to keep quiet resulted in rather bland write-ups each week. Even I had to admit that.

Howard's attempts to spice up my work had never succeeded, no matter how much he cajoled and pleaded. The only effect it had was exhausting me so much I could barely drag myself home after spending hours on end with him and his constant attempts to get me to change.

I wasn't too worried that I'd left my father high and dry, though. Even his Halloween extravaganzas only resulted in little more than half the bar being filled. In Sunset Ridge, only sports on the TV brought customers into McGuire's.

As I turned the corner onto Main Street, I saw a crowd of people coming toward me waving the brightly colored yellow and pink streamers my father had been hanging that morning. I recognized one of the partiers as Jenna Teasdale, a girl I'd hung out with in high school and one of Derek's many ex-girlfriends in town. A pretty brunette with long straight hair and a round face, she'd always had a soft look about her. Still as bubbly as she was at Sunset Ridge High, she waved and opened her arms wide to hug me as she and her two male friends approached me.

"Poppy McGuire, your father knows how to party, girl! You missed a good time!" she squealed.

The smell of tequila came off her in waves strong enough to make my eyes tear, so I quickly did my friendly hug thing and backed away. Jenna tore the cheaply made sombrero my father had picked up from the party store from one of the men's heads and planted it onto mine.

"Perfect! Now you can party like we did," she said, slurring the last few words.

"I'm glad you enjoyed yourselves," I said with a smile, genuinely happy my father's attempt to bring some kind of culture to the town had been at least a success to Jenna and her friends. "I'll be sure to tell my father."

"Definitely! He rocks!" she said with a giggle.

The two men gave their stamp of approval for my father's party-giving abilities by yelling and fist bumping, and then the three of them set off stumbling down the street. Just before they disappeared into the night, Jenna waved frantically at me again as she giggled at something one of her friends said. I couldn't help but be thankful they weren't driving since even now that they had walked away the smell of tequila still hung heavy in the air.

Never my favorite poison, I left the stench behind and hurried down the street toward McGuire's to see if anyone else had attended the Cinco de Mayo party. My fears that the whole idea would never succeed were put to rest as I stepped into the bar and saw no less than forty people still enjoying the festivities. Behind the bar, my father stood pouring drinks and joking around like he always did with his customers.

I sat down at the end of the bar near the door and smiled at the sight of him having such a good time. His idea had worked. He caught a glimpse of me as he gave a very attractive woman with short dark hair and big eyes a drink and quickly headed my way.

"Poppy! I'm so glad you were able to stop over. The Cinco de Mayo event is definitely going to be a yearly thing," he announced as he pulled me toward him for a hug.

"That's great, Dad. I can't believe it did so well," I said as I looked around at all the people still there at midnight on a Monday.

"There are going to be some very sore people in the morning," he said with a chuckle. "I'm predicting a difficult fifth of May tomorrow. Want something to drink?"

I held my hand up to stop him before he poured me anything. "No, I'm good. I can't afford to not be on top of my game tomorrow. Howard has been a real monkey on my back lately. By the way, why didn't you have this party on the actual day of Cinco de Mayo?"

He grinned that wide Irish smile that lit up his face and wagged his finger at me. "There's a method to my madness. I figured the people who could come out for a Cinco de Mayo party would probably be heading down to Baltimore for it, so I thought I'd do it one night early and beat the rush. It looks like your father had a good idea this time."

He really was too cute. The woman he'd served before coming down to speak to me was giving him the sexy eyes, so I leaned in toward him and said in his ear,

"You've got an admirer, Dad. You should go down and talk to that lady. She's very pretty."

My father shook his head and looked down the bar at her. Flashing her one of his smiles, he turned back to face me. "So what can I get my daughter to drink tonight? Feel like your usual, or do you feel like getting in the spirit of the night and trying some tequila?"

"Let's stick to a ginger ale tonight. I'm not much of a tequila girl."

"No whisky?" he asked as he moved to get my glass of soda.

"Not tonight, Dad."

He set the drink down in front of me and shook his head. "Soda at a party. You've been drinking the good stuff since you and Alex got together, and now this," he teased. "By the way, where is he tonight?"

I took a sip of soda and smiled. "At work, as usual. I'm going to start calling him the hardest working guy in Sunset Ridge, right behind you, of course."

"He's a good man, Poppy, and there's nothing wrong with Alex being a hard worker."

Whenever my father got the slightest sense that there could be anything wrong between Alex and me, he always defended him. Not that he had to. Nobody knew more than I did how great Alex Montero was. I just wished life in Sunset Ridge could be a little more exciting so we could work together more often.

It had been nearly a month since anything more than some neighbor parking in the wrong spot had been the highlight of the police blotter. Howard truly believed I'd been holding out the good stuff on him and *The Eagle*'s readership, but in reality, there hadn't been any real crime in town in what seemed like ages.

As a result, while Alex and I certainly spent a lot of time together, mostly at my house or his, we hadn't worked on a case in far too long for my taste. Not that I was hoping for a murder or anything like that, but a nice robbery could be good chance for us to get back to solving crimes together.

My father worried about us, so I quickly moved to reassure him. "I know, Dad. I just wish life in this town hadn't suddenly become so picture perfect."

"You should be happy we live in a safe place, Poppy," he scolded me.

The notes of some song from the eighties boomed out of the jukebox suddenly, so I just smiled at his rebuke. Safe, I liked. Boring, not so much.

As if the sound of the song made some people realize how late it was, customers began to slowly leave the bar until only a handful of my father's customers remained. Without all those bodies to absorb the song blaring out of the jukebox, it quickly became impossible to talk at all over the noise, so my father hurried over to the machine to turn it down before it chased every last person out the door.

Walking On Sunshine wasn't a bad song, but that loud it was almost unbearable. By the time he got it to where it wasn't making people's ears practically bleed, it was too late, though. Most of the partiers had headed out into the night, leaving just my father, a few of his regulars who were probably happy to see all the Cinco de Mayo fun finally over, and me.

"Note to self. Make sure to pay attention to the jukebox," he joked as he came around the end of the bar.

I pointed to the empty barstool where the pretty

woman had been sitting. "You chased her away, Dad."

He rolled his eyes and grabbed a cloth to wipe down the bar. "Yeah, yeah. That's how it goes."

From outside, a blood-curdling scream stopped everyone from talking, and I turned to see a young woman with wavy blond hair run through the door with a look of terror in her eyes.

"Call the cops! Someone's dead!" she yelled before racing back outside.

A look of horror crossed my father's face. "Dead? Where?"

Jumping off my barstool, I said, "I'll go check it out, Dad. You call the station."

I ran outside and saw a crowd of people standing around a silver luxury car parked on the street in front of the bar. People spoke in hushed tones and pointed at the car. Pushing my way through them, I got to it and saw a person lying across the front seat. A thin man about six foot tall with short hair, he looked average in virtually every way, except for the fact that he wasn't moving.

"Did someone check to see if he's just passed out?" I asked the people standing around me, searching the group for the answer.

One heavy-set bald man nodded. "I did. He's gone."

"Okay, don't touch a thing. We've called the police, so let's just back away from the car and they'll be here in a minute. Does anyone know his name?"

Nobody answered, and instead of walking away as I'd suggested, people began to inch closer to press their faces to the car's windows, each one asking the same question.

What happened to this guy that killed him?

I saw no blood anywhere around him, and I had to

admit it looked like he was merely sleeping. I didn't want to speculate on what had happened to this poor soul, though. Alex and Darren, the other cop on duty that night, would be there soon, so I'd leave the wondering about who and what had killed him until then.

The police cruiser pulled up to the scene, causing most of the crowd to scatter, and I smiled as Alex approached me. Dressed in his uniform, he looked sharp and in control of the situation. And very sexy. His fellow officer, Darren Harlson, an older officer who had been on the force since Derek joined years ago, followed him. Portly, he always looked a little sweaty whenever I saw him.

Stopping in front of me, Alex smiled. "How did I know I'd see you first thing? I thought you were staying home tonight."

"I decided to see how my father's Cinco de Mayo event went over. Someone found this man. He's dead," I said somberly.

As Darren joined the two of us, he asked, "Did anyone see anything?"

I shook my head. "No. I was inside the bar when the woman came running in screaming about some man being dead outside, so I came out to look as my father called you guys."

He nodded. "I'm going to find out what everyone knows. Which woman found him, Poppy?"

Searching the people who hadn't moved away, I saw the wavy haired blonde standing alone on the steps to McGuire's. "That's her," I said as I pointed in her direction. "She's the one near the door. She looks pretty shaken up."

"Got it."

He walked away to ask her his questions as Alex peered in through the car's passenger side window. "Do you know this guy? I don't recognize him."

Standing next to him, I studied the face of the dead man. Thin and expressionless, he didn't look familiar. "I don't think so. He doesn't look like anyone I've ever met."

Alex turned his head to look at me and grinned. "I think you're slipping, Poppy. When we first met, you knew everything about everyone in town."

I rolled my eyes at his teasing. Anytime I didn't know the complete history of anyone involved in one of our cases, he said the same thing. Usually I reminded him that detecting was part of being a detective, but tonight I thought I'd go a different route.

"You know, I think you've lived in Sunset Ridge long enough to know something about your fellow citizens, Alex. We don't want my vast knowledge of our neighbors to become a crutch for you."

"No, we don't," he said with a chuckle. "Well, since neither of us seem to know who this poor soul is, what do you say we do some investigating?"

He moved around the front of the car to the driver's side as I followed, each of us slipping on a pair of gloves before we touched anything. Alex opened the door and a sweet smell like from a flowery air freshener hit my nose, making me take a step back. Lifting his flashlight, he shined it along the full length of the man's body to examine him for a cause of death, but nothing obvious jumped out. No blood, no gunshot wound, not even a bruise on the man's head indicated what may have killed him.

"What do you think?" I asked after taking a deep

breath and leaning back in to look.

Alex shrugged. "I can't see any evidence of him being shot or stabbed or even hit on the head. There's no obvious signs of a struggle either, and I see no evidence of strangulation. Something killed him, but I think for this one we're going to have to leave it to Donny to find out what."

At that moment, as if on cue, the coroner's van pulled up next to the car and Donny jumped out. Dressed in his usual black dress pants and white dress shirt that begged for a tie he never wore, he walked over to where we stood.

"I was in the middle of something, so I hope this guy appreciates this," he joked in that gallows humor way he did sometimes.

Alex raised one eyebrow and leveled his gaze on the coroner. "You don't have to come on every case, Donny. If I remember correctly, you have assistants in that office of yours."

Donny's eyebrows shot up, making the deep furrows in his forehead even deeper. "Kids who don't know enough who'd call me in anyway halfway through their examination. I might as well be there at the start to make sure the job gets done right."

The kids he referred to had to be at least my age or even older, but since Donny looked to be close to sixty, I guessed someone in their early thirties might seem like a kid to him. The truth of the matter was he loved his job to the point of being a workaholic, so he didn't really need his assistants and their supposed inadequacies to make him come out to a crime scene, even if it was in the middle of the night.

Alex searched the dead man's pockets for

identification and then stepped back away from the car as Donny leaned in to begin his examination, mumbling, "So what do we have here?"

Flipping open the brown leather wallet he'd taken from the man's coat, Alex slipped his driver's license out from behind the clear plastic slot and read the name. "Marcus Tyne, thirty-one. He would have turned thirty-two right after Thanksgiving."

I leaned in and saw Marcus Tyne's license picture of him wearing a big smile. Poor guy. He looked happy. Reading his address, I saw he lived in Millville, an even smaller town than Sunset Ridge a few miles away.

"That's why I didn't recognize him. He's not from here."

Alex closed the wallet and looked down at me with a skeptical expression. "I still say you're slipping, Miss McGuire."

"And I say you're slacking off on this whole detective thing, Officer Montero."

He chuckled like he always did when I teased him right back. I liked when we could be lighthearted like that. Some people might think it tactless since a man lay dead just a few feet away, but like Donny's gallows humor, our joking around was just our way of keeping our sanity on cases like this.

But I saw the smile slide from his face and before I could ask what was wrong, Alex said, "I need to know if Marcus Tyne was at McGuire's tonight, so we need to talk to your father."

We headed into the bar and found my father sitting alone staring up at the baseball game playing on the TV. He wore a worried expression and sighed when he saw us come through the door.

"Hi, Joe," Alex said as he sat down and took his notebook and pen out of his shirt pocket.

My father turned on his barstool and forced a smile. "Hi, Alex. I can't believe something like this could happen right outside my bar. Do we know who the man was?"

"Marcus Tyne. He was from Millville. Did you know him?"

Shaking his head, my father sighed again. "The name doesn't ring a bell. To be honest, I only really know the names of my regulars, so if he wasn't in here a lot, I probably wouldn't know his name. What did he look like?"

Alex handed him Tyne's driver's license. "Do you recognize him as someone who was in here tonight?"

"Yeah," he said, nodding. "He might have been in once or twice before too."

As Alex jotted down notes on my father's answers, I said, "Just tell us whatever you can remember, Dad."

He pressed his lips together and took a deep breath before he let it out slowly. "I want to say he came in around ten. Let me see. What was he drinking?" After a few more moments, he continued, "Bourbon. I got this new bottle of Gold Label the other day and he saw it on the wall behind the bar and specifically asked for it."

Looking up from his notes, Alex asked, "Was it just you behind the bar tonight?"

My father smiled at me and nodded. "Yes. My go-to girl was busy, so I had to man the bar alone."

"Okay. How many drinks do you remember serving him?"

"Two, and now that you mention it, he seemed to get drunk pretty fast on just two bourbons. I mean, he was a skinny guy, but two drinks doesn't usually level a grown man of any size. I poured him a cup of coffee, but I don't think he drank much of it before he left."

"What time was that?" Alex asked as he wrote down two drinks and coffee.

"I can't be sure, but I want to say before eleven."

Looking up, Alex stopped writing. "Why before eleven?"

"I had a big crowd come in right around that time, and I don't think he was still here by then."

"Okay. Did anyone talk to him or buy him anything to drink?"

My father thought for a few seconds and shook his head. "I don't remember him spending time with anyone while he was here, but I didn't see him leave. I can't be sure because it was so busy, but he only had those two drinks and a few sips of coffee. That I know."

Alex looked up and down the bar and then returned his attention to my father. "I'm guessing the coffee cup has already been washed?"

Nodding, my father said, "Yeah. After he left, someone else sat down where he'd been, so I cleared away the cup."

"I'll take it anyway. There might be some evidence left behind that can tell us what killed Mr. Tyne."

I held up my hand to stop my father from getting up. "It's okay, Dad. I got it. I'm wearing gloves, so I'll bag it."

Heading around the bar, I saw a single coffee cup sitting alongside the sink. Alex handed me a plastic evidence baggie and I gingerly dropped it in before handing the bag back to him.

He looked around me toward the shelves of bottles

on the back wall and pointed at the Gold Label bourbon. "I'm going to have to take the bottle too."

Satisfied he'd gotten all he could from my father, at least for the moment, Alex stood and gave him a friendly pat on the shoulder. "Thanks, Joe. I'll be in contact if I need anything more."

I followed my partner outside and saw Donny had left with the body and Marcus Tyne's car had been towed away. Darren stood speaking to a couple I didn't recognize a few yards away.

Stopping at the bottom of the stairs, Alex turned around and took my hand. Giving it a gentle squeeze, he said, "Stay with your father, Poppy. We can start working on this case together tomorrow, but for now, he needs you more. I'm going to go back to the station for a little bit and see what I can find out about Marcus Tyne. I'll let you know what I learn when I see you at The Grounds tomorrow morning."

"Okay. I guess our plans to spend some time together after your shift are foiled again, huh?" I said, unable to hide my disappointment at us not being able to be together for a third night in a row.

He nodded, looking as unhappy at the disruption of our plans as I was. "Pretty much, but we do get to work together on a case again."

I looked down into his deep brown eyes and wished we were alone so I could show him how much I missed us being together the past few days. Even though it wasn't strictly allowed since he was on duty, I leaned toward him and kissed him softly on the lips.

He pulled away quickly before anyone saw, and I said, "That's a down payment. You can collect the rest tomorrow night."

Alex gave me one of those sexy grins that never failed to make my stomach flip and winked. "I'll see you tomorrow morning at nine."

"Okay. I'll be the woman at the back table waiting for her partner."

He nodded and before he walked away, he whispered, "Love you."

Just as he turned to leave, I mouthed those same words back to him. As I watched him walk away, I thought about how much I looked forward to us working together again. We hadn't had too many cases since we'd finally admitted how we felt about each other, and this murder case would be different than any other we'd worked together before.

But that would have to wait until tomorrow. For now, my father needed me.

Chapter Two

AFTER SITTING WITH my father for about an hour, I walked home and tried to get some sleep, but the events of the night made that next to impossible. After tossing and turning for nearly three hours, I decided my mind was too awake and got dressed to go to the station. Alex had messaged me that he'd be there all night filling in for another officer, so by five am I was walking toward Main Street and the Sunset Ridge police station.

As I passed my father's bar, I remembered Howard would be expecting me for another of our meetings about how to improve things, as he liked to term his attempts to cajole me into giving away details the police preferred to keep from the public. He'd have to save up all his convincing for another day, though, because after I wasn't up for it today.

I quickly left a voicemail on his office phone and told him I'd be writing from home for a few days because of the murder. He'd likely start bouncing in his chair at the news that there had been another murder I'd hopefully report on since I'd become the de facto journalist in charge of bringing those stories to the public whenever they happened since I began working with Alex a year ago.

As I turned into the police station, I mumbled to myself, "I need a raise."

I nearly ran into my least favorite Sunset Ridge cop, Stephen, and as usual, he returned my hello with a sneer I still didn't think I deserved. I'd asked Alex half a dozen times what the guy's problem with me could be, but he claimed to have no idea. I didn't necessarily think he was lying as much as disinterested in the whole thing.

Pushing past my awkward encounter, I headed toward Alex's office and found him behind his desk staring at his laptop. Hunched over after hours on duty, he looked tired, and I wished I could step behind his chair and massage the worry out of his broad shoulders.

"Hey, you. That's some stress you've got going on there," I said with a smile as he lifted his head to look at me.

He looked at his watch and then leaned back in his chair. "Five o'clock in the morning? Something tells me you didn't get much sleep last night. Everything okay?"

I sat down in the chair in front of his desk and sighed. "I'm fine. I just can't get my mind to shut off. It's probably because my father looked so upset when I left him last night. Even after I thought I'd made him feel better about things, I still couldn't convince him that everything was going to be okay."

Alex gave me a supportive smile. "He's going to be good, Poppy. Your father is a tough guy, and he has you by his side. He'll bounce back from this."

His bouncing back wasn't all I was worried about. What if people in town shied away from the bar because of all that had happened?

"I know he will, but that bar is everything to him, Alex. Murder has a way of making people skittish. I'd hate to see him lose his livelihood because of this."

Shaking his head, Alex smiled. "See, I've found murder to have the exact opposite effect on people. Instead of them avoiding where it happened, they seem to flock to it. It's some kind of morbid curiosity in the human psyche that makes them want to rubberneck at anything having to do with death."

"Well, I just hope all of this doesn't hurt him either way."

"I think he'll be okay, Poppy. Want to hear what I found out about our victim, Marcus Tyne?"

The mere mention that he had some news already on the case cheered me up. "Hit me with it. Let me guess. He was the bagman for a mafia family that finally caught up with him last night after he turned state's evidence and ended up in the witness protection program."

With every word that came out of my mouth, Alex's expression morphed into one of complete confusion. Finally, he narrowed his eyes to squints and shook his head. "A bagman?"

"Yeah. I think I heard it on Law and Order a few times."

"Uh, no. I don't think he was a bagman for anyone. And by the way, I think your imagination is starting to get the best of you."

I shrugged at his disdain for my colorful ideas. "Fine. Give me the less interesting version then."

Alex rolled his eyes and then began explaining what he'd learned about Marcus Tyne in the past four hours. "I took a ride out to his house in Millville, but it was dark. I didn't find anyone there. I haven't found any evidence that he was married, so it might be that he lived alone."

"Jeez, that just makes me sad. He lives alone in a house in some tiny town and then dies alone behind the wheel of his car. That's so depressing."

"That wasn't his car, though," Alex said correcting me, as if that was the salient point in my statement.

"That's even worse. Whose was it?"

"I don't know yet, but I do know more about Marcus. He was arrested once in the past year because of a domestic dispute with a woman named Angela Touring. She lives here in Sunset Ridge. Do you know her? She's around your age."

Quickly, I ran that name through my mental Rolodex and came up with nothing. Her name didn't ring a bell from anyone I remembered from high school. "Nope. I really am beginning to slip, aren't I?"

He grinned at my weak attempt at humor. "Not to worry. I'll still work with you, even if there comes a time when you don't know anyone in town."

I raised my eyebrows in disbelief at the sheer madness of not knowing a single soul in town. As if there could ever be a time when everyone in Sunset Ridge was a stranger to me.

"Well, regardless, she's from here and she called the Sunset Ridge police about eight months ago saying Tyne attacked her when she demanded he leave after they had an argument. Derek took the call and went out to her house to find she had a black eye. So he drove out to his house in Millville, but Tyne swore he never hit her and she attacked him."

"Okay. So he got arrested for beating her up. I'm starting to feel slightly less depressed about his life and death."

Alex raised his hand to stop me from condemning Marcus Tyne too quickly. "Not so fast. He was arrested and brought in because she wanted to press charges. But then a few days later, she recanted and claimed she mistakenly ran into a door, which gave her a black eye. With her refusing to say he hit her, the charges were dropped."

None of that made me think he didn't hit this Angela Touring person. "So maybe he did and maybe he didn't hit her. Did anything else ever come of it?"

Glancing over the sheet of paper in front of him, he shook his head. "Not as far as I can see. There was never another domestic call from her. If they stayed together, they found a way to make it work."

"Or she was just biding her time until she found the perfect moment to find a way to kill the abusing bastard."

Alex's eyebrows shot up into his forehead. "Whoa. Talk about putting the cart before the horse. You've got the guy marked as an abuser and this Angela Touring woman marked as a murderer. Anything else you'd like to share about this case?"

He was right. I was letting my vivid imagination run away with me. "Okay. Forget all of that. I was just playing around. So what do we do now?"

"I think we need to speak to Miss Touring, once it's a more reasonable hour. In the meantime, I called Derek to find out what he can tell us about the Touring-Tyne case, so until he arrives, we wait."

"Want to go over to The Grounds and wait there?" I asked, already jonesing for my morning caffeine fix.

Alex screwed his face into a scowl. "I can't. Darren had to go deal with some problem up on Colonial Drive, so I'm the only show in town until he gets back or Derek comes in."

"What about Stephen?" I asked, nearly hissing his name.

"He's not on duty tonight," Alex explained, ignoring the distaste that hung off his name when I said it.

That meant we were waiting on Darren to return because since Derek became chief, he didn't seem to know where the police station was located before nine in the morning. I didn't relish the idea of going without coffee for another nearly three hours, though. That sounded like torture.

Standing from my seat, I pointed toward the street and said, "I'll do a coffee run. Want anything to eat too?"

Alex's eyes lit up at the mention of food. "Yeah, I could really go for a cherry danish this morning." Reaching into his pocket, he took out a twenty and handed it to me. "And make the coffee a large. I think I'm going to be up way past my bedtime today."

I took the money from his hand and stuffed it into my purse. "I was going to treat this morning. You know, since I'm all antsy to get my morning caffeine fix on."

My offer to buy his breakfast earned me another scowl as Alex shook his head like he disapproved of my suggestion. "Hurry back, though. Just the mention of that cherry danish has my mouth watering."

"Got it. A vat of coffee Alex style and a cherry danish. I'll be right back."

I jogged over to The Grounds and got there just as Pam, one of the owners, unlocked the front door. Especially chipper for so early in the morning, she smiled when she saw me bounding toward her and welcomed me into the shop.

"Poppy! You're up early today. I usually don't get to see you anymore. How have you been?" she asked as I walked through the door.

I followed her toward the register as she slipped the white apron with blueberry juice stains over her head and tossed it onto the counter on the wall. "I'm over at the police station waiting for Derek to get to work, so I had to come over and get my morning fix and some danishes."

For a moment, confusion filled her green eyes, and she stared at me as if she was waiting for more information. When I didn't continue, she said, "I didn't know you and Derek were…you know…together."

Laughter exploded out of me, and I waved the mere suggestion that I could be with Derek away. "No, I am not with Derek Hampton, Pam. We're just friends, like we've always been."

Embarrassed at her mistake, she blushed bright red and smiled. "Oh, I'm sorry. I heard you were dating one of Sunset Ridge's finest, so when you mentioned that you were waiting for Derek, I just put two and two together. Silly me."

"No, well, you heard right, but not Derek. I'm dating Alex Montero."

Pam's eyes grew wide and she cooed, "Ooooh, the dark haired one I hear used to be a Baltimore detective? Jennie says he's the cat's pajamas with feet."

Her description of Jennie's assessment of Alex made me giggle. I loved that expression because my mother used to say that about people she really liked, and to hear someone say that about him was just too cute.

"He is pretty great, I have to admit. I'm here for him

too this morning. The two of us need some caffeine to keep going. He's been up all night, and I got next to no sleep after what happened next to McGuire's."

"What happened?"

I gave her a vague explanation of Marcus Tyne's death, careful not to let any specific details about the case slip. I'd worked with Alex long enough to know what I could and couldn't say.

Pam shook her head and knitted her eyebrows in worry. "What's this world coming to? I remember when Gerry and I first moved here you could sleep with your doors unlocked and not worry one bit."

I remembered Sunset Ridge like that too, but I was a little girl back then. The town had changed in many ways, but in the ways that were most important, like knowing your neighbors and the people who ran the coffee shop you depended on, it was still the same small town I'd grown up in.

Pam made our coffees and rang them up, along with the two cherry danishes, and after wishing her a great day, I made my way back across the street to the police station just as the sun peeked above the horizon. By the looks of the sunrise, it would be a beautiful day.

I just hoped we'd get to enjoy some of it as we worked to figure out who had killed Marcus Tyne.

Derek stood just inside the doorway to Alex's office blocking my entrance, so I cleared my throat and he turned to face me with a look of surprise in his eyes. "Did I end up hiring you, Poppy? It's barely six am. What are you doing here?"

Sliding past him, I handed Alex his coffee and danish before sitting down to enjoy mine. "I'm delivering for The Grounds now. What do you think I'm doing here? Someone died right outside my father's bar, Derek. I'm here to help Alex find out who did it."

A sly smile made the corners of his mouth inch up. "And you didn't bring any danish for me?"

I took a sip of coffee and laughed. "I didn't even think you'd be out of bed this early, to be honest. You're not exactly an early bird anymore since you became chief, you know."

"As I was telling Alex here, I wasn't even asleep when he called. That shows you how much you know, Poppy."

Derek was in rare form this morning, so I figured I should focus on my breakfast and let Alex do all the talking. It never helped to aggravate the chief, even if he had been my friend for nearly my entire life and had been crushing on me for nearly as long.

Alex swallowed a bite of his breakfast and asked, "So do you remember anything about Marcus Tyne from that arrest eight months ago?"

"I remember he swore up and down he never hit that Touring woman. Other than that, he seemed like a decent guy. You know, the type you'd sit next to at the bar while you watched the game. I don't know of any reason anyone would have to kill him."

"What about Angela Touring?" Alex asked. "Do you know if they stayed together after that incident?"

Derek shook his head. "I think she left town after that. I just know she never called again after that one time."

Reading off the police record, Alex said, "She lived at 210 Crimson Drive, so I think Poppy and I will take a ride over there after we finish here and see if she knows anything about Tyne's death or who might have wanted to kill him."

"Sounds good," Derek said, nodding his approval of Alex's plan. "Let me know what you find out. In the meantime, I'll let you know if Donny sends any details on the preliminary autopsy my way."

He turned to leave, but I said, "You know, you're pretty alert this early in the morning, Derek. Who knew you were an early bird?"

Looking back at me, he smiled and threw me a look I would have sworn was intended to be flirty if I wasn't with Alex. "There are a lot of things you don't know about me, Poppy. Lots of things."

Before I could ask what since I couldn't think of one thing I wouldn't know about him, he walked away, leaving me wondering what he meant and what that look meant. I turned to ask Alex if he'd seen it, but he'd already begun filling out one of the many forms the department required him to complete at the end of each shift.

"Are we doing this now?" I asked, sure he meant we'd go see Angela Touring later in the day after he grabbed at least a short nap since he'd worked the overnight shift.

Alex looked up at me and nodded. "Now's as good a time as any. Might as well take care of this while the caffeine is doing its job because I figure I'm going to be crashing in a few hours.

I tipped the paper cup up toward my mouth to take a sip of my coffee and stood up ready to go. "Okay, partner. Let's go!"

Chapter Three

"DID DEREK SEEM odd to you?"

Alex stopped at the red light a block away from the police station and turned to look at me. "Odd?"

"Yeah. Strange, like he wasn't acting like himself."

He thought about my question for a moment and shook his head. "No. He seemed like he always does. Like Derek."

Alex turned back to face the road and when the light turned green, he began driving again toward Crimson Drive. I wasn't as sure as he was about Derek, though. Something about him felt different this morning.

As we rolled past a smattering of people out on the streets of Sunset Ridge so early in the morning, I said, "I think there was something up with him. I can't put my finger on it, but he was…odd."

"Odd? I think you're seeing things that aren't there, Poppy. He seemed like he always does, except earlier than you usually see him. Maybe that's what felt so odd. You don't often see Derek before nine am, do you?"

Something in Alex's voice sounded strange now too. I turned to look at him and saw a tiny smile tugging the corners of his mouth up. Had he just slipped in some kind of sexual innuendo about Derek and me?

"If you're asking me if I've ever seen him first thing in the morning, like right after he's rolled out of bed, then the answer is no, although there was this one time in high school that I saw him in the woods without his pants on."

I made that sound far more interesting than it had been in reality, but the effect was just as I expected. Alex looked over at me with an expression I could only describe as curiosity mixed with irritation I suspected was borne out of jealousy.

That's what he got for dismissing my suspicions about Derek so quickly.

"Do I want to know why you saw Derek without his pants on in the woods?" Alex asked, each word dripping with the very irritation I'd sensed in his face.

"No," I said with a chuckle. "But all of this is getting us off the track. You didn't sense something different about him today?"

"Nope."

Now I was getting irritated. Alex usually enjoyed my observations, or at least found them entertaining. Now he just seemed disinterested. "Well, I think something's up with Derek. I think he's hiding something."

"I think what you think is up is actually just Derek acting like himself when he's forced to come to work before nine in the morning. Do you think we can talk about this case now?"

I silently resolved to figure out what Derek was hiding and said, "Sure. What is there to talk about before we get to speak to Angela Touring? Did Donny find out what killed Marcus Tyne and you've been holding out on me?"

Once again, Alex turned to look at me, but this time

I got the furrowed brow look. "You're in a strange mood today, Poppy. Is everything okay?"

His question caught me off guard. I was the same as I always was. That he could think I was acting strangely but Derek was being his same old self baffled me. If anything, Alex should know me better than that by now.

Looking out the window, I said, "Nothing strange about me. I'm my usual inquisitive self, just like always."

An uncomfortable silence settled in between us when Alex didn't respond to my claim of acting like I always did, and by the time we reached 210 Crimson Drive, I had to admit things with us felt strange this morning too.

Maybe he was right. Maybe it was me. I hadn't gotten enough sleep, so maybe my perception of things was a bit off.

"Ready?" he asked as he parked the car.

I turned in my seat to face him and touched his arm as he turned the car off. "I didn't mean anything when I asked if you were holding out on me. I mean, if that's why you think there's something strange about me this morning."

He smiled sweetly, like what I'd said charmed him in some way. "I know you're worried about your father, so I just chalked it up to that. I do have to admit that I had a feeling you were upset with me last night, though."

"Why?" I couldn't imagine why he'd think I was angry with him, of all people, last night.

Frowning, he said, "Because I couldn't show you how much I wished I didn't have to go back to the station to work this case. I saw the look on your face when I didn't kiss you back outside McGuire's."

I waved away his worry, even though I liked that he had been concerned about not giving in to public displays of affection. "No, it's okay, Alex. I shouldn't have kissed you like that anyway. You were working and I know how important it is to keep our professional lives and personal lives completely separate."

"So we're good?" he asked, his dark eyes full of hope.

"Of course. In public, we're all about the job. In private, we're all about each other. So let's go talk to Angela Touring and see if she can help us figure out why anyone other than her would want Marcus Tyne dead."

We got out of the car and began walking up the sidewalk toward her ranch style house. He rang the doorbell, and stared straight ahead as he asked me, "So you've already decided she's our first suspect?"

I saw the hint of a smile as he waited for her to answer the door. Always ready to jump to conclusions, I had decided she had to be our first suspect in the death of the man who had given her a black eye a few months ago. It seemed like a rational idea, and it wasn't like it was chiseled in stone.

If I was wrong, then so be it. No harm, no foul.

"Of course. She called the police on him because he hit her. Hell hath no fury like a woman scorned, or in this case, a woman punched in the eye. Until I hear something to the contrary, she's suspect number one."

Alex rang the doorbell again and looked over at me. "Eight months is a long time to wait for revenge, don't you think?"

"Revenge is a dish best served cold."

"You're full of pithy sayings today, aren't you?" he asked with a chuckle.

I had to laugh. I didn't intend on sounding like a fortune cookie, but it had come out that way. "It's the lack of coffee. I'm usually on my second cup after being up this many hours in the day. I'll get better once the caffeine tank is filled."

He opened his mouth to say something, but at that moment the door opened and a woman with a brown chin-length bob and big, wide eyes stared out at us through the screen door.

"Yes?"

Angela Touring had a severe look to her. With a long face framed by a hairstyle that hit at the pointiest part and only served to accentuate her naturally angular look, she reminded me of a runway model, only not as striking so much as jarring in her appearance. Below the neck, she looked far more feminine with a curvy figure that didn't seem to fit her face at all. All in all, Angela Touring was physical contradiction.

Alex looked through the screen at her and said, "Hello, Miss Touring. I'm Alex Montero with the Sunset Ridge police and this is Poppy McGuire. We'd like to speak to you about Marcus Tyne."

Clearly unsure why we were standing on her porch asking to talk to her about her ex-boyfriend so early in the morning, she hesitated for a moment before pushing open the door and standing back to let us in. We walked into a midcentury home with modest but completely forgettable furnishings. Nothing stood out from the beige walls to the tan carpet to the bland landscape framed pictures that hung on the walls.

Alex and I stopped where the living room met the dining room, and Angela joined us so the three of us were standing clustered awkwardly in the space. She didn't appear to want to offer us a seat at first, but after a few moments of staring at one another uncomfortably, she finally extended her arm toward the dining room table and said, "I guess we should sit down. Please feel free."

We each took a seat at the tiniest table with four chairs I'd ever seen, and as Alex and I pulled our chairs in our knees smashed into each other. I stifled the urge to cry out in pain while he winced for just a second before turning to the business at hand and taking out his notebook and pen.

"Miss Touring, I'd like to know if you still see Marcus Tyne, romantically or otherwise," he said, beginning the interview with a direct question. Clearly, he didn't think he had to charm Angela Touring.

I didn't think he had to either. While she was stark looking and hadn't said much yet, I had the sense she was someone who preferred to be forthright. No need for a smarmy approach with her type of woman.

"I don't," she said tersely. "Not in any way, shape, or form. I haven't seen him for about six months."

The words came out like I imagined a drill sergeant would say them. Tight, succinct, definitive.

Alex wrote down a note that said "Haven't seen him in 6 mos" and looking up from his tablet, asked, "Have you had any contact with him at all in that time?"

Tightening her lips, she shook her head. "No, I haven't, Officer Montero."

Angela Touring had taken Joe Friday's admonition to heart. She was all facts and nothing more.

"What did Mr. Tyne do for a living?" he asked, looking at her like a friend would who genuinely wanted to know the answer.

Maybe he did think this situation called for some charm.

"He owns a small antiquing business he runs out of the back of his home," she said, parsing out the information Alex sought with an eyedropper.

As Alex continued to ask her questions to elicit some details about our victim, I looked around the nondescript house and felt the blandness begin to press down on me. Living in a place like this would make me never want to come home. There was nothing cozy or welcoming about this house. It felt like a showroom for those who wanted someplace to live that lacked any hint of inspiration. Sparse seemed the best adjective for her style of decorating. Or maybe Spartan.

My gaze drifted over to an end table near the large front window that held the only picture not hung on the walls. Trying to avoid being caught studying her home, I turned away from her and squinted my eyes to see what the image in the frame was.

Interestingly enough, it was a picture of Angela Touring and a man, but what man? I couldn't make him out from where I sat in the dining room.

Looking around again, I saw no evidence a man lived in the home or any that a man frequently visited there. Curious, I took advantage of an awkward break in Alex's questioning to ask her if I could use her bathroom to see if I could find any proof a man spent any time in there.

She pointed at the wall behind me and said, "First room on the right."

Quickly, I hurried off to the bathroom and saw there was no way any man spent any considerable time in that house. No shaving cream, razors, after shave, or cologne in the vanity, and only one toothbrush stood in the holder next to the sink. In the linen cabinet, towels and sheets sat folded in perfect squares, even fitted sheets, which made me wonder if Angela Touring was some kind of demon since I'd never met anyone who could successfully fold a fitted sheet properly.

I flushed the toilet to complete my lie and walked out to see Alex already standing next to the table. Angela remained seated and looking up at him like she couldn't figure out why he was still in her house.

"Thanks," I said with a smile and received the tightest one in return.

Without waiting for Alex, I began walking toward the front door to get a better look at that picture on the end table, and lo and behold, there in that gold frame were Angela and a very happy Marcus Tyne standing in front of a Ferris wheel at what looked like the Sunset Ridge fireman's picnic and carnival held each August.

As Alex followed me toward the door, Angela asked, "What is all this about, Officer Montero? Is Marcus in trouble again?"

I turned to see him stop and slowly spin around to answer her, but instead he asked another question. "Did he often get into trouble, or was the problem you two had what you're referring to?"

For the first time since we arrived, Angela's expression looked upset. Standing from the table, she shook her head violently. "I didn't mean that I thought he'd hit another woman or anything like that. That's not what I was saying at all. I just wondered if he'd gotten into trouble."

"You said again, Miss Touring. I just assumed you were referring to the dispute you two had that ended up in you calling the police eight months ago."

She shook her head again, making her bob swing

around from one side of her jaw to the other. "No, that's not what I meant at all. Marcus just had a tendency to get in trouble is all I meant. He didn't try to, but it somehow followed him."

"What do you mean?" Alex asked as the two of us inched back toward her.

"Nothing. Nothing at all."

Her tone had returned to that clipped one she used before, and I sensed there would be no more information coming from her. To be honest, I wasn't sure there was any more to get. I may have been wrong about her being suspect number one in this case. She didn't seem to have seen the victim in a number of months, and other than her appearing to be upset about the dispute she'd had with him that resulted in Derek coming out to see her, she was practically emotionless about Marcus Tyne.

Not exactly a woman crumbling under a guilty conscience.

"So what is all of this about? Why are you asking about Marcus if he isn't in trouble?" she asked, looking first at Alex and then to me for the answer.

"I'm sorry to have to tell you this, but Marcus Tyne was found dead early this morning."

Angela Touring recoiled and then covered her face with her hands before running out of the room. We waited a few minutes for her to return, but she never did, so we left without saying another word.

As we drove back to the station, Alex said, "That was strange, wasn't it?"

Strange wasn't the word for it.

"Did you notice she wasn't crying when she ran out of the room?"

He turned to look at me and nodded. "I thought it seemed a little overdone. She was like a robot the whole time I was asking her about him, and then suddenly, she was overwhelmed with emotion. It all seemed very staged."

"Definitely. And did you notice the picture on the end table near the window?"

A blank expression settled into his features. "No, I didn't see any picture but the ones on the walls."

I wanted to celebrate that I'd seen something he hadn't, but I didn't. Alex wouldn't have minded, but I kept my rejoicing to myself.

"Oh yeah. And it was a picture of Angela and our victim looking as happy as two peas in a pod."

He stopped the car at a red light and smiled. "Good job, Poppy. So a woman who called the cops on a man for hitting her eight months ago and claims she hasn't seen him in six months keeps a picture of her with him out in the open in her living room?"

"Exactly. I checked the bathroom for any signs of a man living there before I was able to get a good look at who was in that picture and I found nothing to say Angela either lives with a man or has a man over regularly. I mean, what man would be okay with dating a woman who keeps a picture of her with someone else out for anyone to see?"

Alex pulled the squad car up to in front of the police station and put it in park. "I had a feeling that was what the sudden need to use the bathroom was all about."

"I'll go even further," I said. "Women who don't still feel something for a man don't keep their picture up after the relationship is finished."

He turned off the car and sat back against the seat.

Running his hands along the steering wheel, he said, "Well, I'm beginning to think you may have been right thinking Angela Touring could be our first suspect."

Thrilled at my success on the case so far, I said, "How about we head over to The Grounds and talk about it over a cup of coffee? And we can discuss our trip too."

Alex's eyes lit up at the mention of our trip to the Outer Banks we had planned for the third week of July. We hadn't chosen a hotel yet, and if we expected to get a room for that week, we needed to within the next few days.

"Sounds like a good idea. I just want to see if Stephen is still around and if he found out whose car Marcus Tyne was found in, so let's go in and then we can head across the street."

The thought of being on the receiving end of another of Stephen's nasty glares made my stomach clench, so I begged off joining him in the station. "I'll grab us a table and our coffees while you deal with him. See you in a few?"

Alex gave me a knowing smile which made me wonder if he had any idea why Stephen had a problem with me, but I didn't care enough to ask again. My day was going great so far, and I wasn't going to let some guy and whatever issue he had with me ruin it.

"I'll be there in a couple, but you better make my coffee black this time. Lack of sleep is catching up with me."

I got out and leaned against the side of the car as he closed his door. "Black it is. See you in a few, and this time we have to decide on a hotel, Alex. No more dragging our feet."

He threw his head back and laughed. "Everything else might be dragging on me today, but I promise no dragging my feet. I still say the one with the jetted tub sounds good."

"And I say the private bungalow sounds good. So you see, we're still at an impasse. That's why we have to talk about it and decide today."

Alex began walking toward the station, nodding. "Then that's what we'll do. Just give me five and I'll be there ready to fight for that tub."

I watched him until he entered the building as I imagined how incredible it would be to enjoy that jetted tub with him. Seated behind me with his strong arms around my shoulders as I rested my head on his chest and those jets pulsed warm water against our bodies.

Walking across the street to The Grounds, I had to admit he might not have to fight very hard at all for his choice.

Chapter Four

THE LULL BETWEEN the early birds and the crowd getting their coffee on their way to their nine-to-five jobs gave me the chance to snag our usual table at the back of The Grounds, and after getting my usual dark roast and Alex's black coffee, I took a seat facing the door to wait for him. As I stared off into space, the noise of fellow customers chatting at nearby tables faded away until I became lost in my own head about our upcoming vacation to the Outer Banks.

Our first official trip together as a couple.

In some ways, it wasn't that big a deal. We'd been dating for months and spent time together nearly every day, but we'd never gone away from Sunset Ridge for longer than a few hours and never for anything but investigating a case.

When I gingerly brought up the subject of us possibly taking a trip a few weeks ago, I hadn't actually expected him to say yes, to be honest. A true homebody, Alex liked spending time at his house or mine, and even though he rarely denied me dinner at Diamanti's or one of his old favorite restaurants in Baltimore, the fact remained he preferred to stay in rather than going out.

Taking a trip couldn't have been more out of the

house, so I had expected to have to plead my case, but he surprised me by saying yes before I'd even gotten the entire question out of my mouth.

Now we just had to choose a hotel so I could make the reservations, but despite giving him a hard time about his choice, I had to admit now that I thought about the two of us in that jetted tub maybe that wasn't a windmill worth tilting at. A private bungalow certainly could be nice, but the room he wanted wasn't going to exactly be roughing it.

And what we could do in that tub definitely made me more amenable to the idea.

"Poppy McGuire, as I live and breathe."

A familiar voice from not long enough ago tore me out of the fantasy my mind had been busy constructing of Alex, me, and that jetted tub, and I looked up to see none other than the man who had been my fiancé before he cheated on me with a grocery checkout girl from Savings King while he was supposed to be looking at the bed and breakfast we wanted to honeymoon in.

Jared. My ex. The man who had humiliated me and would forever be on my list of people I hoped Karma would exact swift and painful retribution on.

I craned my neck to look up at his face, and to my disappointment, I saw he still looked as good as he always had. Tall with light brown hair and blue eyes, he'd been the hot jock in high school, and even now in his thirties, he still hadn't shaken that look. My gaze drifted downward, and I noticed he was just as tan as he'd always been. Jared looked like he had just returned from a week in the tropics where he did nothing but lay out on the beach and down umbrella drinks.

Why did he have to be standing there in the coffee

shop I liked to think of as my turf in the town he'd run away from with Cicely, that mousey checkout girl?

"Jared, what are you doing here?" I asked, not even feigning an attempt at being polite. He'd lost the chance to have me be gracious when he cheated on me.

"It's nice to see you too, Poppy. I'm back in town now. I see you're still the same girl you've always been."

I knew what he meant by that. Small. A nobody. Someone who would always be from Sunset Ridge and nothing more.

"Yes, I'm the same woman I've been for years," I said, correcting him. Girl? What was this? The 1950s? Would he be smacking my behind when I walked away too and making some comment about how he'd like to get with that, like I was some inanimate object?

My terse response didn't deter him from continuing the conversation, and he sat down in Alex's seat. "I was hoping we could call a truce. Do you think that's possible? I mean, we are grown adults and we're going to have to live in the same town, so can't we be civil to one another at least?"

Live in the same town? Was he planning on staying in Sunset Ridge? Why?

Determined to make it look like it still didn't bother me that he'd basically left me at the altar for another woman, I shrugged off the idea of a truce. "It's not necessary. I hold no grudge against you, Jared. I wish you all the happiness you deserve."

And scorpions to stalk you like prey wherever you go.

He smiled, showing his perfectly white teeth made even brighter by the color of his sun-kissed skin. "I'm happy to hear that. I think it might make you happy to know that Cicely left me a few months ago."

I nodded and struggled not to grin like I so desperately wanted to. Karma inflicting its painful justice had always been my fondest wish for Jared, and to hear that wish had actually come true made me want to celebrate.

But I didn't because no matter how much I still wished those scorpions would nest in his shorts and torture him, I wasn't cruel. At least not outwardly.

"I'm sorry to hear that," I said, not meaning a single word.

He smiled again and stared across the table at me. "You always were too good for me, Poppy. I know that now. I guess you can say I was a fool back then."

For a moment I wondered if I was supposed to disagree with him. I had a feeling only a saint would be able to do that, and I was no saint.

The nice person who I wished could go away at that moment so the person with the snappy comebacks could show her face took over my brain, though, and I said, "Well, it's all water under the bridge now. I wish you nothing but happiness, Jared."

Perhaps if I said that for another hundred years I might be able to convince myself I actually believed a word of it.

"You're too sweet, you know that?" he said in a voice that had something underneath it. Was he flirting with me?

I took a sip of my coffee and moved Alex's in front of me. I didn't know why, but I needed Jared to know I was waiting for someone.

He looked around at the people filing into The Grounds and chuckled. "This town never changes. Look at these people."

I scanned the room and saw exactly what he saw, but to me, it wasn't something to be laughed at or scorned. The Grounds' customers were small town people just like me, and while they drove me crazy sometimes, at the end of the day, I was one of them.

Explaining to him just how wrong he was to discount us ran through my mind, but what would be the use?

So I said nothing. Jared wasn't worth the effort.

We sat in silence as the coffee shop filled up with the nine-to-fivers grabbing their morning coffee on their way to work, and I saw more than one woman eye him up and then look at me like I was some lucky girl to be sitting there with such a good looking man. At one time in my life, that would have been important to me. Jared's boyish charm and athletic look had initially attracted me to him, and even after I realized he wasn't much more than those traits, I still liked how it felt to be with him.

Now it meant nothing that those women thought I had snagged myself a hot guy because I had something better. I had a hot guy who was even more than just what the world saw.

"So I guess you're not going to ask me what I'm going to do now that I'm back in good old Sunset Ridge," he said, tearing me from my thoughts of the past.

"I can't imagine you'd be here for very long since you don't like much about the town or the people who live here."

My indictment of his opinions surprised him, and he quickly moved to defend himself. "That's not true. Well, not entirely. I like some people here. You, my parents,

Derek. In fact, I hung out with him last night. It was like old times. Remember those days?"

So that was why Derek had been acting so strangely earlier.

What I remembered about those days and the old times Jared referred to amounted to very little I wanted to think about. He and Derek had been drinking buddies since high school, and that never stopped, even when he and I began dating. Too many times I'd sat waiting for him when we were supposed to go out because he'd been out carousing with the current chief of police. Not exactly my fondest memories.

"Derek's the chief of police now, so I can't imagine it was really like old times."

Jared laughed like I had said something amusing. "You don't know Derek as well as you think you do. Trust me. We had a good time."

I looked toward the front door of The Grounds hoping to see Alex but only saw the steady stream of people coming in for breakfast.

Beginning to feel like I was trapped in a conversation that would never end, I mumbled, "I'm sure you did."

"We ended up at the Madison last night, and I heard something very interesting about you," he said in a singsong voice, making me cringe at what he could have heard. Late night drunk talk at the local diner never amounted to anything good.

Trying to ignore him, I said, "Oh yeah?" and hoped he'd get the hint I didn't give a damn about what he'd heard about me. He didn't.

"Yeah. I heard you're helping the police solve crimes these days. I couldn't believe it. My Poppy doing the amateur sleuth thing. I told the woman who said it there was no way, but she swore up and down it was true, and even Derek said you were."

I took a sip of my coffee and wished for this whole thing with Jared to end. "How nice that I'm the talk of the Madison in the middle of the night."

"She also said you were an old maid in training, but I know that's not true. Not you, Poppy."

His smirk told me he was mocking me, but as much as I wanted to smack that stupid expression right off his face, I kept my cool and shrugged again, feigning disinterest. "I wouldn't put much stock in what anyone has to say about anyone in this town, Jared. You know how it's a hotbed of gossip. I'm sure once everyone finds out Cicely dumped you for another man that's all the busybodies around here will want to talk about."

My arrow hit its mark, and he winced like he was in pain. He hadn't mentioned anything about why that checkout girl had left him, but I assumed if she was the type to run off with someone else's fiancé, then she was the type to cheat on that same guy. Once a villain, always a villain.

And I wasn't an old maid in training, thank you. If Alex would finally get to The Grounds, I'd be able to show Jared that.

Since he hadn't, though, I had to defend my own honor. "I have been working with the police on cases. I'm pretty good at it too. My partner says I have natural detective instincts."

That I hadn't been able to figure out that Jared was a two-timing bastard who was cheating on me until he ran off with another woman seemed to show otherwise, but I'd take Alex's word for it that I had some skill at investigating crimes.

"Partner?" Jared squinted like he didn't understand the meaning of the word. "Do you mean like a life partner? Have you changed teams, Poppy?"

God, what had I ever seen in this guy? How had I ever been able to overlook the fact that he was as dumb as a bag of hair? Had I truly been so shallow that his looks had blinded me to how stupid he was?

I opened my mouth to explain exactly what I meant by partner, but thankfully, I saw Alex walking toward us, saving me from having to bother. He cocked one eyebrow when he noticed someone sitting in his seat and strode confidently through the crowd of people to stand next to the table.

Alex normally looked attractive, but I secretly loved that he was wearing his police uniform, which made him look downright incredible. The women who had been admiring Jared forgot all about him and focused their attention on the gorgeous cop glaring down at my ex.

Jared looked him up and down before a worried expression settled into his features, probably because he was guilty of some crime he thought he'd been clever enough to cover up. "Can I do something for you, officer?"

"You can get out of my chair," Alex said in the authoritative voice he only used with suspects who chose to give him a hard time. The tone of it resonated in the air around us, music to my ears.

"Jared, this is my partner, Alex," I explained as he looked over at me for some help with what had quickly become an awkward situation, thanks to Alex's almost rudeness.

From above us, Alex added, "And I'm her boyfriend. Now get out of my seat."

I loved how he didn't ask who Jared was, as if that information didn't matter to him at all. I suspected it did, if his behavior was any indication, but Alex had a way of masking his feelings better than anyone I'd ever met. Usually that trait of his bothered me, but at that moment, I loved him even more for it.

Jared practically jumped up from the chair, explaining as he did how he was just leaving anyway. "Nice meeting you, and Poppy, it was nice seeing you again." Then he flashed me a smile and added, "I hope we can catch up more next time."

He made a beeline for the door as Alex sat down and silently began to drink his coffee. I couldn't tell if he was angry, as his knitted eyebrows suggested, or just being his usual quiet self, so I began to make small talk about the crowd thinning out around us, to which he only smiled occasionally or nodded.

At least I got a smile.

After a few minutes of listening to the conversations of people around us about the weather forecast and if traffic would be detoured yet again that day because of road work on Main Street, I couldn't stand the silence between Alex and me anymore.

"So I guess you're probably wondering who that was?" I blurted out, the words tumbling out like wild animals sprung from cages.

He didn't respond but simply looked across the table at me with those dark brown eyes that seemed devoid of any reaction at all.

"That was Jared Cooke. My ex. Fiancé. My ex-fiancé. The one I told you about who cheated on me with the checkout girl at Savings King when he was supposed to be checking out the bed and breakfast we were considering for our honeymoon and then ran off with her."

The words all came out so roughly, as if some couldn't wait to find their way out of my body and others had to be ripped out, clinging to my tongue to avoid being said.

"I know who he is. Derek pointed him when he saw him come in here as he was keeping me in front of the station to talk about the Tyne case," Alex said calmly, almost like he didn't care, which seemed at odds with how he'd acted when he first saw Jared sitting there with me.

"Oh. Well, I didn't ask him to sit with me. He invited himself over. If it was up to me, I'd never speak to him again. He's the last person I'd want to see, to be honest."

Alex nodded but said nothing, leaving an empty space in the conversation I felt compelled to fill with more explanation. "I really thought I'd never have to see him again. I'd wished for nothing more. Well, that and for scorpions to crawl into his underwear and sting him unmercifully."

When I finished, I realized my shoulders were sitting somewhere just south of my earlobes. Nothing like seeing the ex to stress you out. Pushing them down to where they belonged, I sighed, but then Alex reached across the table to take my hand in his and smiled at me.

"Things are different now, Poppy. You're with me, we're happy, and we're planning our first trip away together. By the way, have you come around to my idea of the hotel with the jetted tub and fireplace in the room?"

With every word that came out of his mouth, I felt

my stress melt away. Smiling for the first time since before Jared interrupted my fantasy of Alex and me in one of those tubs together, I said, "It's going to be summer. I can't imagine we'll need a fireplace in the middle of July."

He winked and said, "We will after we get out of the tub and lay around naked."

My eyes grew as wide as saucers, and I looked around to see if anyone else had heard what he'd said. The grin on his face looked full of mischief and way too sexy for early morning at The Grounds.

"I'm not used to you being so…"

I didn't know how to finish that sentence. Alex and I had certainly moved past the point where I wondered if we'd ever sleep together, but we hadn't gotten to where either one of us mentioned it so openly, except when we were in private.

"Everyone knows we're together, Poppy. I doubt they think we get together at night and play Scrabble. We're two consenting adults."

"Sitting in the town coffee shop talking about taking a bath in a jetted tub, drying off in front of a fireplace, and sex," I whispered. "This is Sunset Ridge, Alex, and I was the latest addition to the old maids club until recently."

"Well, they're going to have to go on without you because you're with me now."

I truly loved him and how he could make me feel better, even after having a run-in with the one man who had made me doubt myself more than anyone else in the world. "So what about this hotel choice? No bungalow?" I asked with a smile while secretly dying to get to the hotel room with that tub now.

His phone vibrated against his hip, and he lifted it to see who'd messaged him. "The great hotel debate will have to wait. I know who the owner of that car is and we need to go talk to him."

He stood to leave and tossed his coffee cup in the nearby garbage before pointing to my cup. Handing it to him, I smiled as I watched him throw mine away.

When he pressed his palm to my lower back to guide me out of the shop, I quietly said, "You win. We'll go to the hotel with the tub and the fireplace."

Smiling, he whispered in my ear as we walked through the line leading to the register, "I knew if you thought about it you'd come to see it was a good idea."

I had a feeling when I saw the triumphant look he wore that he had known all along I'd end up agreeing with him.

Chapter Five

"SO WHO IS this Gerald Engels guy?" I asked as we drove down Main Street to the very man's house at 317 Sycamore Street on the outskirts of town past the Hotel Piermont.

Alex had said his name as we walked to the police cruiser but hadn't said another word about him. He likely assumed I knew who he was, but the name didn't sound familiar to me. He really had to stop thinking I knew everyone in town. I mean, I did know a lot of Sunset Ridge's citizens, but that didn't mean I knew everyone who lived there.

My question was met with silence, so I asked again, this time with frustration tacked on to every word. "Alex, are you going to tell me who Gerald Engels is? And please don't say you thought I'd know who he is."

He stopped the car at the last traffic light in town where Serpentine Road met Sycamore Street and stared straight ahead for a moment before saying, "He's the owner of the car Marcus Tyne was found dead in."

Okay. So why all the pregnant pauses and strange silence?

"That's good to know. But is there something wrong that you're not telling me? You don't look very happy about going to speak to him," I said as the light turned green and we turned onto Sycamore.

Alex shook his head, quickly dismissing my concerns. "No, nothing's wrong."

But I knew differently. I'd spent enough time around him to know when something wasn't right with my partner. Maybe he thought going to see Gerald Engels would put me in danger. Our victim had been found dead in his car. Maybe Engels was the one who killed him.

So I tried to ease his mind about that possibility. "You know, I can stay in the car if you think this might be dangerous. I don't want to, but if it would make you feel better about things, I'm fine with it."

I didn't like the idea at all, to be honest, but if that made the worried look leave his face, it was a small price to pay.

He looked over at me and smiled. "I'm not anticipating any problems when we interview Gerald Engels, so you don't have to sit in the car, Poppy."

"You don't? Don't you consider this Engels a suspect since Marcus Tyne was found dead in his car?"

Alex's smile spread across his face. "Not necessarily. It would seem to me that if someone wanted to murder Mr. Tyne, the dumbest thing to do would be to make his own car the murder scene. I don't know Gerald Engels, but I'm not assuming he's that stupid."

I thought about this line of reasoning and couldn't disagree. That would be pretty dumb to leave that kind of clue right back to you, if you're the murderer. But if he wasn't worried going to see Engels would be dangerous, why was he acting so strange?

"Okay, Alex, let's lay our cards on the table. What is

up with you?"

Stopping the car in front of a small, white house, he put it in park and turned to look at me with an expression that told me he had no idea what I was referring to. "Nothing's up, Poppy. What are we laying our cards on the table about?"

Frustration settled in and I threw my hands up. "You've been acting weird this whole ride. Is this because of seeing my ex?"

He shook his head, but his mouth turned down slightly into a frown. "No. I took care of that. At least I think I did."

"Then what's going on with you? You've looked worried the whole time we've been in this car, and if it isn't that Gerald Engels could be a dangerous murderer, albeit a sloppy one, then what's with the worried face?"

Alex brought my hand to his lips and pressed a kiss to my palm. "I don't know what you're talking about, Poppy. My face is just like it always is. I think you're reading into things that aren't there."

That was the second time in one morning he'd said that. Now I knew something was wrong. Whenever he told me I was reading into a situation too much, it never failed that later he admitted something had been wrong but he didn't want to talk about it. Alex Montero was nothing if not reliable in his reactions. I just didn't know what he was reacting to at the moment to upset him.

But there was no point in talking about it now. When he was ready to discuss whatever the problem was, he would. I'd learned that much from being around him for the past year.

So I let it go, knowing we'd talk about it sometime in the near future.

"Okay, you're probably right. You know how I am. I love to see things that aren't really there. It's my active imagination."

That actually came out a bit more snide than I'd intended, but he didn't react to my sarcasm and instead nodded like he approved that I'd given up for the moment. "Good. Now let's go in and see what Gerald Engels can tell us about why Marcus Tyne would be lying dead in his car early this morning."

We walked up the creaky wooden stairs that led to the equally rundown wrap-around porch to the Engels' residence, and Alex knocked on the front door. As we waited in silence, I wondered how long it had been since the house had been taken care of since the paint on the door had practically all peeled off and the same thing had begun on the house itself. Gerald Engels clearly wasn't a man who took care of where he lived.

After a few minutes of waiting, Alex knocked again, this time much harder. I wondered if anyone was home, so I looked in through the front windows that desperately needed a good cleaning and saw the TV on. In a chair nearby sat a man.

"Someone's in there. I can see them. Maybe they can't hear you knock. Bang a little harder," I said as I watched the man just sit staring at the TV.

Alex did as I suggested and slammed his hand against the door three times. Thinking out loud, I said, "If he can't hear that, maybe he's dead too."

Just then, I saw the man stand up slowly from the recliner and begin to make his way toward the front door. Joining Alex, I said, "He heard that one."

"Good. I was beginning to think we had a second crime on our hands."

The door opened and there in front of us stood a man who looked to be slightly shorter than six foot with disheveled brown hair and in clothes so wrinkled they looked like he'd worn them for days. Worst of all, his eyes had a vacant feel to them that unnerved me.

"Gerald Engels, I'm Officer Alex Montero and this is Poppy McGuire. We'd like to talk to you for a few minutes about Marcus Tyne."

The mention of our victim's name elicited no reaction whatsoever from Mr. Engels. He simply stared out through the screen door at us and then turned around to walk back into the house.

Alex and I looked at each other completely baffled at his behavior. "Do you think he's drunk or high?" I asked, trying to come up with some reason for what had just happened.

"I have no idea, but I want to find out," Alex said, opening the front door. "You might have been right about the danger, though, so stay alert, Poppy. Okay?"

His concern for me filled his dark eyes, but I wasn't worried about what would happen so much as curious about why Mr. Engels seemed so out of it.

Following Alex into the house, I saw what might be considered a pack rat's home. Knickknacks and collectables cluttered shelves and anywhere there may have been an open space. The only spot spared was on top of the TV. Some things looked old, like the dozens of jelly jar glasses my grandmother used to have from the 1970s that lined the countertop in the kitchen.

This place certainly wasn't like a usual bachelor pad I'd ever seen.

Gerald Engels had returned to his brown recliner to watch some show about fly fishing. At least that might have explained the vacant look he wore when he answered the door.

"Mr. Engels, I'm Officer Montero and this is Poppy McGuire. Are you okay?" Alex asked as he positioned himself between the man and the TV to block his view.

But still Gerald Engels didn't react in the slightest.

"Sir, is there something wrong?" he asked, louder this time.

Finally, the man looked up at Alex and the fact that he had two people standing in his living room registered in his brain. "Who are you?" he asked slowly.

Alex pushed down his frustration and once again explained who we were before saying, "We need to speak to you about your car, sir."

Gerald Engels looked up at him, his mouth hanging open. "My car?"

"Yes, your car. Where is your car, Mr. Engels?"

"My car? What car?"

"Your car, a 2010 Acura TL. Do you know where that car is? Was it stolen because we have no record of it reported stolen?" Alex said as Engels tilted his head and stared toward the TV.

He seemed truly lost about what Alex kept saying. "I think he's trying to watch his fly fishing show through your legs."

Turning around, Alex shut off the TV before asking Engels once more, "Sir, are you okay? Do you understand what I'm saying? We're here about your car, your 2010 Acura TL."

Still the man didn't respond, so I said, "Let me try."

I crouched down next to the recliner and asked, "Are you okay, Mr. Engels? Is there something wrong?"

After a second or two, he looked down at me with a

vacant stare and slowly shook head. "I don't think I am."

Gently, I touched his hand and asked, "What's wrong? Did you take something?"

In a quiet voice, he said, "I don't know where I am."

I looked up at Alex in surprise and saw his shock at Engels' answer. Something was definitely wrong with him.

In my sweetest voice, I explained, "You're at your house, Mr. Engels. This is your house."

He slowly turned his head and looked around like everything in the room was foreign to him and said again, "I don't know where I am."

I looked up at Alex and said, "I think we have a problem here. He doesn't seem to know what's going on."

Alex asked, "Gerald, do you know what day it is?"

He opened his mouth and then closed it before opening it again, like he wanted to say something but couldn't. "I don't feel well. I have a headache. I feel sick."

I leapt to my feet, suddenly worried something bad could happen to this man if we didn't get him to a doctor immediately. "We need to take him to the hospital, Alex. Something's very wrong with him, and I don't think we have time to wait for an ambulance."

Alex sprang into action, lifting Gerald Engels out of his chair and steadying him on his feet. Barely able to walk, he leaned heavily on Alex as the two of us helped him out to the police cruiser and put him in the back seat. I hopped into the passenger seat as Alex turned on the flashing lights and pressed the gas to the floor.

We raced down Sycamore onto Serpentine Road through the red lights near the Hotel Piermont and all along Main Street as I watched Gerald Engels get progressively sicker. Worried we wouldn't get him help in time, I said to Alex, "Can you drive faster? I don't think he's going to make it."

"Poppy, I'm going fifty already. The people in this town aren't used to lights or sirens meaning anything, which makes racing through town twice as hard since I have to keep an eye out to make sure I don't run anyone over. I'm going as fast as I can."

I heard the fear in his voice that I felt too. Gerald Engels seemed to be fading away right before my eyes, and I didn't know why or how to stop it.

He looked like he would pass out at any second, so I took his hand and held it as I tried to keep him calm. "It's okay, Gerald. We're taking you to the hospital. You're going to be okay. Just stay with me, all right? Stay with me and try to keep those eyes open."

"I don't know…I don't feel right," he mumbled as his eyelids fluttered closed.

"I think he passed out!" I yelled in a panic. "Are we almost there yet?"

Alex cut the tires hard to the right to turn onto Anderson Street where Sunset Ridge Regional Hospital sat at the very end of the road. Squeezing Gerald's hand, I tried to get him to look at me. If only he could stay awake just for a few seconds more.

"Gerald! Stay with me!" I yelled into the backseat. "We're almost there. Stay with me!"

His eyes flew open, and he clutched his chest as he cried out, "I can't breathe! I can't breathe!"

Just then, Alex slammed on the brakes and the car skidded to a stop in front of the Emergency Room entrance. He and I jumped out, and while he ran to get someone to help us, I tried to soothe Gerald's fears.

Sitting next to him in the backseat, I stroked his arm as he continued to complain he couldn't breathe. "We're at the hospital now. They're going to take care of you. Just stay with me and you'll be okay, Gerald."

Two orderlies ran out to take him into the Emergency Room, leaving me standing at the car exhausted. I didn't even know Gerald Engels, but the thought of him dying bothered me. I began to choke up, and when Alex came back to the car, I turned away so he couldn't see how overcome the whole situation had made me.

He put his hand on my shoulder and quietly said, "He's going to be okay. You did great, Poppy. You really did."

I tried to will the tears away, but it was no use. They rolled down my cheeks as I wiped them away and made excuses for my emotions. "I'll be okay. I just guess it was all a bit much."

After I took a deep breath to calm my nerves, I turned around to see him smiling at me. "You were fantastic with that whole thing, you know that?" he said sweetly.

"I just hope we got there in time, Alex. Can we go in and see how he's doing?"

"Sure."

As we walked into the ER, I asked him, "Do you think whoever killed Marcus Tyne tried to kill Gerald too?"

"I don't know, but something happened to him. I want to know what."

A crowd of hospital personnel in blue scrubs raced past us toward one of the patient rooms as a voice on the intercom announced, "Code Blue ER! Code Blue ER!"

"What's a code blue?" I asked, hoping it wasn't for Gerald Engels.

Alex pulled me toward the wall as doctors and nurses tore down the hallway toward that same room. "It's a code for cardiac arrest," he said somberly.

I looked down toward that makeshift room just as a nurse yanked the curtains closed around it and my heart sank. What had happened to make him so sick so quickly? We'd just been talking to him at his house a few minutes before and now he may have been lying on a hospital gurney in cardiac arrest.

Choking up from emotion again, I pushed down everything I felt and followed Alex as he walked to the nurses' station at the far end of the room. I couldn't fall apart every time something terrible happened if I wanted to continue working on cases with him.

"We just brought Gerald Engels in. I need to know when he's stable enough to talk," Alex said to a harried looking woman with three pencils stuck in her disheveled blond bun as she hung up the phone that immediately rang again. Handing her his card, he added, "Please contact me at this number."

She took the card and nodded as she answered the phone. "Okay, Officer Montero. I'll make sure you know when he's able to talk to the police."

I needed to get out of that ER before my nerves frazzled to nothing. All the beeping noises and people yelling for assistance as others ran by us made me wish for the quiet and solitude of my cozy little house at that moment.

Pushing out past people as they rushed in, I finally made it outside. I inhaled a deep breath of air and closed my eyes, thankful to be out of that place.

Alex came up behind me and touched me gently on the arm. "You going to be okay?"

I looked at him and forced a smile. "Yeah, I'll be fine. That was all just a lot, sort of like sensory overload for a minute there."

"Let me take you home, Poppy. I can work the details of the case for the rest of the day, and if Mr. Engels is okay to talk anytime soon, I'll be sure to let you know so you can come with me when I speak to him."

"What happened to Gerald, Alex? Did the same thing that killed Marcus Tyne get to him?" I asked as we walked to the squad car.

"I don't know what happened to him, but I know this. We need to find out from Donny right now what happened to Marcus Tyne because if it's some kind of public health issue, we can't let this get away from us."

"Public health issue?" I asked as we got into the car. "What are you talking about? I thought we were going with the idea that Marcus Tyne was murdered."

Alex started the car and pulled away from the curb. "We were. We still are, but I can't rule out that whatever killed him might be the same thing that just landed Gerald Engels in the hospital, and that could be something entirely different than murder."

"Like what?" I asked, my heart pounding in my chest at the thought of some kind of epidemic in Sunset Ridge.

His eyebrows knitted, Alex shook his head. "I don't know, Poppy."

"Well, I'm not going home then. If you can work without sleep, I can work through getting all emotional. Let's go see what Donny has to say about what killed Marcus Tyne."

Chapter Six

Donny poked his head into Alex's office to announce that he had nothing definitive to report. "Before you start asking me what killed Marcus Tyne, I should tell you I don't know."

Both Alex and I looked at him with disappointment. What was the point of making us wait three hours to tell us he had no idea what had killed our victim?

"Would you like to come in, or is this your new way of dealing with the police, Donny? Taking to doing drive bys instead of your usual detailed explanations of things nobody really understands?" Alex asked with a smile to temper his sarcasm brought on by lack of sleep.

The coroner shrugged. "I like to keep you guys on your toes. No, but really, I don't have anything to discuss yet. Nothing definitive."

"I'll take anything, Donny. Just give me something to work with."

With a sigh, he nodded and took a seat next to me in front of Alex's desk. "My preliminary examination tells me the man died of organ failure, specifically his kidneys shutting down, in addition to congestive heart failure with cardiogenic pulmonary edema."

"That sounds awful," I said as I imagined how much

pain Marcus Tyne must have been in from all of that.

Donny looked at me and frowned. "I'd say that's a good way to put it. Certainly not the way I want to go, I'll tell you that."

"Me neither. It sounds like a terrible way to die."

"If I have my way, I'll just go in my sleep. Peaceful and quiet. I like that idea," Donny said with a satisfied grin, like he'd thought quite extensively about his exit from this world.

"I agree," I said. "I don't like to think about my own demise, but if I have to go, I'd like it to be painless and peaceful."

"Oh yeah, painless is important too. I forgot to mention that. Definitely don't want to be in agony in my last moments on this earth."

Alex cleared his throat, making Donny and me stop talking and turn to face him. "Have we covered all the details of your death wishes? So now can get to the guy who actually died? You know, our victim?"

"Sorry," I mumbled.

"Yeah, sorry Alex. It's just that as I said when I first got here, I don't really have anything definitive yet."

"Well, what killed him? Were any of those things you mentioned deadly?" Alex asked with an edge to his voice that told me his frustration with this case was increasing by the moment.

Donny shook his head. "He went into cardiac arrest, but everything in this guy seems to have been shutting down. I don't know what would have made that happen yet."

"Everything? What can do that to the human body?" I asked, wondering if Alex's thought about a public health emergency had been more on the mark than I'd initially believed.

For a moment, Donny considered my question, and then he answered, "Well, that's an interesting question. Anyone at the end of their life and dying from a disease like cancer will experience a failure like that, but I didn't find any evidence that your victim was suffering from any cancer. Things like hemorrhagic fever and plague can have similar effects, but—"

Before he could continue, I interrupted him. "Plague? Like the Black Death in Europe in the fourteen century plague? You can't be talking about that, Donny."

I looked across the desk at Alex and saw his eyes nearly bugging out of his head. Just the word plague made the hair on the back of my neck stand up.

But the coroner didn't seem as traumatized by the mere mention of a disease that had wiped out upwards of half the population of Europe at one time. Touching my arm, Donny tried to calm me.

"I'm not saying that it was the plague, so don't worry just yet. I just used it as an example of what could cause organ failure as extensive as I saw in your guy. But for what it's worth, the bubonic plague still exists today in the twenty-first century, even here in the United States. Mostly in the southwest. It's also been found in Russia and in China in the past few decades."

"I just want to make sure I have this straight, Donny," Alex said calmly. "You aren't saying this is plague, right?"

Donny waved his hands in front of him as if to erase any mention of plague. "No, no. Don't worry. I don't think we have any variety of the plague on our hands. That's not what I was saying. I was just offering it as an example. There's no need to press the panic button here."

Both Alex and I took deep breaths and let them out slowly. So it wasn't plague, but what killed Marcus Tyne by causing his organs to completely shut down?

"Is there anything else other than cancer or something on a biblical level that could have killed him?" Alex asked with a glimmer of hope in his eyes.

Donny shrugged. "Poison might do it. It would depend on what he was given, but some poisonous substances can cause the body to react like your victim did."

Smiling, Alex jotted notes down in his tablet. "Poison. Good. Okay, poison is something to go on, at least. It's not bubonic plague, so I'll take it for now."

The coroner nodded and stood from his chair to leave. "When I have a cause of death, you'll be the first to know, unless this is some kind of contagious disease we're dealing with, which means you'll be more like the twentieth person to find out after the CDC and the Feds. I'm telling you now, I hope it isn't that because I don't need those people swarming my morgue."

The happiness drained from Alex's face at Donny's mention of a contagious disease. "You just said it probably isn't plague and now you mention the CDC? What are you doing to me, Donny?"

Throwing his head back, he laughed at the reaction he'd gotten from Alex. "I love seeing you guys overreact. Don't worry. I'm putting my money on something other than contagious disease. I don't know what yet, but I'll let you know what I find after a few more tests."

He turned to leave and Alex said, "Hey, the guy whose car we found him in was just admitted to the hospital after we found him at his house. He seemed confused and right before we got to the hospital, he said he couldn't breathe. We heard it announced that they had a Code Blue right after they took him in. I think he went into cardiac arrest."

Donny looked at each of us and sighed. "Another cardiac arrest. That's not good. Hopefully, he recovers so he can give us a hint as to what happened. If not, he's going to be next on my table, so I better get back to the lab now."

We sat in silence as all of what Donny had told us sunk in. Bubonic plague? Poisoning? It all seemed so impossible to be happening in Sunset Ridge.

Alex typed something into his laptop and shook his head as he read what appeared on the screen. "I thought he might have been wrong about the bubonic plague here in the US, but he was right. There were four deaths so far this year, all in New Mexico and Arizona."

"Yet another reason why I love living right here in Maryland. No scorpions, hundred degree heat, and now no plague."

My lame attempt at humor made him smile. "I think I'd have to second that emotion. I could probably handle the heat, but no thanks on the scorpions and plague."

Leaning back in his chair, he folded his arms across his chest. "I wonder if this is some kind of food poisoning or something like that. But what kind of food poisoning causes organ shutdown so pervasive?"

I thought back to the last time I had food poisoning. I'd eaten undercooked chicken at a barbeque, and for nearly twenty-four hours after, I suffered terribly. I thought I might never get to leave my bathroom again.

"All I know is that food poisoning makes you wonder

if you're going to die while you're in the middle of it," I said as my mind replayed those horrible hours of that night.

"I know that. I've had food poisoning a few times, but never did it get so bad that I was in danger of dying. Maybe being dehydrated but not dying," Alex said.

"Then I doubt it was food poisoning that killed our guy. Maybe some other kind of poisoning, though."

Alex's eyebrows raised into his forehead. "Been reading Agatha Christie lately, Poppy? Are you suggesting a good arsenic poisoning right here in little old Sunset Ridge?" he asked facetiously.

He enjoyed making fun of my reading choices since they tended toward the older mysteries. He preferred more modern day books, and more than once he'd had a laugh at my bookcase full of the oldies, as he liked to call them.

I liked the term classics myself, and even though many of those stories' settings were very different from the town we lived in, the methods and styles of the detectives were just as good as any of his newer fictional investigators.

"No, I wasn't, Alex, and it isn't like poisoning someone with arsenic is impossible today. For someone who chastises me about jumping to conclusions too often, you seem perfectly fine with discounting this idea very easily."

My defense of such an old school method of poisoning someone amused him, and he laughed out loud at me. "My apologies, Miss Marple. I guess I better get prepared for an onslaught of doilies in this case."

I leaned forward and perched my elbows on the edge of his desk. "I'll have you know, Mr. Montero, that arsenic was found in dangerously high levels in wine just last year. Discount it as much as you want, but it could be what killed Marcus Tyne and nearly killed Gerald Engels."

Still doubting my thesis, he grabbed his pen and scribbled something in his notebook as he corrected me. "That's Officer Montero, Miss Marple."

I craned my neck to look at what he'd written and saw it said *Poppy loves arsenic*.

"Funny. Real funny."

I sat back in my seat, disgusted at how easily he dismissed my idea. Alex usually seemed so open minded when it came to my suggestions, but clearly this one didn't get the benefit of the doubt.

His expression slowly morphed into one far more serious than my sulking warranted, so I asked, "What's wrong?"

Sighing, he said, "Something just occurred to me. Marcus Tyne was at McGuire's Monday night. I'm wondering if Gerald Engels was too."

"Why?"

Alex hesitated for a moment and then said the one thing I hadn't thought of in all of this. "Because if he did, that's a connection I'll have to investigate."

As the possibility of my father's bar being even more involved in this case wound its way through my mind, my stomach tightened. What if both men were at McGuire's? What if they both drank the same thing there and...?

I couldn't finish that thought.

"Poppy, don't jump to conclusions. I'm serious. I can see by your face what you're already thinking. Don't."

"What if they were poisoned there, Alex? That will

devastate my father. How could that happen?"

The horror of someone dying outside his bar had shaken him to the core. What would happen if that man had died because of something he'd consumed in McGuire's? I didn't think he'd be able to handle it.

In a stern voice, Alex said, "I told you not to jump to conclusions. We don't know what killed Marcus Tyne yet. We don't even know if Tyne and Engels were at any of the same places that day. All we know is we have one victim, Poppy. Concentrate on that."

I couldn't, though. Every horrible possibility ran through my head as I sat there. If we found out that both men were at McGuire's Monday night, my father's business might be shut down for days or weeks even as the investigation worked its way through suspects and clues. That bar was his life. He devoted every second of his day to that place.

"That bar is all he's had since my mother died, Alex. He'd be brokenhearted if he had to close, even if it was just until the investigation was over."

"Poppy, I severely doubt anyone died from anything they had at your father's bar. Please don't worry prematurely. Let's find out what Donny has to say first before you get worried about Joe."

I took a deep breath and tried to calm down, but it was no use. Hanging my head, I said, "I don't know what my father would do without that bar. I know it sounds silly, but I think he lives for that place."

"Look at me, Poppy."

After another deep breath, I did as Alex wanted me to and lifted my head to look at him. His usually stoic expression had been replaced by the look he always gave me when he knew I was unraveling. His brown eyes seemed softer and more caring when he looked at me like that.

"I want you to go spend some time with your father this afternoon. I promise I'll call you when Donny gets me any results, but I think it would do you some good to be with him today."

"I don't know, Alex. He's going to know I'm upset about something. I don't think telling him about it would do any good for me or him."

"Then don't tell him. Why don't you go out for a bite to eat with him or you two do something together you haven't done in a while? I know he loves a pick-up game of basketball any time he gets the chance," Alex said with a smile.

My father did love to get outside and shoot hoops on his day off, but I'd never been very good at basketball. It had been over a decade since I'd even touched one.

"Maybe. I'm just not sure I can hide what I'm thinking."

Alex laughed out loud at that idea. "Poppy, you have the opposite of a poker face. I don't think you've ever had an emotion that didn't show all over your face. So no, I don't think you can hide anything, but maybe you two spending some time together will take your mind off things for at least a few hours."

I had to admit he was probably right. Until Donny got back to him with some information about Marcus Tyne's cause of death, all I'd be doing was waiting around and worrying.

"What about you? You've been awake for almost twenty-four hours. You must be exhausted."

Alex waved away my concern. "I'm fine. Maybe I'll catch a nap while I'm waiting for Donny to call. I don't have a shift tonight, so I can catch up on sleep then."

The dark circles under his eyes told the real story, no matter what he claimed. A workaholic, if I knew him, he'd probably catch his second wind once Donny gave him his preliminary report and launch into the investigation full steam ahead, sleep or no sleep.

"You know, Donny has your cell number. You and I could go back to my house and you could grab a nap there. You aren't on the schedule today, so it wouldn't be breaking any rules."

A sly smile spread across his lips. "I'm not worried about breaking any rules. You know how I am with a case. I won't be able to sleep at your house anyway. Too many distractions."

"Are you calling me a distraction?" I asked with a smile. "Because if you are, that might be one of the nicest things you've ever said to me."

Rolling his eyes, he pointed toward the door. "Go. Take a few hours to spend time with your father while I sneak a nap in my chair here. I'll call you as soon as Donny calls me."

I got up from my seat, accepting that I wouldn't be able to change his mind on this issue. "Fine. I'm going. I wouldn't want to be a distraction to you while you're trying to work. Or napping."

He shook his head and smiled. "You're my favorite distraction, Poppy. Tell Joe I said hi and I'll be in for Thursday's Orioles game."

"I beat out this season's sport? I must be doing something right," I joked as I left.

I heard him chuckling as I walked down the hall toward the front door of the station, but for all my joking around, I couldn't help but worry that when Thursday came around for them to hang out at McGuire's to watch the baseball game that the bar would be closed and my father would be stuck in the center of our investigation of Marcus Tyne's death.

Until that happened, though, I had to push my worries out of my mind if I was going to spend time with my father. Alex had been right when he remarked about me not having a poker face. My mother always said I wore my emotions and my heart on my sleeve.

I couldn't let my father see how worried I was about him and this case. That would only make him wonder if he truly was to blame for that man's death. That I'd never believe, no matter what Donny or Alex or anyone said.

No amount of evidence would ever convince me that my father had any part in Marcus Tyne's death. Donny could run every test known to mankind, and it wouldn't matter if every single one showed he'd died from something he drank at McGuire's. I still wouldn't believe my father had done it.

Joe McGuire was capable of many things, and I knew he wasn't a perfect man. But he wasn't a murderer, and no one would ever be able to convince me otherwise.

Chapter Seven

MID-AFTERNOON ON A Tuesday had never been a busy time for the bar business in Sunset Ridge, but when I walked into McGuire's after leaving the police station, I stopped dead at the sight of my father all alone there. Everything I feared this case would do to him had already begun.

"Hey, Dad!" I said in my cheeriest voice as I hopped onto a barstool. "What's new?"

He tore his attention away from the replay of some baseball game and looked over at me. Smiling as always, he walked down to where I sat. "Poppy! I didn't expect to see you sitting there. No work at any of your jobs today?"

"I told Howard I'd be working from home for a couple days, and Alex is waist-deep in paperwork, so there was nothing for me to do with him today either. So I figured I'd come see how my favorite guy is doing."

My father looked around his empty bar and shrugged. "I'm okay. Things seem a little slow today, but I'm sure they'll pick up."

Joe McGuire, the eternal optimist.

"I bet it will. It's not like you're always slammed in the middle of the day on weekdays, right?" I asked, truly hoping the answer would be no.

He shook his head and lifted the coffee pot to offer me a cup. "Usually only my regulars are here around this time, but between doctors' appointments and handling the chores their wives give them each day, that varies too."

I slid off the stool and came around the back of the bar to take the pot from him. "Let me get that, Dad. I don't need you to wait on me. You want a cup?"

"No, no. You know I don't handle the caffeine as well as you do, sweetheart. I'll stick with my water," he said with a smile, stepping around me while I poured myself my third cup of coffee for the day.

As he sat down at the bar, I suddenly had an idea. "Hey, Dad, why don't you take the day off? I'm already back here ready for when anyone comes in, and you know you can trust me to run the place like the well-oiled machine you've made it. Why not take a mental health day? You could go see a ball game. Are the Orioles in town?"

Without even having to think about it, he shook his head. "Nope. They're doing a three-game stand in New York this week. I don't want to take a day off anyway. I have things I have to do here."

I looked up and down the bar and saw a spotless work area. "Like what? You've gotten this place to the point where it practically runs itself. Working here is more socializing than anything else."

My father knew I was right. Despite that, he waved off my protests. "Well, I have to put the air conditioners in my windows upstairs. That's something I have to do here. So you see, I can't take a mental day."

Chuckling, I corrected him. "A mental health day,

Dad. A mental day is something entirely different. So go do things in your house and I'll stay here and man the bar. If there are any problems, you'll be right upstairs. I promise to come get you if I need you."

He tilted his head and stared at me for a moment, like he wanted to figure out what I was up to. "What's this all about, Poppy? My birthday isn't for another five months, so I know you're not trying to give me the bum's rush so you can plan a surprise party for me. So why are you so eager to see me anywhere but right where I belong?"

I turned away to avoid the intense gaze of his blue eyes and looked up at the baseball game playing on the TV. "I'm not trying to do that, Dad. I just figured I'd offer to watch the bar so you could have a day off. Just trying to be a good daughter."

"You're always a good daughter, sweetheart, but I get the feeling you're treating me with kid gloves because of what happened last night. You don't have to, though. I'm fine. Really."

As he talked, I watched the right fielder catch a ball and throw it on a frozen rope to the second baseman to get the runner out just in time. I'd spent countless hours with my father watching baseball when I was a little girl. The skill and talent of the players and how pure the enjoyment I got from watching them always impressed me. I'd gotten that love of the sport from him.

Now that he needed me for the first real time since my mother died, I couldn't even convince him to take a day off and get away so he wouldn't have to witness the demise of his business.

I watched the game for another few seconds as I considered telling him the truth, but he beat me to it.

"You don't have to worry about me or this bar, Poppy. Whatever happens, we'll both get through it just fine."

Again with the optimism.

Turning around to face him, I saw he truly believed he'd weather this storm like he'd done all the others. I only wished I could be that sure.

"I'm just worried about you. That's all. I don't want you to have to sit here all alone if no one shows up today because of Marcus Tyne's death right outside the bar."

My father took hold of my hands and smiled like what I'd said had any good to it whatsoever. "Honey, I've gotten through lots of ups and downs in this town. When I first opened this bar, the very women who meet in my back room every second Tuesday of the month started a petition to close me down. Sunset Ridge's very own temperance movement."

This news stunned me. I'd never heard anything from him or my mother about the town busybodies trying to get rid of the bar.

"I can see by the look on your face that you're surprised. Don't be. Your father's much tougher than you think he is. I fought those ladies tooth and nail for months at council meetings where they threw everything from the Bible to ridiculous antiquated town ordinances at me, but I stood strong. And in the end, people in Sunset Ridge came to understand I wasn't trying to open a den of inequity or anything more than just a place where people could have a drink and watch some sports."

My father never ceased to amaze me. Shaking my head, I smiled as I imagined him going up against those nosy women and their hypocritical attacks. I knew why they didn't want any bar in town. They worried their husbands would have someplace they'd rather be than at home with them listening to their hurtful gossip about everyone else in town.

"I had no idea, Dad. I always thought McGuire's had been a staple in town since you won it off Campbell Grave in that poker game."

"No, and when I won it the ladies were in the middle of doing their best to shut him down too. I guess I inherited the issue with them when I won this place."

Leaning over the bar, I kissed him on the cheek. "I just worry about you. You're my father, so I don't want anyone to hurt you or this bar because I know how much it means to you. That's all this was."

"Well, you don't have to worry. I'm a resilient guy, Poppy. You don't live as long as I have without growing a thick skin. I know how the people in this town can be. I've seen it firsthand. At first, many people didn't dare come here because those women threatened them with their fire and brimstone about the evils of alcohol, but they came around in the end because I stuck to my guns. Then when your mother died, many of the people who acted like they wanted to throw themselves into her grave with her basically disappeared right after the funeral and even though I needed to work more than ever before to take my mind off everything, many days and nights this bar was empty."

"I didn't know, Dad. I'm sorry."

"It's okay, Elizabeth. I had you, so I didn't need anyone else, as it turns out. But I want you to remember something. This bar isn't my life. It's where I work, but I've done this long enough that if I had to give it up tomorrow, I'd be okay. I've squirreled away enough money for retirement, and although I'd miss my regulars who are more friends than customers, I'd be fine. We'd just have to see each other in other places in town. So don't worry about me."

Taking one last sip of coffee, I realized I'd been all wrong about things. My father had everything in perspective, like I wished I could. He'd be fine, and if McGuire's suffered because of the Tyne investigation, he'd weather that storm like all the others.

If he could get through the self-appointed morality police in town, he could handle a little downturn in business until people moved on from the newest crime in Sunset Ridge.

"I love you, Dad. You're my idol, you know that?" I said as I came around the bar to hug him.

He squeezed me tightly to him and kissed my cheek. "Thank you for worrying about me, honey. You're sweet."

I pulled back from him and smiled. "I guess I better go since I'm obviously not needed here. Maybe Alex needs me with the case."

"How is that going, by the way?"

"We're still waiting on the autopsy results. Donny seems to be having difficulty figuring out what killed Marcus Tyne, but from what he says, whatever it was caused every one of his organs to shut down."

My father recoiled at the sound of what poor Marcus Tyne had gone through before he died. "Oh, God."

"I know, but don't think about it. I'll let you know what I find out from Alex once the coroner contacts him. Until then, I'm going to go home and do some work for Howard so he doesn't have any reason to give me a hard time when I go back to the paper tomorrow."

Two of my father's regulars appeared in the

doorway as I turned to leave, and from behind me, he said, "See? Nothing to worry about."

I waved goodbye and said, "Yeah, yeah. Talk to you later, Dad!"

Maybe there was something to that eternal optimism thing after all.

*   *   *

EARLY WEDNESDAY MORNING as I sat at my little kitchen table enjoying my first cup of coffee for the day, Alex showed up ready to tackle the Tyne case. Practically bounding through my door, he sat down across from me and placed a sheet of paper down between us.

"The results are in. Are you ready to start investigating this case?"

Looking down at my pale blue and white shorts with clouds and sheep on them and the matching blue t-shirt I'd worn to bed the night before, I could honestly say I was the furthest thing from being ready. On top of what I was wearing, I hadn't even showered yet, so my hair looked like something may have begun to build a nest in it overnight while I slept.

"Uh, no, but how about you tell me what killed our victim while I enjoy my coffee and then I'll do my best to hurry so we can get out there and solve this case?"

Alex's eyes scanned me from head to toe. "Okay, you have a point there, although I think those might be the most adorable pajamas I've ever seen on an adult. They might make our suspects want to answer my questions more freely because you just look so cute wearing them."

Leveling my gaze on him, I shot him my "It's early, so jokes aren't really going to work" look. "Funny. So what did Donny find out?"

"Antifreeze," Alex said as he sat back against the wooden chair and folded his arms across his chest.

I heard the word but couldn't understand what he meant. Was this some cop keyword or lingo like ten-four or B and E?

"What? What does that mean?"

He slid the sheet of paper toward him and began reading. "Ethylene glycol was found in deadly amounts in the victim." Alex looked up and tilted his head left and then right. "It says a lot more and I paraphrased, but what killed Marcus Tyne was antifreeze."

Immediately, I understood how bad this could be for my father. "Antifreeze? That means it had to be put into his drink."

The implication seemed to be lost on my partner. "Probably, but I'm sure it could be found in something like soup or pudding."

Wide awake now, I jumped up from the table and tossed the rest of my coffee into the sink before quickly rinsing my cup. I turned around to see Alex studying Donny's report, as if he hadn't just practically indicted my father with his announcement.

"How can you just sit there like that after what you just said?" I asked, my panic spiraling out of control.

He looked up at me completely confused by my question. "What do you mean? This is good news, Poppy. My guess is this is what made Gerald Engels sick too. You remember, Gerald, the guy whose life you basically saved? What's wrong?"

Barely fighting back the tears, I explained, "Marcus

Tyne was found dead right outside McGuire's, and now you tell me he was poisoned by someone putting antifreeze in his drink? Alex, isn't it obvious? All the signs point to my father as a suspect!"

Hearing me spell it out, Alex instantly stood from the table and came over to take me into his arms. As I reveled in the feel of him holding me even as my emotions ran wild, he said quietly, "Poppy, that isn't obvious to anyone but you. I promise you it didn't even cross my mind. Your father isn't a murderer and he had no reason to spike a stranger's drink with something that would kill him. I'm more interested in Gerald Engels, to be honest, since it was his car that Marcus was found dead in."

I looked up at him, hoping I'd see in his face he believed what he'd said. Searching his dark eyes, I saw his words were genuine. "I'm just worried about my father. Nothing like this has ever happened, and when I was at the bar yesterday, it was practically empty. I don't want this to hurt him or his business."

Smoothing my messy bedhead hair back from my face, he smiled down at me. "I don't think you have to worry about that. I passed McGuire's when I was driving home last night and the place was packed with cars all over the place on the street. I was surprised one of his neighbors didn't call the cops on him."

Packed? That seemed odd since the beginning of the week was generally the bar's slow time. "Tuesdays are never a busy night there. Maybe he got some spillover from his Cinco de Mayo promotion."

"My guess is it had more to do with our victim than the fifth of May. People are nosy and probably wanted to be at the place where someone died."

"That's awful!" I said in horror at the very idea of that kind of rubbernecking.

"That's how people are, Poppy. You know that. Think of every crime scene we've ever been at and think about the crowds that form outside. Craig's job on the force is probably the most secure of us all because he's the guy who has to deal with keeping the onlookers back away so we can do our job. It's human nature to want to know, especially about the gruesome parts of life."

I didn't want to talk about this anymore. Just the thought of people wanting to get some kind of thrill from being close to where someone died bothered me.

Pulling away from Alex, I shook my head. "People disgust me sometimes."

He slid his arm around me and drew back into him. "Speaking of people, have you heard from Jared since you saw him at The Grounds?"

Now I saw in his eyes genuine jealousy. He waited for me to answer his question, but I couldn't help but think he looked cute in that shade of green.

"No, why would I?"

Honestly, I doubted my ex would bother to take the time to contact me again after the cool reception I'd given him the day before.

"Because he seemed pretty interested in catching up again," Alex answered, parroting the exact words Jared had used as he left us sitting in the back of the coffee shop.

Pressing my hands to his tan Henley and loving the feel of his muscular chest beneath it, I smiled up at him. "I don't care about Jared. I only care about the incredibly sexy Sunset Ridge policeman standing right in front of me."

"Oh yeah?" he teased with a sparkle in his eye at my compliment.

"Yeah, and you know what? I've never seen you jealous like this. It think it might make you even cuter, if that's possible."

Alex wrinkled his nose and shook his head. "Jealous? No way."

I stood on my toes and kissed him softly. Still touching his lips with mine, I said, "You have no reason to be jealous."

Cradling my face, he nodded. "I'm the furthest thing from jealous, but I can't deny he has that look I'm sure many women like—the athletic, high school jock look."

"I prefer retired Baltimore cop now small town guy look better. Plus, you possess so many things beyond looks that he'll never have."

"Like?"

As the worry about my father returned, I hung my head. "Like you actually care when I'm upset about something."

He gently lifted my chin so I was looking up into his brown eyes full of worry about me and kissed me sweetly on the lips. "Don't worry about your father. He's going to be fine. As far as I'm concerned, he's not even a consideration for my list of suspects. Since I know he won't be on yours either, it's nothing to even waste time thinking about."

"Okay. Well, I better get ready so we can this investigation going, right?"

Alex slid his hands down my neck and let them rest on my shoulders, and his expression changed like he had other things on his mind. "The hospital said we wouldn't be able to speak to Gerald Engels until this afternoon, so

I think we have a few minutes to spare."

"Don't you think we should get moving on the case, though?" I asked, feigning innocence about what he truly wanted.

"I'm not officially on the clock until three this afternoon…"

He didn't bother to finish his sentence, and he didn't have to. As he pressed a kiss onto my mouth so long and deep it made my toes curl, I knew exactly what he meant.

Chapter Eight

ALEX AND I arrived at the hospital to see Gerald Engels after they notified us he was awake and alert enough to talk to the police. As we rode up to the third floor, my partner remained silent as he stared straight ahead into the silver paneled elevator door, like he had something on his mind.

"Everything okay?" I asked, lightly touching his forearm.

He turned to look at me and nodded. "Yeah. I'm just hoping to hear something from Gerald Engels that helps us get this case moving. I don't think I've ever had a case that seemed to stop before it ever got started like this one."

"Well, it did take Donny longer than usual to figure out the cause of death this time. There wasn't much we could do before we knew what had happened to Marcus Tyne, but now that we do, I'm sure things will get rolling and we'll have this case solved in no time."

Alex raised his eyebrows in surprise. "That's very optimistic for you, Poppy."

I thought about my father's never-ending belief that good things were right around the corner and smiled. "You act like I'm always a glass half empty kind of girl.

I've been known to think on the bright side every now and then."

"Oh, I know. It's just that over the past year you've gradually become more jaded like me."

The elevator stopped, and I elbowed him gently in the side. "I think you're a bad influence on me, Officer Montero."

As the doors opened, he smiled and shook his head. "Not me. I'm just a cop doing my job. I can't help if my experience rubs off on you because you're my partner."

He stepped out into the third floor beige painted hallway and motioned with his head toward Room 319 as I followed. Nudging his shoulder with my fingertips, I said, "I'm coming, Mr. Glass Half Empty."

We walked halfway down the hall to the nurses' station and stopped so Alex could flash his badge to the woman standing there before asking to speak to Mr. Engels' doctor. The nurse, a tall woman with a tight black bun knotted on the top of her head, paged Dr. Carter and told us he'd be along in a few minutes.

I hadn't been on that floor for long before it began to make me uneasy. Never a fan of hospitals or sick people, I'd grown to hate them during my mother's illness. I couldn't count the number of times I visited this place with its white tile floors and neutral colored walls. After a while as she grew sicker and sicker, each time blended into the others.

Since then, I'd avoided anything to do with doctors or hospitals, if I could help it. The few times I'd had to accompany Alex here were the exceptions to a rule I intended on keeping forever. All hospitals reminded me of death.

My mother's death.

Alex lightly pushed on my upper arm, so I turned to face him, not realizing how long I'd been lost in thought about my hatred of hospitals. "Hey, you faded out on me for a moment. You okay?"

"Yeah," I said as I nodded a few too many times. "I'm fine."

Studying me for a second, he asked again, "Are you okay? You don't look right."

"I'm fine." Looking up and down the hallway, I asked, "Where's this doctor? I feel like we've been here for a while already."

"If a while is less than five minutes, then yeah, we've been here for a while. What's going on with you, Poppy?"

I stopped searching for this Dr. Carter and saw Alex staring at me with concern written all over his face. Clearly, I wasn't masking how much I hated hospitals as well as I thought.

"I'm good, Alex. I've just never been a fan of hospitals. Or doctors. Or anything involving sickness. I could never be a nurse. God help me, that job sounds like something straight out of Dante's circles of hell."

My explanation did nothing to ease his worry about me, and he softly touched my arm. "You don't have to stay here if it's a problem. I can handle talking to the doctor and Gerald Engels. We can meet at The Grounds after and I can tell you everything that happened."

As much as I didn't want to be in that place, I hated the idea of shirking my responsibility to Alex even more. Shaking my head, I remained resolute in my plan to stay right there and deal with my issues.

"I'm fine." As I repeated my lie, I saw a short, round, balding man wearing tiny round glasses and a white doctor's coat walk toward us with a determined look on his face. Reading his nametag, I pointed behind Alex and said, "I think this is Dr. Carter now."

I wanted to add just in the nick of time since any more discussion of my problem with hospitals and I would have done something stupid like lash out at Alex. I'd done that far too many times to my father on those countless visits to see my mother as she slowly wasted away in that hospital bed that would end up being the last place I saw her alive.

Alex spun around to see the doctor and extended his hand to shake his. "I'm Officer Alex Montero and this is Poppy McGuire, Dr. Carter. We'd like to speak to you about your patient, Gerald Engels."

He adjusted his glasses and nodded as he extended his arm out to the right toward the nearest room next to the nurses' station. "Let's go in here. We can talk in private in this room."

The three of us sat down around a table in what looked like a breakroom for the staff, and Alex took out his pen and pad. "Doctor, we were the people who brought Mr. Engels in. I'm investigating the murder of his friend and need to know what made Mr. Engels sick enough that he went from appearing slightly drunk to being deathly ill between the time we met him at his house and the time we got him here to the hospital. We weren't with him for more than fifteen minutes, tops."

"Antifreeze, Officer Montero. Gerald Engels was suffering from Ethylene glycol poisoning."

Alex's eyes lit up as my heart began to beat wildly, and he asked, "Doctor, could someone accidentally ingest this Ethylene glycol?"

Shaking his head, Dr. Carter frowned. "No, I would

say that's highly doubtful."

After he wrote a few notes about accidental poisoning being unlikely, Alex asked, "How could someone drink it then without knowing?"

"It can taste sweet, so it could be put into a drink and someone wouldn't know. Then it's downhill from there. Pets often die from drinking even a small amount of antifreeze off the ground underneath cars. It's sweet, so they lap it up and then nothing can be done to stop the effects."

Without another word, Alex stood from the table and announced, "I need to make a call, doctor. Please excuse me."

Then he walked out of the room, leaving me there with Dr. Carter. Sure I'd be on the verge of a panic attack at any moment if I didn't keep my mind preoccupied, I asked him, "Would antifreeze work in any drink?"

He scrunched up his face as he thought about my question and finally said, "It might. The sweeter the drink, the better."

As all my worries about my father began to flood my mind, I asked, "Would it work in alcohol like whisky or bourbon?"

"It would work well in sweeter alcoholic drinks, especially bourbon or rum. They would mask the taste of the antifreeze."

My heart sank at his answer. Someone had poisoned Marcus Tyne and killed him, and then they'd poisoned Gerald Engels and nearly killed him. Two victims of antifreeze poisoning. Two men who may have been drinking at McGuire's.

"One more question, doctor. How much would have

to be put into someone's drink?"

"Well, it depends. As little as a third of a cup can be deadly. Mr. Engels didn't ingest that much, thankfully, but you saw the effects of less than that amount on the human body. It's a nasty poison."

My stomach twisted into knots at every word. Had someone somehow gotten behind the bar at McGuire's and slipped the poison into the drinks? How could that have happened? I knew my father ran the bar like everyone who came in was a friend of his, but who in Sunset Ridge would want Marcus Tyne and Gerald Engels dead and my father blamed for their murders?

Alex opened the door, and peeking his head in said, "Dr. Carter, I'd like to see Mr. Engels now. Poppy, let's go."

Something in his tone sounded off, like he suddenly was worried about me again. I joined him out in the hallway as the doctor escorted us to Room 319, but Alex said nothing as we walked there.

Had he learned something even worse than what we already knew in that phone call he made?

Gerald Engels sat in his hospital bed watching the TV perched near the ceiling across the private room, and when the three of us entered, he didn't seem to recognize anyone but the doctor. Not that I needed him to know that I'd saved his life, but I figured he'd at least remember me from the day before as I tried to calm him on the ride there.

Dr. Carter turned toward us and in a low voice said, "Try not to keep him too long with questions. He needs his rest."

Alex smiled and nodded before looking over at the man who'd become our second victim. "Gerald, do you remember me? I'm Officer Alex Montero and this is Poppy McGuire."

He looked at us for a long moment and then shook his head. "I'm sorry, I don't remember you, Officer Montero." Focusing on me, he smiled. "I know you, Poppy, from your father's bar."

"You don't remember us being at your house yesterday?" I asked while I tried to recall when I'd seen Gerald at McGuire's. As much as I thought back to my shifts there for the past few months, I didn't remember ever seeing him before we met the day before.

Pen and notepad in hand, Alex walked around the bed and leaned against the wall nearest Gerald. "Do you remember where you were yesterday? Can you retrace the steps of your day for me?"

"I worked till noon on a spinning wheel I've been cleaning up, and then I went to McGuire's for a drink right after the bar opened, and then I went back to work."

He sounded so sure of where he'd been, but there was one huge problem. We'd seen him at the same time he thought he'd been at the bar.

I looked over at Alex to see if he'd picked up on that detail. After jotting down a word, he shot me a look of recognition and then looked back at Gerald. "Mr. Engels, there's a problem with that timeline. We saw you right after noon and you were at home sitting in your living room."

Shocked, he opened his eyes wide and shook his head in disbelief. "What? Are you sure? I could have sworn that's what I did."

Needing to know what he drank at McGuire's, I asked, "Gerald, what did you have at the bar?"

"A bourbon. My friend Marcus had told me about this new bourbon Joe had gotten—some gold label stuff—and after only having a taste the night before, I wanted to try it again."

Alex wrote down his answer and asked, "About Marcus. How did he get your car Monday night?"

"I told Marcus he could drive it home since I wasn't feeling too well and I didn't want to drive. I figured if I walked home and got some fresh air, I'd feel better. Marcus said he felt a little woozy too. I guessed we both caught a bug or something. Why? Did he have an accident?"

"Do you remember what else you had to drink or eat yesterday?" Alex asked, completely avoiding having to tell Gerald about his friend's death.

"I had a soda from my refrigerator right before noon and a couple cups of coffee and a blueberry muffin that morning for breakfast," he answered after thinking for a few moments.

"How can you remember that but not remember anything else about your day?" I asked, seizing on what I saw as an inconsistency in his answers.

Gerald smiled at me. "I'm afraid I'm a very boring person. You could ask me what I had any day and that would be my answer. Coffee and a blueberry muffin for breakfast and a soda right before noon. Every day like clockwork."

"Where did you have the coffee and muffin?" Alex asked. "At home or at a restaurant?"

"The Grounds. I like the taste of their coffee better than the stuff I make at home. What's this all about?" he asked with fear in his eyes.

Alex looked over at me with a look of resignation

and then cleared his throat as he told Gerald about his friend. "I'm sorry to tell you this, but Marcus Tyne was murdered Monday night and found in your car outside McGuire's. He'd been poisoned just like you were with antifreeze."

Gerald's expression filled with anguish. "Marcus? Dead? That can't be. I just saw him Monday night. Who would do this to him?"

"And to you," I said quietly, not wanting to upset him. The fact was, though, someone had poisoned him just like they had his friend.

Gerald's shock morphed into sadness, and he hung his head. "And to me," he said in a low voice.

"I know this is very upsetting, and I apologize, but any help you can give us will be appreciated. Do you know anything about where Marcus went Monday?"

"I think he was working—he worked with antiques like me—before I picked him up and we went to the Madison Diner for dinner and then to McGuire's."

Alex drew an exclamation point in the middle of the page he'd been taking notes on, a sign something had struck him as important. Folding the pad up, he put it back into his jeans pocket and pressed a smile onto his face.

"Thank you very much, Mr. Engels. I'm very happy to hear you'll be fine. You're a lucky man. If it wasn't for Poppy springing into action and taking care of you as I drove you here, you'd probably be dead."

His matter-of-fact way of telling him who had helped him while declaring how close he came to death made Gerald sit up straighter, and he after his brain had processed what Alex said, he looked over at me.

"Thank you, Poppy. I don't know how I'll ever

repay you for this," Gerald said with tears in his eyes.

"There's no need to repay me. Just get better, and the next time I see you in the bar, you can buy me a drink. Deal?"

A broad smile spread across his face. "Deal."

Before we left, Alex said, "We'll probably have more questions as the investigation continues, but I hope you feel better soon."

"If you have any more questions, you know where to find me," Gerald said with chuckle.

Alex and I walked out of the hospital room, and we barely made it to the elevator before I asked, "What was the exclamation point for in your notes? What's going on?"

His expression fell, and he pressed the button for us to go to the ground floor. Sighing, he said, "It's not just McGuire's we have to worry about now. It's The Grounds and the Madison Diner too."

"What do you mean?" I asked, not understanding.

The elevator jolted to a stop, and before the doors opened, he said, "Marcus Tyne may have been at all three places the day he died. That means he could have consumed the poison at any one of them, so all three will have to be checked."

A few people waited for us to exit, and as we walked out toward the squad car, I asked, "What does checked mean?"

"Donny and his people are going to have to get samples from each place, and I expect the health department is going to have to get involved too. We need to find out where Marcus Tyne and Gerald Engels were slipped that antifreeze."

I stopped at the car and took a deep breath. The

coroner and the health department getting involved in this case meant my worst fears were about to come true.

My father's bar would be shut down.

Alex tapped on the roof of the car and shook me from my terrible thoughts. Looking over at him, I saw the regret in his dark eyes.

"I still don't think you have to worry, Poppy. I know what you're thinking, though."

"That my father's going to be devastated?"

"I'm sure Donny's tests will prove beyond a shadow of a doubt that the antifreeze wasn't put in either man's drink at McGuire's."

"I hope you're right. I just don't know how it could have happened. My father said he worked behind the bar alone Monday night for the Cinco de Mayo party."

I thought back to him asking me to bartend that night. "If only I hadn't been so selfish and begged off helping him, a man might be alive now, Alex, and my father wouldn't have to have his business closed."

"Don't say that, Poppy. You're not to blame for anything that's happened. Your father would tell you the same thing. Let's get back to the station and get working on who might have wanted these two men dead."

I closed the door and slumped against the seat. "I just realized something, Alex."

As he started the engine, he looked over toward me and asked, "What's that?"

Staring out the front window, I closed my eyes. "It's not just my father who's going to suffer because of this case. Pam and Gerry at The Grounds depend on that business to live, and the people who run the Madison only have that restaurant. These aren't chains and big businesses, but mom and pop places. They can't afford to be shut down for days or weeks. This could really hurt them and my father and even the town."

Alex shifted the car into drive and began heading back to the police station. In that calm voice filled with strength I'd come to depend on, he tried to reassure me. "Then we better get this case solved quickly. Don't worry, Poppy. We'll do it."

It's not that I didn't believe him when he said that. I just worried that no matter how fast we worked to clear all three businesses, it might be too little, too late.

Chapter Nine

A LEX FOLLOWED ME into McGuire's and sat down at the end of the bar as I looked for my father in the stockroom. I found him piling boxes one on top of another, clearly keeping himself busy to take his mind off everything.

Sticking my head in, I said, "Dad, Alex and I are here to talk to you about the case. Do you have a minute?"

Lifting a box over his head, my father grunted as he stacked it up next to the ceiling. "Sure. Just give me a minute, okay?"

I headed back out to take a seat next to Alex and saw my father had done some serious cleaning behind the bar. Every night, he wiped the area down, so it wasn't like it was ever dirty at the start of the day, but now the whole thing looked clean enough to eat off of.

"My father's scared. I can tell," I whispered in Alex's ear.

As usual, he tried to calm my nerves. "Everything's going to be fine, Poppy. He shouldn't be worried."

The door to the stockroom closed, and my father appeared looking as chipper as ever. "I didn't expect to see you two here this morning. I don't really expect to see anyone much during the day."

"I just have a few questions, Joe. We've found a second person who was poisoned by antifreeze. A man named Gerald Engels. He says he was in here Monday night and then Tuesday afternoon. Do you recall that?"

My father took a deep breath and blew it out slowly, puffing out his cheeks. "The name doesn't ring a bell, but remember, I only really know my regulars."

"He seemed to know who I was, Dad, so I think he might have been in here at least a few times. A little shorter than Alex with light brown hair. Messy hair."

My description of Gerald Engels wasn't exactly the best. To be honest, although he knew me, I still didn't recall seeing him until that day at his house.

"That could be any one of a number of people, Poppy," my father said with a smile. "He said he's been in here a lot?"

"Not a lot, but he knew me from here, so I must have waited on him a few times for him to remember me."

Alex and my father each smiled, and turning toward me, Alex said, "I think you underestimate yourself. I wouldn't think he needed to see you more than once to remember you. You make quite an impression, Poppy."

Rolling my eyes, I tried not to laugh as my cheeks warmed from blushing at his compliment. "Well, regardless, he had been in here before. I haven't worked behind the bar since the middle of April, so that gives us something to go on."

"What do you mean something to go on?" my father asked, confused about why it would matter when Gerald Engels had been in the bar before that week.

"I just meant that might be helpful for you to

remember who he was. He works with antiques and lives out on Sycamore, if that jogs your memory any."

He shook his head and sighed. "It doesn't. I don't remember him being in here at any time."

Disappointment settled into Alex's expression. Frowning, he nodded. "Okay. Then I guess it's not worth much telling you he came in especially on Tuesday to have a taste of that gold label bourbon he'd tried the night before with Marcus Tyne."

Shrugging, my father seemed frustrated. "I wish I could help you more. I just got that bourbon in last week. It's good stuff."

Alex sighed his own frustration. "Do you remember if you served that to anyone else?"

My father nodded. "I might have. It was so busy in here on Monday that I can't be sure."

From behind me, I heard voices and turned to see three official looking men walk into the bar. They introduced themselves as from the Frederick County Health Department and then said the words I'd dreaded hearing since we first found out Marcus Tyne had been in McGuire's the night he died.

"Until the investigation is complete, your bar is going to have to be shut down, Mr. McGuire. We need to take samples of everything your customers may have eaten or drank in the past three days, so if you can cooperate, we'd appreciate it."

I watched as my father pointed to where the liquor was kept and explained about the beer and soda taps, all the while hating that he had to go through this. Alex silently pulled me off to the side as the men began their work.

"This is only until they test for antifreeze, Poppy.

After they find out it wasn't here that either man was poisoned, your father will be able to open back up," he said quietly as I stood there stunned.

"Look at him, Alex. He's terrified. They don't mean to look like the gestapo, but they come in here and announce they're closing him down until further notice, so of course he's scared."

As I said that, the health department workers thanked my father for his cooperation and told him they'd find him if they needed any more help. It wasn't a very subtle way of saying to go away and let them do their job.

He walked out from behind the bar, and I saw in his hunched shoulders the effect this had on him already. Taking his hand, I gave it a supportive squeeze and forced a smile. "This won't take long and then you'll be open again and watching baseball with your friends, Dad."

Nodding, he clearly didn't believe that any more than I did. "I'm okay, honey."

But I knew he was anything but okay.

"I'm going to see if there's anything in the stockroom they'll need. I'll give you a call later, okay, sweetheart?"

He kissed me on the cheek and walked away as I watched heartbroken for him. "I hate this. I hate feeling helpless. This can't ruin his business. I can't let that happen."

Alex said nothing for a few moments and then as he watched the three men begin to take samples from every open bottle, he said, "I'm more concerned with what the health department finds, to be honest. They aren't going to care if he didn't know the drinks were poisoned or not."

"He can't afford to pay a fine," I said, concerned about my father's welfare even more now.

Stepping in front of me so I couldn't watch what they were doing behind the bar, he said, "Poppy, if they find the antifreeze was in something here, it won't be just a fine he has to deal with. Then it will be criminal charges."

"No! Alex, that can't happen. My father would never hurt anyone like that. Never!"

How could he say something like that? There was no chance those men had been poisoned here. No chance.

I stood there staring at him, shocked he'd even thought that, as his phone began to ring. Answering it, he said, "Hang on, Donny. Let me put you on speaker."

Guiding me to the back of the bar, he placed the phone in the center of one of the tables, and we sat down to listen to what the coroner had to say. My heart sat in my throat waiting for any word that he knew where the antifreeze had come from.

"I just got the call that the health department didn't find any evidence of antifreeze anywhere at The Grounds or the Madison Diner," Donny said somberly. "I know a team is at McGuire's right now. If I hear anything, I'll be sure to let you know."

"Okay, thanks Donny," Alex said before ending the call.

We sat there in silence as the reality set in. What if they found something at McGuire's and thought my father intentionally tried to poison two people?

I saw my father coming toward where we sat and took a deep breath to calm myself. I couldn't let him see me fall apart or he'd know something was really wrong. I didn't want him to worry about this yet. Not yet. There was still a good chance that the tests would show there was no antifreeze here either and the two victims had been poisoned somewhere else.

At least that's what I prayed would be the case.

He stopped beside the table and looked down first at me and then Alex. "Those don't look like good faces. Did something happen?"

"Dad, don't worry. It's going to be okay," I quickly said before Alex could tell him the bad news.

He looked at Alex. "My daughter is trying to protect me. How about you give it to me straight?"

"It's nothing definitive, Dad."

Putting his hand up to stop me, he shook his head and directed his attention toward Alex. "I don't need you to sugarcoat it. You have a job to do, so what's going on?"

With sadness in his eyes, he told my father the truth, even as I struggled not to break down into tears.

"I just got a call about The Grounds and the Madison Diner. They found no traces of antifreeze at either one."

"Okay," my father said after taking a deep breath. "I guess that means we just wait for the results from here now."

"Joe, no matter what the tests say, I can promise you we'll find out who did this. I want you to know that."

All the energy seemed to leave my father's body, and his shoulders hunched even more. "I know, Alex. I know you will." Turning to look at me, he said, "I think once they leave, I'm going to go upstairs to try to get lost in a western and forget about this until I hear one way or the other. You can see yourselves out, right?"

Standing, I hugged him tightly and promised we'd

get to the bottom of this case quickly. "Don't worry, Dad. You and your regulars are going to be yelling at the Orioles before you know it."

He cradled my face in his hands like he did when I was a little girl and pressed a tiny kiss on my forehead. "I know, Poppy. It will be okay. I know I didn't put antifreeze in anyone's drink. The truth will come out, and I'll be back behind that bar like I have been for all these years. I'll talk to you later, okay?"

"Okay, Dad. Call me if you need anything. I mean, anything at all."

Even as he put on a brave face and promised he would call, I knew inside the fear of what those health department guys would find when they ran their tests was tearing him up. He walked away toward the stockroom again, and I collapsed into my chair, terrified at what would happen if they found antifreeze anywhere here in the bar.

Alex gently touched my arm and motioned toward the door. "Let me take you home, Poppy. There's no point in waiting here. As soon as Donny hears something, he'll call me, so we might as well wait at your house where you can relax."

I didn't argue, even though I wanted to. I wanted to scream at the top of my lungs that anyone who could even consider the idea of my father poisoning someone was out of their mind crazy. That my father would sooner hurt himself than see anyone else suffer.

But what was the use? I couldn't do a damn thing until those results came back and we had something to go on. Even knowing all three businesses had no hint of antifreeze would help because then we'd know something, at least.

Until then, I'd have to accept feeling helpless.

ALEX AND I sat quietly at my kitchen table, neither one of us wanting to talk about the case but having nothing else on our minds. Well, that's all I could think of. I had a feeling Alex was worried about me more than the case. He never got upset about cases. For him, they simply required the methodical approach he always used to get to the truth.

For this case, though, I wasn't sure I'd be able to do that. There was too much at risk for me.

"We must be missing something. We don't know much about Marcus or Gerald, and I bet the answer lies with them," I finally said, unable to stay silent any longer.

"I don't think you're wrong, but we can't investigate anything until we get those results, Poppy. Let's just wait for them to come back and then we can move on this."

Frustration overwhelmed me, and I exploded. "I can't relax. My father is being railroaded by someone, Alex! I can't relax!"

He reached across the table to hold my hand, but I pushed him away and jumped up from my seat to pace across the room. "You can't imagine what this feels like. My father needs me and I can't do anything for him because I'm sitting here trying not to dissolve into a puddle of tears like a little girl."

Immediately, I knew I'd said the wrong thing. The look of pain told me I'd been thoughtless again. Alex knew all too well what it felt like to be powerless when someone you love was hurt. How could I be so insensitive?

I sat down and held my hand out to touch his. "I'm so sorry. I didn't mean it like that. I know you know exactly how I feel."

He nodded, accepting my apology even as the hurt remained in his eyes. "I do, but I know it's different because he's your father. We're not giving up, Poppy. I just suggested taking a little time to get our heads clear for when we get the results of the health department's tests."

Standing, I walked around the table to wrap my arms around him and rested my head on his shoulder. "I'm sorry, Alex. I'm not being very professional with this case at all. I just want to clear my father's name and have everything go back to the way it used to be for him. That bar is all he has, and I don't know what he'll do if he loses it."

Alex kissed the top of my head and said sweetly, "That bar isn't all he has. He has you, Poppy. That's far more important than some building or some business."

I looked up at him and sniffled. "He's got the best cop in Sunset Ridge on the case too, so I'm not worried."

"Don't lose faith in us. I know this case hasn't been like our usual cases, but we've been hampered by the science with this one. Once all that is out of the way, we'll find out who's behind Tyne's murder and Engels' attempted murder and your father will be back to the way he's always been."

That was the first time he'd described what happened to Gerald Engels that way. "I guess that was attempted murder. I don't know why I hadn't been thinking of it like that all along."

Alex smiled and kissed me lightly. "Because you've

been thinking like a good daughter."

I stood up and walked over to the refrigerator to get a drink of iced tea. "Well, the time for that is over. Once Donny and the health department guys get the results, no matter what, I need to be thinking like a detective. My father's counting on us, and I'll be no use to you if I keep missing the big picture."

ALEX HAD RETURNED to the station to check out what connections there existed between our two victims other than their friendship and interest in antiques, so I decided to take a walk to clear my head.

All Thursday afternoon, the buzz around town centered on how McGuire's, The Grounds, and the Madison Diner would be closed until further notice. Rumors spread like wildfire that all three had been victims of a cyber-attack, some kind robbery spree, and the strangest one, that Diamanti's owners had committed some kind of sabotage to all three businesses to help bring more people into their restaurant.

Seeing people milling around The Grounds like zombies desperate for their caffeine made me chuckle until I remembered Pam and Gerry were losing money every minute they had to keep their doors closed, even though the coroner and health department had finished their inspections.

The police department didn't want to cause a panic by announcing that antifreeze had poisoned both Marcus Tyne and Gerald Engels, so the absence of the truth further added to the gossip around town. Mayor Sanders and his wife Christine quickly set up an impromptu garden party at their Victorian Row home for the citizens of Sunset Ridge, offering coffee and soft drinks along with sandwiches and donuts from the Savings King, a wise move to take the citizens' minds off what they imagined may be happening as they watched teams of health department workers parade in and out of each business along Main Street.

For everyone else, the whole event became just another reason for the people of Sunset Ridge to come together and share gossip about others, but even as I tried to remain strong, I worried about my father.

He'd always been the strong one I could lean on when things got tough, and now everything he'd worked for was under attack. His bar. His livelihood. His reputation in town. Alex was right that he had me, but those other things mattered to him. He'd spent much of his adult life as the owner of McGuire's, and one terrible act by someone hell bent on murdering Marcus Tyne and Gerald Engels could take everything away from him.

I couldn't help but wonder if the person responsible knew that and had chosen my father intentionally. Was my father meant to suffer too, or was he just a convenient patsy?

Chapter Ten

THE SOUND OF Alex's phone tore me out of a dream that disappeared from my memory almost as soon as I opened my eyes. He slowly slid his arm out from underneath me and reached over to the nightstand to answer the call as I mourned the loss of him holding me.

"Hello?" he said in a groggy voice while he scrubbed the sleep from his face.

Whoever had called didn't say much before Alex pressed END and dropped his phone back down onto the nightstand. He pursed his lips and made something like a grunting noise. If dissatisfaction had a sound, that was it.

"What's going on?" I asked as the last remnants of sleep faded from my brain.

"Nothing. Just work. I have to get to the station."

He slid out from underneath the covers and walked toward the bathroom before I could ask what they could possibly need him for at seven in the morning after he'd worked no less than fifteen hours a day all week. Throwing the covers off, I padded across the room and stopped to lean against the doorframe to the bathroom as he brushed his teeth.

"Do they think you wear an S on your chest, Alex?

You're working yourself too much."

Leaning over the sink, he spit out the toothpaste and finished rinsing before turning his head to look at me. "Working a lot isn't the same as doing a good job."

I saw the frustration written all over his face, so I took him into my arms and hugged him close. "Whatever's going on, it will be okay."

Secretly, I prayed that the call he'd gotten wasn't to tell him that the antifreeze had been found in anything the health department had taken from McGuire's. Was that why his mood had turned sour so suddenly?

I stepped back and searched his face for the answer to my unspoken question but found nothing to tell me one way or the other. Without a word, he kissed me tenderly on the lips and then pushed past me to finish getting ready to leave.

"Did they find something at McGuire's, Alex? Is that what's going on?"

He finished tying his shoes and sat up on the edge of the bed. Shaking his head, he said in a low voice, "No. That call was about Gerald Engels. He's taken a turn for the worse."

"What? The doctor said he'd be fine when we were there to see him. What happened?" I asked as my emotions began to overwhelm me. I barely knew Gerald, but something about saving his life made me feel like we'd been friends for years. The idea of him dying now made my heart contract.

"I don't know. I didn't want to tell you just in case…"

Alex let his sentence trail off, but I knew what he meant. "I can't believe he's not getting better. I want to come with you if you're going to see him."

He stood from the bed and walked over to me. "I'm not, Poppy. I'm just going to the station now. There's nothing for us to do at the hospital now. I'll call you later, okay?"

Hanging my head, I thought about how true that statement was. There was nothing we could do for Gerald. This time, we couldn't race through town or hold his hand and tell him everything thing would be okay.

"Poppy, look at me."

I lifted my head and did as Alex commanded. "You don't have to tell me. I know."

He cupped my chin in his palm and leaned in to plant a soft kiss on the center of my lips. Smiling, he said, "I just wanted to say I love you and I'll see you later."

Surprised since I'd expected him to once again remind me that I had done all a person could to help Gerald Engels, I smiled at hearing him say those words I so loved. "Oh. I thought you were going to say something else."

"What else is there to say after you wake up next to the woman you love?" he asked with a sexy grin. "But I don't want you to worry about Gerald. You did a great thing for him. Don't forget that."

"I know. I just can't believe he's having a setback. I was so sure he'd be okay now."

Opening his arms, Alex said, "Come here."

I fell into his embrace, loving the feel of his arms around me once again. I rested my head against his chest and whispered, "Please tell me there will be some good news today. Just a tiny bit of good is all I ask."

"I second that idea," he said against the top of my head before he kissed me again. "I better get going. I'll call you when I hear anything, Poppy."

"Okay." As he let me go, I hoped we'd both get our wish. "I'm going to be working from here today, so call me on my cell."

"Will do," he said with a smile and then disappeared down the stairs, leaving me standing in my bedroom debating whether I should drive two towns over to grab a coffee or make myself a cup at home.

The mere thought of getting ready for the world and having to drive that far for caffeine when I had some waiting for me one floor down made the choice easy. I was too loyal to Pam and Gerry at The Grounds anyway. If they weren't open, then my kitchen would be where I got my morning go-go drink from.

AN HOUR LATER, I had that much-needed caffeine coursing through my veins and energy to tackle my work for the day as I tried not to think about Gerald Engels a few miles away at Sunset Ridge Regional. What I didn't have was any interest since I had to write a piece on the upcoming Founders' Day celebration yet again. Year after year, I produced the same article because my boss had whittled down my options on what I could write about to one topic.

How wonderful the Founders' Day celebration was for the town.

Any deviation from that very narrow idea and the dreaded red pen came out. I'd tried a few years ago to inject some journalistic attempts at changing the narrative slightly, but he'd sliced and diced that article until all that was left was the basic cheerleading piece he thought was appropriate.

I hadn't even made the article realistic, never mind negative. I'd included some references to the history of the town's founding, but Howard said the past bored people. I'd tried to show him how the entire event was indeed historic in nature, but my explanation fell on deaf ears.

"No history, Poppy. Live in the now," he said, waving his arms for flair. As if empty platitudes meant anything to our discussion.

But I'd obeyed his orders, so now once again, my yearly Founders' Day Is Coming! Are You Ready? piece was due and I had to fight every instinct in my soul to write something interesting for *The Eagle*'s readers.

Not that Howard actually expected me to change much of anything from years past. I suspected he'd be just fine with me submitting the exact same article from last year as long as I made sure to change the dates of the event. As he liked to say every chance he could, "Facts are what keeps our newspaper a vital part of this town."

Facts. Clearly, my boss and I had different definitions of that word.

My fingers hovered over the letters on my keyboard, ready to do their job just as soon as my brain sent the signal for them to type the words. Nothing came to me, though, except the case of the antifreeze poisoning that had already killed one man and might result in the death of yet another soon.

Needing to know his condition, I called the hospital and asked for Dr. Carter. Thankfully, he remembered me, and even though I knew he legally couldn't tell me much, I had to ask.

"I heard Mr. Engels had taken a turn for the worse

this morning. I was just hoping to find out if he's doing better, doctor."

The phone fell silent for a long moment, and then he said, "I can't really say anything about his condition since you aren't technically the police and you aren't family, but I know you were the one who was responsible for getting him here in time the other day, so I can say this. We're still watching him and hoping for improvement. I hope you can understand."

The news didn't brighten my spirits like I'd hoped it would, but it could have been much worse. Dr. Carter had given me something to hope for, so I thanked him and said goodbye, even as I prayed his patient would begin to improve.

I hung my head in sadness at the thought that even after our attempt to save him, Gerald might still die. This case had gotten under my skin. Now I worried about him and my father, who at any moment could find out somehow antifreeze had gotten into one of the drinks at McGuire's.

My phone rang, tearing me out of my thoughts, and I answered it to find my boss already talking when I said hello.

"...the garden party in April. I loved it! The readers loved it! Do you know I got four letters telling me how much we should include more of that kind of writing in the paper, Poppy?"

"Hi, Mr. Fleming. How are you?" I asked, feeling like I'd come in at the middle of our conversation.

"I'm a little worried, to be honest. Do you know why that is?"

I hated when he did that. Like he was a professor and he thought quizzing me was the way to talk to me.

"I'm not sure. You were talking when I answered my phone, so I'm wondering if I missed you saying what's making you so worried."

Yes, there was a touch of smart ass in that answer, but I knew he wouldn't pick up on it. He'd already moved on to what he'd say next as soon as the last word of his question left his mouth.

"The police blotter, Poppy. Why didn't you include anything about Marcus Tyne being found dead outside of your father's bar? *Eagle* readers deserve to know, Poppy."

He sounded like the drool was practically spilling out of his mouth at the mere thought of a salacious story for his beloved police blotter.

"It's an active investigation, Mr. Fleming. I can't release any information without the approval of the police while the case is still in progress. If I did, they wouldn't let me know another thing and your police blotter would become a weekly list of parking violations, if I was even that lucky."

A grunting noise came through the phone followed by Howard conceding I had a valid point. "I see what you mean. Okay, but as soon as that investigation is over, I want all the pertinent details in the blotter. The people of Sunset Ridge deserve to know the facts, and it isn't enough to have a headline or two in the paper. The police blotter is the official record of this town, Poppy."

Somehow I doubted that to be true, but there was no point in debating the issue with him. Better to just agree and hope to be left alone.

"Will I have your Founders' Day lead-up piece on time?" he asked, switching topics as I'd hoped.

"Yes, sir. I just finished putting the final touches on

it," I lied.

"Is it as good as always?" he asked.

I knew what that really meant. Was it similar to the past articles he'd approved?

With as much enthusiasm as I could muster for selling out, I said, "Yes, it is. You're going to love it. It's just what you want."

"Excellent. Just excellent. That's good to hear, Poppy."

The way he said that I couldn't help but imagine him sitting behind his desk and steepling his fingers as he spoke. Chuckling, I said, "I better go now, Mr. Fleming. I have some work to do and I want to catch up with the police chief today too."

Howard loved to hear I spoke to Derek, as if that was some monumental achievement. I'd know the guy since grade school. I could likely just show up at his house in my bathrobe begging for a cup of sugar in the middle of the night and he wouldn't blink an eye. But to my boss, speaking to the police chief meant something entirely different, apparently.

"Oh, okay," he said reverently. "I won't keep you then. Please tell him how wonderful we all think he's doing."

"I will, sir. I'm sure Chief Hampton will appreciate that."

"Fine then. I'll see you in your office soon?"

That was Howard's passive-aggressive way of telling me he wanted me working in my office more often. I found it strange that someone who could be so unrelentingly aggressive on some issues turned into the kind of boss who didn't feel comfortable telling me to come into the office.

I used it to my advantage, though, so I had no reason to complain.

"Absolutely. I'll see you bright and early Monday, Mr. Fleming."

His happiness came through the phone loud and clear. "Wonderful! And Poppy, I want you to think of some ideas for a piece on the antiquing craze in the area. That man's death made me realize we really should do something on that. I think our readers will love it."

And right then and there he returned to the unfeeling man I'd so gotten used to in the past few years. Nothing like capitalizing on another person's untimely demise.

"Yes, sir. I'm on it."

My boss's phone call brought my mind back to the case, and I looked at the time to see only an hour had passed since the last time I checked. With every minute that ticked by, the chances that my father would be implicated in this crime became more and more likely, at least in my worried mind.

I couldn't stay cooped up in my house all day waiting for Alex to call with the results of those tests or I'd go stir crazy. I needed to do something to take my mind off this case, but what?

Whenever my mother could, she liked to go on picnics. She claimed there was no way anyone could be in a bad mood sitting on a blanket spread out on the ground eating things like fried chicken and cole slaw. Looking out the window, I saw a perfect day for a picnic. I could grab some food, a thermos of iced tea, and a blanket and then all I'd have to do was convince Alex to join me.

I just hoped it worked and I could get my mind off

waiting for those test results from the health department and news from the hospital.

Armed with all the fixings necessary for a picnic lunch, I grabbed my purse and headed out the back door only to find Jared waiting on my porch with two cups of coffee in his hands. With a smile, he extended his arm to give me one, but I shook my head.

"What are you doing here, Jared? Why are you lurking on my back porch in the middle of the day?" I asked sharply.

Giving me the puppy dog eyes that had always worked on me when we were together, he said, "I hoped you'd accept my apology."

"You didn't do anything wrong the other day that you have to apologize for. I really need to get going. I have plans."

He stepped in front of me to block my path and smiled. "I meant I really wanted to apologize for what I did. You know, with Cicely. I'm sorry, Poppy. I was a fool and never should have left you."

The picnic basket suddenly felt like a lead weight in my hand, so I rested it on the arm of an Adirondack chair and corrected him. "You didn't just leave me. You cheated on me with some tart from the grocery store at the very bed and breakfast you were supposed to be checking out for our honeymoon and then ran off with that Savings King chick Cicely leaving me to cancel our wedding."

He actually looked like hearing the laundry list of his offenses bothered him. With a sheepish look, he said, "I know. I was stupid. I want to make it up to you."

Then before I could refuse, he touched my arm and looked into my eyes in that way that never failed to make me melt inside all those years ago. "Let me take you out to dinner tonight. It can be like old times. I know how much you like Diamanti's."

But that was then and this was now, and I wasn't doing any melting as he tried to convince me to do what he wanted. I couldn't deny Jared was still so very smooth and before Alex came along I might have fallen for his charm, but no more.

"I don't think Alex would appreciate me going to dinner with my ex, but thanks. You don't have to do anything, Jared. I'm happy now, so I wish you well. Right now, I need to go and meet my boyfriend for lunch, so have a good day."

Jared stood staring at me with his mouth hanging open, likely shocked that I didn't fall at his feet as I always had before. He didn't get a chance to say another thing before I bounded down the stairs to my car. Throwing the picnic basket in the back seat, I sped out of there as quickly as possible so I didn't have to deal with any more of his attempts to woo me back.

For the first time in days, a tiny part of me felt incredible. If it weren't for the fact that my father remained in the middle of a murder investigation and the man I helped to save barely clung to life, it would have been a terrific day.

I found Alex hunched over his laptop scowling at what he saw on the screen. Flush from my personal victory and hoping to put the terrible events of the past few days out of my brain for at least a few minutes, I swung the picnic basket from my arm and tried to tempt my workaholic cop boyfriend to tear himself away from his desk.

"There's a picnic waiting for us, Alex, so what do

you say to lunch in the park near Candy's Cuts?"

"I really should be doing work," he said as he leaned away from his computer, looking exhausted at only noon.

Clearly, I'd have to put more effort into persuading him.

"It's a beautiful day and a beautiful woman is dangling a picnic basket in front of you, so you have to give in and go with her. You need a break from all this as much as I do, so come on."

Slowly, a smile spread across his lips. Nodding, he stood and came around his desk to take the basket from me. "I can't say no to you, Poppy. You're too convincing."

Squeezing his forearm, I teased, "I am, so let's go and for the next thirty to sixty minutes we'll enjoy a nice lunch on a blanket on the ground on this beautiful May day and pretend everything's perfectly fine."

He looked down at me, arching one eyebrow skeptically. "Is everything okay, Poppy? You seem different."

"I am different, but I'll tell you about that at another time. Right now, that beautiful day is waiting, so let's go."

Alex didn't press me for what had changed to make me different, thankfully. I'd give him all the details about how I'd finally seen karma at work with Jared later, but for now, I just wanted to enjoy lunch with the man I loved.

Chapter Eleven

SEATED ON THE white and blue checkered tablecloth I'd spread out on the ground under a large oak tree, we enjoyed the warmth of the beautiful spring day as we ate our ham and cheese sandwiches I'd packed after a quick check of the refrigerator showed me I didn't have any chicken to make my mother's famous friend chicken recipe. A few yards away, a little boy pulled clumps of grass up and tossed them behind him as his mother watched.

"This was a good idea, Poppy," Alex said. Pouring himself a paper cup of iced tea, he added, "Just what I needed after spending hours in the office."

"When you aren't even supposed to be working," I said, giving him a look that conveyed I disapproved with how much time he spent at the station.

Alex leaned back on his hands and shook his head. "I didn't feel right not doing something on this case, even though we're stuck in a holding pattern until those damn test results come back."

Although I wanted to remind him that actually being at the station meant he was, in fact, doing something, I sensed he wouldn't take my teasing well, so I asked, "Did you find anything that could help us understand what's going on?"

"No," he answered with a heavy sigh. "Other than that problem last year with Marcus Tyne, neither man seems to have been on the police radar or anyone else's, for that matter. It's like they suddenly appeared at McGuire's Monday night just in time for everything to happen. I hate to say it, but I'm baffled."

"And those test results aren't going to solve that," I said before taking a drink of tea.

"I know. All that will do is tell us where they may have ingested the antifreeze, although if it's at your father's bar, that's going to make it twice as hard since he had all those people there that night."

I liked that he used the word if when he referred to the bar. The possibility that the health department's tests would likely show Marcus Tyne and Gerald Engels drank the poison at McGuire's made my heart skip a beat every time I thought about it, but I knew it was just a matter of time before I may have to deal with that reality and what it would do to my father.

Out of the corner of my eye, I saw Derek walking toward us. He wore a stern expression, which made me wonder if Alex was about to be dressed down for spending time in the park when he should be back at the station working on the case. If Derek planned to give him a hard time, I planned to mention the fact that Alex wasn't even scheduled this morning if he didn't say it first.

"Enjoying the park, you two?" the chief said as he stopped at the edge of the tablecloth and looked down at us.

"Hi, Derek. Fancy meeting you here," I said with a smile, ready to get serious if I needed to.

He smiled and shook his head like I'd said something crazy. "I hear you saw your ex since he's back in town, Poppy. I would have mentioned something to you if I thought he planned to go anywhere near you. I hope you know that."

Surprised at his admission that he'd spent time with Jared, I said without missing a beat, "I would hope so, Derek. I mean, the guy might be a good guy to you, but what he did to me, one of your friends, wasn't okay at all."

Derek understood my jab and nodded, as if to say he knew he deserved that. Turning to face Alex, he said, "I remembered something I think might be helpful to your case. Mind if I crash the party?"

"Sure. Join us. I think we still have some iced tea left," Alex said as he moved over to let his chief sit down between us.

I opened the picnic basket and took out the last ham and cheese sandwich. Handing it to Derek, I said, "Please, eat something too."

He looked down at the wax paper square I held in my hand and then looked up at me. "Did you make this?"

Dropping it in front of him, I said, "Yes. Don't act so surprised. It's a sandwich, Derek, not duck a l'orange."

"I'm just not used to this Poppy McGuire. You're practically Betty Crocker."

Alex chuckled at Derek's ribbing of me, but that was okay. I could handle the chief.

"It's a sandwich. Don't get yourself all turned around. Ham, cheese, and mustard on bread is nothing that incredible. I have far more impressive skills you never notice."

As Derek stuffed his face with the sandwich I'd made for our picnic, Alex quickly said, "On that note, let's talk about what you remembered."

"I think he's occupied right now," I joked as Derek tried to swallow the giant bite of ham and cheese he'd just taken.

Downing a big gulp of iced tea, he said, "I knew you'd ask me something as soon as I started eating. Okay, I remembered something from the Tyne-Touring case this morning in the shower that I think might be useful. She was seeing someone else when she was seeing Marcus Tyne, a guy named Frank Mitchell. Interesting thing is, Frank is a mechanic over in Millville."

Alex and I looked at each other like we'd just heard the answer to the sixty-four thousand dollar question. "A mechanic?" I asked as he jotted down the man's name and details in his notepad.

"A mechanic," Derek answered with a grin. "Mechanics work with antifreeze, don't they?"

"They do," Alex said as he stood up and began cleaning up the remains of our picnic.

I tugged on the tablecloth to get Derek to move, but he waved me off. "Leave it. I'm going to enjoy a few minutes of this beautiful day. Let me know what you find out."

The sight of him lounging out in the middle of the day in the park dressed in his black police uniform made me smile. Derek certainly knew how to handle the stress of his job the right way.

"Okay. I'll get the tablecloth later. Do you want us to leave the thermos? I think there might be some iced tea left."

Alex handed it to me, but Derek shook his head.

"No, I'm good. I'm just going to sit here and watch that kid tear up the grass."

I turned to see the little boy had cleared out a patch of lawn nearly a foot wide in front of him and wondered if having a policeman watching him now would end his destruction of the park since nothing his mother had said had done it.

"Try not to scare the kid to death, Derek," I said as we began walking to the car. "You don't want to scar him for life."

He didn't bother answering me, instead choosing to lean back on his elbows and close his eyes to bask in the sun of the early May day.

AFTER A FEW phone calls between Alex and Craig back at the station, we learned that Frank Mitchell worked as a mechanic at Millville Motors. We rolled up to the garage that sat at the end of a dead end street eerily named Cemetery Street despite the fact that a quick glance around the area showed no cemetery anywhere nearby.

The building, an old cinderblock structure with three garage doors in the front, had cars parked haphazardly all around it. Some looked like they'd been there since the disco era. I saw a rusted pale blue Ford Pinto with black and white fuzzy dice hanging from the rearview mirror parked alongside an old black pickup truck that resembled something Dorothy's uncle drove in the Wizard of Oz.

"No cemetery for people but maybe the name refers to this junkyard they've got here," Alex said with a smile as I pointed at the cars parked on the side of the building.

"Weird. It's like the original kind of hoarding. Guys with cars. I don't get it."

"That's because you're not a car person. The Pinto isn't much to think about, unless you want a car that catches on fire and explodes, but I bet there's a gem somewhere in the middle of that mess," he said as he craned his neck to see further into the lot of dead cars.

"You're not like that, though. You've got your Mustang, but it isn't like you keep cars parked on your front lawn and work on them every so often."

Alex chuckled. "I could be that kind of guy, I think. It would just have to be in the backyard."

I stopped as we reached the door to the building, horrified at the thought of a junkyard anywhere near any house I lived in. "You're kidding, right?"

With a wink, he moved around me and opened the door without answering my question. I filed away my concern about his car hoarding tendencies and walked into the garage to find the junkyard outside was nothing compared to the mess inside.

"Whoa," I mumbled as I stopped short near the door and turned to look at Alex. "How does anyone work here? Do they just drop them from the ceiling into their spot every morning?"

Everywhere auto parts lay strewn across the floor. Next to the outer walls, parts sat in boxes stacked on top of one another, some piles ten and more high. Alex pointed toward where a makeshift path had been created and motioned for me to follow him.

We stepped carefully around car parts until we reached the middle bay where a big burly man in greasy brown coveralls and a dingy white t-shirt stood under a car perched above his head. He didn't notice us approach him, and as we moved closer to where he worked, he cursed loudly and threw a wrench down onto the floor.

"Son of a bitch!" he barked as the tool went skidding into a nearby pile of auto parts.

Alex cleared his throat to alert him to our presence and said, "We're looking for Frank Mitchell. Can you tell me where we can find him?"

The man wiped his greasy hands on his chest and then touched his unkempt beard as he sneered at us. "You're looking at him. What do you want?"

I couldn't help notice his fingernails. Filthy like he hadn't washed his hands thoroughly in ages, they instantly made me think his thick fingers and big hands could hurt someone. Maybe even kill someone.

Alex flashed his badge and told him who we were like he always did, except he added where we were from this time since we were in Millville. Frank Mitchell's response set the tone for what I had a feeling would be a difficult discussion.

Shrugging, he shot Alex a look of disgust and then turned to look at me with an even worse look, like he detested my mere presence there. Then he bent down to pick up the wrench he'd slammed into the floor and returned to working on the exhaust of the car above him.

"We're here about the death of Marcus Tyne. Do you know anything about that, Mr. Mitchell?" Alex asked far more politely than the man deserved.

Frank's hands stilled and he turned to look at us, his eyebrows lifted in surprise. "So that son of a bitch is dead? I guess what they say is true. What goes around comes around. Good."

With that, he returned to twisting the wrench and mumbled something about Karma.

"You don't seem very broken up about it. Is that because Angela Touring was dating Marcus at the same time she was dating you?"

Frank sensed the edge I heard in Alex's question. His entire body stiffened and then he slammed the wrench into the frame of the car. "If you're saying she was cheating on me, you got it wrong. I left her, so take your theories and stick them—"

I cut him off. "So she was cheating on Marcus with you?"

Furious at what I said, he barked, "Angela wasn't cheating on anyone. I left her, so your timeline is wrong, lady. She was free to date whoever she wanted to. She wasn't my problem anymore. She was his."

Jotting notes in his tablet, Alex asked, "Where were you all day Monday, Mr. Mitchell?"

Calm again, Frank shook his head. "Right here. All day. Until around nine at night. So now that you know that, you can leave."

"Is there anyone who can vouch for that time frame?" Alex pressed.

Frank pointed the wrench toward the office a few feet away. "My boss. He'll tell you exactly what I just told you, so go talk to him."

And with that, Frank Mitchell turned away and the interview ended. I wanted to ask more questions, but Alex stopped me with a gentle touch to my arm.

I followed him to the office and said, "I had a few more things to ask him. Why did you stop me?"

Alex stopped outside the office door and shook his

head. "There was no point, and I didn't want you to get hurt. Frank there is a bit volatile, and I don't relish the idea of fighting him because he's a hothead."

"You underestimate me," I said with a smile. "He's big, but I bet he's slow compared to someone my size. He'd probably get tangled up in car parts and fall right on his ugly face. And then you'd get to arrest him."

Alex rolled his eyes. "You're going to give me cardiac arrest talking like that. How about we avoid as much violence as possible, Poppy? I like you in one piece, just the way you are. My getting to arrest him wouldn't make up for what may happen to you."

He was so cute. I winked at him, charmed by his chivalrous attitude. "Always my hero. Okay, we'll do things your way. I'm not a big fan of broken bones anyway, although I do have to admit I like the image of Frankie boy there taking a tumble onto a floor full of metal parts."

After knocking and hearing a man yell for us to come in, we walked into a smaller version of the garage area we'd just left. An old wooden desk sat back toward the wall, surrounded by more boxes of auto parts. Only the space in front of the desk remained free of the piles of parts, but there were no chairs for anywhere to sit like in most offices. We met Frank's boss, an equally big and burly man named Ralph Burns. I expected him to be like his employee in temperament too, but to my surprise, he only resembled Frank on the outside.

"Mr. Burns, I'm Officer Alex Montero and this is Poppy McGuire, my partner. We're here about a murder that took place in Sunset Ridge. I need to know if you can verify what your employee Mr. Mitchell said about when he worked this Monday."

Ralph Burns spun around in his chair to grab a time card from a shelf behind him and set it down on the desk in front of him. "I can't imagine Frank being involved in anything like murder. He's just not that kind of guy."

Neither Alex nor I replied to his defense of the angry man we'd met a few minutes earlier. For me, I'd already begun formulating a theory that included Frank Mitchell as the main suspect in our case. The guy clearly had anger management issues, and just the mention of Angela Touring had made him practically foam at the mouth.

Ralph scanned the time card and then looked up at us. "He punched in at seven am and didn't punch out until nine pm."

Alex wrote down the times and looked at him in disbelief. "Is that a normal workday? It seems like a long time to spend under a car."

Ralph nodded. "It is. He's got house and car payments now, so he's working all the overtime he can."

"Are you sure he didn't leave this building during that whole fourteen hour period?" Alex asked as I replayed Ralph's answer in my mind.

"Yep," Ralph said with a nod.

I jumped on his use of the word now in regards to Frank's mortgage and car loan. "What do you mean now he has those payments? Why does he have to work so much?"

"Because his soon-to-be wife likes nice things," he answered matter-of-factly.

Both Alex and I looked at each other with intense curiosity, and Alex asked, "Who is his fiancé?"

"Angela. Angela Touring. They're supposed to get married in July, assuming they don't break up again."

As Alex feverishly jotted down Ralph's answers, I asked, "When was the last time they broke up?"

Ralph sighed like the answer he had to give was something exhausting to him personally. "Saturday. He came in here screaming and yelling about her wanting things she shouldn't want that night. When I saw him on Monday morning, he was no better. Still ranting on about how Angela thought she was someone better than who she really was. I think things are better now because on Tuesday afternoon he was back to talking like they were two bugs in a rug."

I nudged Alex as he finished writing and whispered, "Two bugs in a rug. Did you see an engagement ring on her hand the other day?"

He didn't answer my question. Instead, he thanked Ralph Burns before hurrying me out of the building to the car, practically pushing me out the door. I suspected he didn't want me asking Frank's boss any more questions, but why?

"What's with the bum's rush?" I asked after the door to the garage closed behind us.

"Nothing. Get in the car. We have somewhere to go," he said, again rushing me.

I did as he commanded, but he needed to give me more than nothing as an answer. When he didn't say anything else within a few minutes, I turned toward him and said, "So we're sticking with nothing. Okay. Want to share with the class where we have to go?"

"I'd rather hear what you think of everything that happened back there, to be honest, Poppy."

"Well, for starters, I think Frank Mitchell could easily kill someone considering his temper. He's a nasty guy, and having a woman cheat on him wouldn't sit well with someone like him."

"Agreed," Alex said in a low voice as he turned onto the road back to Sunset Ridge. "Definitely not a nice guy. I'm not sure he's a murderer, but I wouldn't be surprised if he was, although I can see him beating the hell out of someone rather than poisoning them."

"Hey, why didn't you ask about the antifreeze while we were there? You didn't ask Frank or his boss."

The corners of Alex's mouth hitched up slightly into a sly smile. "Because I didn't want to tip them off so they'd have time to get rid of evidence."

"Why would they have time to do that?" I asked, confused.

Alex looked over at me, tilting his head and giving me a look that said he thought I should know the answer to that question. "Because I didn't have a search warrant. If I brought up the antifreeze and couldn't do anything about it other than ask questions, if Frank's guilty, he'd get rid of any evidence as soon as we left."

"Ah. Okay. So are you thinking Frank is a suspect?"

"Maybe. I'm guessing you think he is?"

I had to laugh. Of course I did.

"Yep. I think Angela and Frank both had something to do with Marcus Tyne's murder. I'm guessing when she and Frank broke up over the weekend, she turned to Marcus and Frank found out."

Alex turned the car toward Angela Touring's house and smiled. "Then let's see if we can find out if you're right."

Chapter Twelve

MY HUNCH ABOUT Angela and Frank seemed entirely plausible, even if Alex appeared skeptical. That's just the kind of detective he was. I respected that, but for me, I preferred to go with my gut.

That it meant jumping to conclusions drove him crazy, although he'd been getting better with my flights of fancy in the past few months. It was true they often didn't pan out, but nobody got arrested simply on my hunches, so it wasn't like anyone got hurt.

Except my ego every so often when Alex chose to rub it in that my guess as to who the guilty party was turned out to be completely misguided. That didn't matter to me, though. Each of our cases served as another chance for me to hone my detecting skills, so making mistakes didn't faze me in the least.

And if Alex had a good laugh at my theories, at least it meant I got to see him happy.

We pulled up to Angela Touring's house and saw her car in the driveway. "Good, she's home. I want to find out about this engagement of hers to Frank Mitchell," Alex said as he shifted the car into park.

"I wonder why she didn't mention that the first time we spoke to her," I said as we walked up the sidewalk to her front door.

"And why didn't she have on an engagement ring," Alex added.

He knocked on the front door as I tried to imagine Angela Touring with Frank Mitchell in any kind of romantic way. The thought boggled my mind. One look inside her house told anyone with working eyes that she liked her surroundings neat and tidy. I couldn't fathom how someone like that could tolerate those filthy fingernails of Frank Mitchell's and that disgusting beard of his.

I shivered just thinking about him putting his hands on a woman, and Alex turned to look at me. "You okay?"

"Just thinking about Angela and Frank together. Yuck."

"Yuck?" he asked with a chuckle. "That doesn't sound very professional, Poppy."

I shrugged. "Okay, how does revolting sound? Repulsive? Nauseating?"

As he considered the alternatives I'd offered to describe the two of them in bed together, Angela opened the door and stared out at us with a frightened look in her eyes. "Hello, Officer Montero. This really isn't a good time."

Alex opened the screen door slightly to let her know we wouldn't be run off that easily. "This won't take long, Miss Touring. We just want to clarify a few things we've found in our investigation so far."

She hesitated for a moment and then finally relented. "Okay, come in, but I am in a hurry."

We walked into her spotlessly neat house and followed her to the dining room where we'd all sat together the last time we were there. Beside the table were two large pieces of black luggage and a smaller matching bag.

So that's why she was in a hurry.

"Are you leaving to go somewhere?" Alex asked with a glance down at the bags.

"I just need to get away for a little while," she said sheepishly, avoiding meeting either of our gazes.

"Is this because you're in mourning over Marcus Tyne's death?" he asked sharply.

Angela reacted to the mention of her ex-boyfriend's untimely demise the same way she had after we'd first told her about his murder. Covering her face with her hands, she hung her head and ran out of the room.

This time we weren't buying that act, though.

"I'm betting she thinks we're going to leave like last time," I said in his ear as we both looked down the hallway toward the room she'd run to.

"I bet, but those crocodile tears don't have the same power the second time that they had the first," he said with a confident grin.

We waited a good five minutes before she returned to the dining room, and the surprised look on her face said she hadn't expected us to still be there after her performance. She stammered out, "Oh...I thought...I assumed you had left. I'm sorry...I just get so upset when I think about poor Marcus."

Alex remained silent and studied her, so I took my opportunity to question her. "Yeah, about that. We just met your fiancé, Frank Mitchell, who by the way didn't seem too broken up about poor Marcus's death. I guess since you cheated on him with our victim that's to be expected, though. Congratulations on your engagement.

He's a real prize."

Angela's eyes opened wide at hearing we found out about her and Frank Mitchell being together. "Engagement? What are you talking about?"

Shaking his head at her tired act, Alex said, "There's no need to pretend, Miss Touring. We know all about your love triangle and how you and Frank are scheduled to marry in July, assuming you don't break up before then."

I watched as Alex explained the charade was over, but Angela didn't seem to understand she didn't have to pretend to be surprised anymore. In fact, if anything, she grew more confused than shocked as she listened to him.

"Frank and I aren't engaged. I don't know where you heard that from, but we're the furthest thing from getting married in July or any other time, for that matter. We broke up months ago after he found out I was cheating on him with Marcus."

Alex turned his head to look at me and raised his eyebrows. Her story intrigued him as much as it did me. "So if you two aren't engaged, why is Frank telling his boss that's the reason why he needs the overtime? We heard he had bills to pay and a house to afford for his fiancé, which his boss claimed was you."

Unexpectedly, Angela burst out laughing. Shaking her head, she said, "Frank work overtime? Are you kidding? Frank hates work. He's one of the laziest men I've ever met. He's a seven to three-thirty guy every day he works. In all the time I've known him, he's never spent a minute more than he has to at that garage. Who fed you this nonsense?"

"Ralph Burns, his boss," I offered as Alex began taking notes on Angela's claims. "He raved about how much Frank wants to work and takes overtime anytime he can get it."

Angela huffed a derisive snort and rolled her eyes. "He's his brother. Of course, he's going to say nice things about him when the police come calling."

"Ralph is Frank's brother?" I asked, remembering how similar they looked to each other even as I tried to wrap my brain around what Angela just said.

I saw Alex write *boss and brother same?* in his notes and look up to listen to Angela's answer.

"Half-brother is more correct," Angela explained. "Ralph was his father's first child and Frank was the bastard he had with a woman he cheated on his wife with. Same father but different mothers. Still brothers, though, not that they are alike in more than a handful of ways."

"Do they get along?" Alex asked.

Angela smiled. "Well enough for Ralph to lie to the cops about Frank. Trust me. There's no way the man I knew would be caught dead working any more than he absolutely had to. It was one of the many things about Frank I grew to hate."

Frank Mitchell's surliness, the unkempt mess of a beard he wore on his face and wiped his hands on, and those disgusting fingernails certainly must have been in the top ten list of those things she hated. His violent temper could be added to that hit list too. In fact, I couldn't think of one thing about Frank Mitchell that could appeal to any woman, much less someone like Angela Touring.

"What about how nasty he can be?" I asked, much to Alex's surprise.

He furrowed his brow and gave me a sideways

glance, but I didn't regret asking the question. If anyone knew Frank Mitchell that way, I suspected it was the woman who had dated him and cheated on him. I had a feeling she'd seen every shade of nastiness from him in their time together.

Alex opened his mouth to say something, but Angela cut him off. "I know all about Frank's meanness. He's not a nice man when he's angry. Trust me."

"So where are you going and why, if it isn't because you and Frank Mitchell just broke up on Saturday, like Ralph told us?" Alex asked.

A terrified look crossed Angela's face. "It's not safe here for me. If Marcus was murdered, then it's just a matter of time before Frank does the same to me."

Her admission surprised Alex. "Are you saying you think Frank Mitchell killed Marcus Tyne? Why? You two broke up months ago. Why would he wait until now to get his revenge?"

"Who else would want to hurt Marcus? He was a gentle soul everyone loved. Well, everyone but Frank."

"Has he threatened you?" I asked her, for the first time believing the possibility that she hadn't been involved in killing Marcus with Frank.

Angela shook her head and frowned. "No, but that's doesn't matter. I know Frank. He's a dangerous man."

"We have no record of him ever threatening you before," Alex said as he flipped through his notes to get to the information Craig had given him over the phone on our way to Millville Motors. "In fact, we have no record of him ever being charged with any violent crimes of any sort."

I heard the suspicion in his voice loud and clear. He didn't believe her story. She knew it too. But I believed her. That crying act had been just that, but the fear I saw in her eyes told me she was truly terrified of something or someone, and I had a strong feeling it was Frank Mitchell.

"He killed Marcus. I know it as sure as I know my name. He told me he would. When I broke up with him to go with Marcus, his exact words were, 'Enjoy yourself while you can because he's not long for this world, Angela.' I knew what he meant."

"It just seems odd that someone so easily angered could put off getting revenge on another man for months," Alex said. "I didn't get the sense that Frank Mitchell lived by the idea that revenge is a dish best served cold. What would have caused him to kill Marcus Tyne now? You two have been broken up for almost as long as he waited, if he in fact killed him."

Angela sighed and sank down into one of the dining room chairs. Her shoulders sagged, and I sensed she was holding back tears. What had Alex said to deflate her like that?

"Miss Touring, if there's something we should know, you need to tell us. Why would Frank Mitchell want to kill Marcus Tyne now instead of all those months ago when he threatened him?"

She sighed again. "That time when I called the police on Marcus? He didn't do anything to me. That's why I didn't want to press charges when the officer came out to talk to me."

"Okay. So why did you break up with him then if he didn't attack you?" I asked as Alex and I waited to hear what could come next in this story.

Angela looked up at me and took a deep breath. She let it out in a rush and said, "Because it was Frank who hit me. I was afraid to tell the police who really did it, but my sister pressured me into calling you guys. I knew what would happen if I told them Frank gave me that black eye. He'd kill me. I was sure of it. So I lied and said Marcus was the one who did it."

"And then he broke up with you because of it," I said quietly, suddenly feeling sorry for Angela Touring.

"Yeah," she admitted with a nod. "I apologized for days, but he couldn't forgive me for lying to the police about him. I told him I didn't have a choice, but he wouldn't hear it. And then when he and I broke up, I thought Frank had gotten his revenge, but that wasn't enough for him. I should have known that. He was too angry when he found out about Marcus and me to just be satisfied with us breaking up."

Alex took this all in and finally said, "If Frank did this to Marcus, you running away isn't going to stop him if he wants to hurt you. Do you have family or friends who could stay with you? Your sister?"

Angela's eyes flashed the terror she felt at his suggestion. "And put her in harm's way? No way. If I stay in this house, I'm a sitting duck, along with anyone else who's here with me. I don't want anyone else to get hurt if Frank decides to look for me, so where am I supposed to go?"

A thought suddenly popped into my brain. "What about the Hotel Piermont? He won't suspect you'll be there, will he?"

"I've never been there, so no, I don't think so."

Alex didn't look too sure about my idea, but I knew she'd be okay there, at least for a few days until we solved the case and hopefully had Frank Mitchell behind bars. "Good. Then it's settled. We'll give you a ride to the Hotel Piermont and you can stay there until it's safe for you to come home."

"But what if he finds me there?" Angela asked, still uncertain merely hiding out at the local hotel would be enough to keep her safe.

"He won't. You just said it yourself. You've never been there, and there'd be no reason for you to stay at a hotel just a short ways away from your house. You'll leave your car here, and for all he'll know, you could be enjoying a few days in D.C. or halfway around the world. As long as he can't find you here, you'll be good."

My reasoning seemed to convince her, even if it didn't have the same effect on my partner, and she picked up her bags to leave. "Okay, but please tell me you're going to get him on Marcus's murder. He didn't deserve an ending like that."

I grabbed one of the large suitcases and headed toward the door. "Don't worry. We'll get him. He's not going to get away with poisoning two men."

From behind me, I heard Angela say, "Two men? Frank killed two people?"

Before I could answer her, Alex said, "No, just one. The other man lived."

"Oh," she said sadly. "I'd hate to know two people suffered because of Frank's rage."

We got her and her luggage settled into the back seat of the police cruiser, and closing the car door, Alex leaned over the roof and gave me a look that said he still wasn't sure this was a good idea.

"I don't think this is exactly what Derek intended when he told us about Frank, Poppy. The Sunset Ridge Police Department isn't in the habit of putting up people at the Hotel Piermont for protection. Who's going to pay for this?"

The thought of who'd pay for her stay had never crossed my mind. "I don't know. Why couldn't the department pay for it? I'd say it's worth it to keep a citizen safe from someone who's going to hurt her. Won't her help in convicting him be worth a few nights at the Piermont?"

Alex's skeptical look told me my argument hadn't convinced him. "That's assuming he's the killer. I'm not entirely sure he is. All we have is her claim that he wanted Marcus Tyne dead. That doesn't explain why Gerald Engels ended up getting poisoned."

He wasn't wrong. Those were valid points, even if I didn't want to think about them because they didn't fit into the theory of the case I'd constructed in my mind.

"But what about his brother lying to us about when he worked on Monday?" I asked, desperately trying to grasp at something to bolster my point.

Shrugging, he appeared unconvinced. "Brothers lie for one another, Poppy. Maybe he didn't want to see Frank get into trouble for something else we don't know about. Maybe he didn't want to lose what looked to be his only mechanic. There could be dozens of reasons why he lied to us that have nothing to do with this case."

Disappointed, I sighed at how easily he'd poked holes in my theory. "Then why did you say that stuff about not letting them know about the antifreeze part of this case before? I thought you were thinking Frank Mitchell had means and motive, and with his brother's lie, he had opportunity if he wasn't at work all day on Monday."

"I'm not saying he didn't. I'm just saying it's not a slam dunk like you seem to think. The issue with Gerald

Engels doesn't fit, among other things. Where during that day or night did Frank find Marcus to slip him the antifreeze, and then when did Frank run into our second victim on Tuesday before we went to see Gerald at his house? It doesn't work if this is just a revenge murder because some guy resented some other guy for stealing his girlfriend. Forget about how long we're supposed to believe a hothead like Frank Mitchell waited to get that revenge."

I frowned, disappointed in myself for not even coming close with my theory this time. I didn't mind being wrong, but I'd missed so many points in my rush to believe that nasty man could be guilty.

"So what are we going to do with her?" I asked, looking down toward where she sat in the back seat.

"We'll have to take her to the Hotel Piermont. I don't see what else we can do. I just wouldn't bet on Derek approving that expense, though. It might have to come out of your pocket, Poppy."

That didn't bother me. I believed Angela's fear of her ex-boyfriend and sympathized with her about it. If Jared was a violent man who terrified me, I'd want someone like me to help if I believed at any moment he could show up to kill me.

"I'm okay with that, Alex. It's the neighborly thing to do, so I'm fine with it."

"You know the price of a room at the Hotel Piermont?" he asked with a teasing look.

He just couldn't forget that I'd been there once. "Not that again. Let it go, Alex."

"I'll let you explain it to Derek then."

"I'll just tell him the truth. We couldn't let her leave town, and she wasn't going to stay here. What other choice was there?"

Alex rolled his eyes and smiled. "At least you didn't suggest she could stay with you. I guess there's that."

I chuckled at his teasing. "After all this time, you're finally getting the hang of this small town thing, aren't you?"

Chapter Thirteen

Fᴵʀꜱᴛ ᴛʜɪɴɢ ᴛʜᴇ next morning, I called the Hotel Piermont and spoke to Angela Touring to make sure she hadn't had any unexpected visitors during the night. Happier than either time I'd spoken to her before, she actually laughed at my mention of the reputation of the hotel and joked her friends would think she was turning over a new wild leaf if they knew where she'd stayed last night.

Satisfied our best witness remained safe and sound, I told her I'd stop by later that day with some magazines to help her combat the boredom while she stayed hidden away. She seemed to appreciate my efforts at being neighborly and thanked me over and over. All in all, my Friday began pretty auspiciously.

I felt pretty good, so I got dressed to go to *The Eagle* for a few hours. Although Howard would be nowhere to be found, I'd be able to tell him I had, indeed, spent some time working in my office on those articles I had due to him by midweek.

Grabbing my purse, I headed for the door as my phone began to ring. I dug it out to see it was Alex and barely answered it before it sent the call to voicemail. The Grounds hadn't reopened yet, and our everyday morning meeting wouldn't happen, so I assumed he wanted to call to talk to me about the case.

It wouldn't be the same without the coffee, but today would be the last day we had to suffer.

"Hey, you!" I said with a smile, happy to hear his voice. "I'm already missing our table at the back of The Grounds."

"Hi, Poppy," Alex said in a low voice far too serious for what I'd just said.

Instantly, I knew something was wrong. "What's happened?" I asked as my heart slammed against my chest.

"I just heard from Donny. He got the results back from the health department's tests."

Hearing those words made my mouth dry up. Swallowing hard, I said, "Oh. Is it good or bad news?"

"The health department found no evidence of Ethylene glycol in any of the alcohol at the bar but they found trace amounts on a single glass at McGuire's."

Each word felt like a nail in my father's coffin. My breath caught in my chest by the time he finished speaking, and my mind whirled with what would happen next.

I grabbed onto the edge of the kitchen table and lowered myself onto a chair as I began to shake. "So what does that mean?"

Somewhere in my brain, I knew exactly what it meant, but because this case involved my father, I didn't seem to be able to accept it.

"I don't have a choice. I have to bring him in for questioning."

"What? It's just a trace found on a single glass. Is that enough to make him a suspect?" I asked, my world spinning out of control around me.

"Poppy, I have to do my job. I just wanted to let you know first. I hope you understand."

I did and I didn't. I knew his job as the officer on this case meant he had to follow every lead he found, and the health department saying antifreeze existed on even one glass from McGuire's made my father a genuine suspect.

But this was my father. Alex knew him well enough to know he could never do anything like poison someone. There had to be some mistake, some reasonable explanation for why that trace of antifreeze had been found anywhere at the bar.

"Are you there, Poppy? Are you okay?" I heard Alex ask as I thought through all the possibilities to show my father couldn't have done this terrible thing.

"Yeah, I'm okay. I have to go, Alex. I understand."

I didn't know if he said anything after that because I pressed END on my phone and tossed it into my purse before racing out the front door to head to my father's. I couldn't bear the idea of him being alone when Alex came to take him in for questioning. He needed me to stand by him now.

My feet couldn't move fast enough, and with each stride, I tried to remind myself he'd need me to be calm. By the time I'd run the three blocks, my lungs ached from running and my legs felt like jelly, but none of that mattered. I needed to be by his side so he wasn't alone in this.

I found the bar door locked, so I quickly ran around to the back of the building to the door that led to his upstairs apartment. That was locked too. Taking out my cell phone, I pressed 1 to speed dial his number, but I hadn't gotten there in time.

After four rings, it went to voicemail and I heard his deep voice intone that same message about calling back as soon as he could that he'd had for years. I'd missed him, and now he likely sat alone in the interrogation room at the police station as Alex prepared to ask him how that poison had ended up on a glass in his bar.

The bar where our murder victim had drank at before he was found dead late Monday night and where a second victim had likely been poisoned too.

As my emotions spun out of control, I ran down Main Street to the police station, praying the questioning hadn't gotten too far yet. My father was far too trusting and wouldn't even consider having a lawyer with him in that meeting. Alex wasn't the villain, but right now, he was a police officer looking to arrest someone for Marcus Tyne's death and being trusting could get my father thrown in jail.

I tore down the hallway to Alex's office and found it empty. My heart sank. He was already in the interrogation room.

Rushing down the hall, I pushed past Stephen, who as usual was glaring at me, and stopped dead at the sight of Derek standing outside the interrogation room watching through the glass as Alex and my father sat at that same table I'd sat at for so many cases. He didn't have the speaker on, so I couldn't hear what they were saying.

"I need to be in there, Derek," I said as he stepped in front of door to block me from going in.

He merely shook his head. "Not this time, Poppy. Let Alex do his job."

I stared up at him in shock, my emotions swirling inside me. "Why are you being like this? My father has always been wonderful to you. Who closed his bar every Friday when you were the quarterback of the Sunset Ridge Knights to cheer you on from the sidelines? Every week."

Derek cupped my shoulders and sighed. "I don't think your father poisoned anyone any more than Alex does, but we need to make sure we dot all the I's and cross all the T's on this one. Alex needs to do his job, ask his questions, and when the real murderer is found, there won't be a chance that they'll be able to say your father is the one to blame."

I began to protest, reminding Derek that I should be in that room not only as Alex's partner but to support my father, but Derek gently held me where I stood. "Trust me, Poppy. I would never hurt you or your father. You're like family to me."

Looking in, I saw my father frown and hated how helpless I felt to protect him. "I want to hear what they're saying then. At least give me that."

Derek didn't fight me on that demand and turned on the speaker. My father's voice came through loud and clear, including the trembling underneath it that told me his first time in the Sunset Ridge police interrogation room terrified him as much as it terrified me to see him in there.

I listened to Alex as he asked what my father had done on Monday. I'd heard him ask that question of suspects so many times before, but now it felt different hearing him say the words to someone I loved.

"Can you give me specifics on what you did Monday? Start with the morning, if you can, Joe," he said in an even voice.

My father nodded and slowly recounted everything

he'd done that day, even as I wished I could stop him.

"I woke up, got ready for my day, and did a quick cleaning of the bar before opening it at eleven. Then I had a few people in during the lunch rush, my regulars who prefer a liquid lunch. The afternoon was slow, so I spent most of it watching TV. At around five, I made myself a frozen pizza in the microwave in the stock room since there weren't any people in the bar, and by five-thirty, I was back behind the bar getting ready for the Cinco de Mayo party that night. I spent the next hour or so hanging decorations and making sure I had enough tequila stocked behind the bar for the party."

Alex took notes on what my father said and then looked up at him as he drew a question mark in the left margin. "Did you leave the bar at any time on Monday day or night?"

"You mean the building or just walk out from behind the bar?"

"Either."

Smiling, my father shook his head. "I didn't leave the building at all once I opened the bar. Leave behind the bar, though? Yeah. I run a small town bar, Alex. I routinely walk out from behind there and leave it unmanned when I don't have a bartender working with me. I've never had a problem. Then again, I should know from Poppy working with you that this town isn't as safe as it used to be."

For a moment, Alex stopped writing in his notebook and I saw his body relax. "I know what you mean, Joe."

I hated listening to my father say all those things. He'd asked me if I'd be able to help him behind the bar that night for his Cinco de Mayo event and without even giving it a second thought, I'd told him I was too tired.

He'd been so understanding and I'd naturally thought he'd get one of his usual bartenders, but now it was so clear to me that if only I hadn't been so busy with my personal life he wouldn't be sitting there answering questions like some criminal.

"We're going to need the names of everyone in the bar that day, Joe."

My father nodded. "It was a busy night because of the Cinco de Mayo promotion I ran, but I'll do my best to try to remember everyone who was there."

"Also, do you remember anything notable about that day? Anything that sticks out in your mind?"

Hesitating, my father finally answered, "No. Nothing. I wish I did."

"Okay. What can you tell me about how well you knew Marcus Tyne and Gerald Engels?" Alex asked as he sat back in his chair and studied my father.

I'd seen Alex do that exact motion before and knew precisely what he wanted to find out. He was watching to see my father's reaction to his question and how he answered it to see if he was lying.

"I barely knew them at all. They weren't regulars, but I want to say they'd come in the bar a few times before Monday."

"And you're sure they were in the bar on Monday?" Alex asked as he leaned forward toward the table.

"No. To be honest, I'm not, but since Marcus Tyne died from antifreeze poisoning and you told me the tests showed a trace amount of antifreeze was found on a glass in my bar, I'm assuming just like I think you are that he was at McGuire's sometime that night."

"But you told me the other day when I asked you about him being there Monday night that you did remember Marcus Tyne being in the bar that night," Alex said, practically pouncing on my father's answer. "You said you remembered serving him that particular bourbon and after two drinks you served him coffee because he seemed very tipsy for just having two drinks."

I wanted to rush into that room and demand he treat my father with more respect. Being interrogated under any circumstances was downright terrifying. Maybe he misspoke the first time or maybe he was just confused because he was sitting in that room being asked questions like a criminal.

"Alex, I don't remember him being there or not being there. He may have been. If I said he was the other day, then maybe I was right then and I'm wrong now. I don't know. The same thing applies for Gerald Engels. I don't remember him being there on Monday night either."

"What about on Tuesday around noon? He says he was at McGuire's drinking bourbon at that time."

My father slowly shook his head. "I don't remember him being there at that time either, and I've asked all my liquid lunch regulars and they don't recall him being there either."

"I'm going to need their names too then," Alex said as he drew another question mark in his notes.

"Okay. I wish I could be more helpful, but I don't remember seeing them together that night. It was very busy, though, so that shouldn't surprise anybody."

I watched as Alex took a long pause before he asked another question. It was his way to set the pace intentionally slow at times during interrogations so suspects felt compelled to fill the dead space in the conversation and hopefully say something they didn't realize would be helpful in the case.

Helpful usually meant incriminating, and I hated that Alex had chosen to employ this technique with my father. It felt unnecessarily sneaky.

At least he hadn't started in with the Gatling gun style questioning. If he did that, I'd have to be held back from charging into that room and demanding he show my father more respect.

Finally, he said, "Okay, Joe. Why do you think the health department found a trace amount of Ethylene glycol on a single glass in your bar?"

My father sighed heavily and hung his head. "I have no idea. I've racked my brain for the answer as to why that would show up anywhere in my place. I haven't changed the antifreeze in my car or Poppy's since last fall, and neither of us has had any leaks lately."

"I told you when we began today that they're over at your apartment now checking for any evidence of Ethylene glycol there. Are they going to find any?" Alex asked with concern in his voice.

Pressing my palms against the window, I fought the urge to slam my hands against it at hearing my father's home was now being investigated too. The rational part of me knew it was the next logical step in the investigation, but the part of me that was Joe McGuire's daughter hated the thought that people were rummaging through his belongings looking for proof that he could be a murderer.

"Poppy, he's just doing his job," Derek said quietly behind me.

I hung my head and nodded, knowing he was right. "I know. I just hate seeing my father sitting in that room being asked questions in a murder case."

Derek gently laid his hand on my shoulder. "Nobody thinks he did this. We have to follow all the leads though."

Suddenly, a horrible thought tore through my brain. Spinning around, I asked him, "But what if the person who did do this isn't found and for whatever reason they find antifreeze at my father's house? You can't do this to him!"

Taking me into his arms, he held me as I fought back the tears at the possibility that my father might actually be charged with Marcus Tyne's murder and the attempted murder of Gerald Engels. That couldn't happen. I wouldn't let it.

"Relax, Poppy. It's going to be okay. We're going to find the killer, and then your father will go back to his life of serving small town drunks and police officers who make him stay open too late."

I looked up and saw him smiling down at me. Leave it to Derek to break the tension by reminding me how he and his friends kept my father's bar open until four in the morning after the last World Series with the promise that if anyone called the police, Derek would make sure the complaint got lost.

"You are really a criminal in disguise, aren't you?" I joked.

He slid his hands down my arms and laughed. "Now you know my secret. It's why the women in this town love me."

Out of the corner of my eye, I saw my father extend his hand to shake Alex's. "All joking aside, Derek, what's going to happen now?"

He looked through the glass and saw Alex and my father stand up from the table. "You're going to take your father back to your house and do your Betty Crocker thing you're so good at now. Have lunch with him and try to put this out of your mind for a while."

A second later, Alex appeared behind us. His frown told me he hadn't enjoyed what he had to do any more than I'd enjoyed watching it.

"Poppy, I need to speak to the Chief for a moment."

"I'm going to take my father home. I'll call you in a little bit."

He shook his head sadly. "Not yet, Poppy."

His answer stunned me. Was he actually holding my father at the police station? Did that mean he intended on arresting him? Just the thought made my heart ache.

I knew I had to accept that Alex had a job to do, so I hurried into the interrogation room and threw my arms around my father. He comforted me like he always did, and holding me tightly to him, he made me believe things would be okay.

"I'm so sorry, Dad. If I had just worked that night when you asked me to, none of this would be happening. You'd be over at McGuire's now, where you belong. If I wasn't so selfish…"

He leaned back away from me and shook his head. "None of that. Everything's going to okay, Poppy. You weren't selfish. You're allowed to have a life other than helping me at the bar, so don't beat yourself up."

"I just want this to be all over, Dad. I want us to go back to our lives, me helping Alex on cases that don't involve my father and you running McGuire's and looking forward to the next time the Orioles are on TV."

He pulled me close and gently pressed a kiss to the top of my head. "Don't worry, honey. I know I'm innocent, so just give Alex a chance to do what he does best."

I looked up at him and defiantly corrected him. "Oh, I'll be working on this case, so it won't be just Alex. Don't worry about that."

My father's expression grew dark. "Are you sure he's going to let you, Poppy? Won't there be a conflict of interest if you're working on this case after what just happened?"

"I don't care. There's too much at risk. I'm going to be working this case just like any other we've had."

Behind me, the door opened and Alex walked in. "Joe, you're free to go, but we need you to stay in town."

The serious tone in his voice struck me as odd, even as we stood there in that room where he'd asked my father questions in a murder investigation. Did he have to be all-business with him?

"Trust me, I'm not going anywhere. Sunset Ridge is my home, so if you need to find me, you know where to look," my father said with far more understanding than I would have.

I glanced over at Alex and saw the concern in his dark eyes. He had a job to do, and at that moment, the job involved looking at my father as a suspect. I understood it. It's just that I hadn't gotten to where I needed to be to accept that fact.

My father took my hand, and we silently walked past Alex out of the interrogation room. He thought I was angry with him. I read it in his face. I wasn't. I just wasn't able talk to him without being upset about the whole situation, and I doesn't want to fight with him, so I remained silent.

He probably liked that since I usually talked too much anyway.

Chapter Fourteen

MY FATHER SAT quietly on the couch in my living room saying nothing as I scurried back and forth from the kitchen getting him a glass of water and a sandwich. I had a sense he didn't know what to say now that he'd promised me everything would be okay.

I set the plate down on the coffee table in front of him and sat down in the nearby chair. "It's ham and cheese, Dad. I make a mean sandwich, just so you know."

He glanced at the plate and shrugged. "Thanks, honey."

After a few moments of waiting for him to pick up the sandwich, I said, "Would you like me to make you something hot? I can do that, if you want. Just tell me what you'd like and I'll make it for you."

With a heavy sigh, he shook his head. "I don't need anything, Poppy. I'm not really hungry, to be honest. I feel like I want to just go home and shut out the world for today, if that's okay."

My heart ached seeing him so defeated. His shoulders sagged and his back hunched like I'd never seen before. I wanted to take him in my arms and hug him tightly to me until the real murderer was found.

"I know, Dad. I figured you'd want to stay here for a while, though. You know, until the police leave your place."

His frown deepened at my mention of them searching his home for evidence. "I'm sure they're gone by now. My home isn't very big."

Nothing I could say seemed to help, but I wanted to do something to take his mind off the events of the day so far, so I asked, "Did I tell you that Howard mentioned to me that he would like me to write an article on the antiquing craze in our area?"

"Oh yeah?" he said absentmindedly, clearly not interested in my upcoming assignment.

Not that I couldn't understand why. The oh-so-scintillating world of antiquing paled in comparison to being accused of killing one man and attempting to kill another.

But I continued to talk, hoping that something I said would take his mind off his troubles.

"Yeah, I'm thinking it might even be something that would allow me to do research in the field. I mean, it's not Woodward and Bernstein with Watergate, but it's something more than my usual pieces about how lovely the grass looks for the spring tea at the current mayor's house or how tasty the pancakes are at the breakfast social the First Presbyterian holds each February."

My father gave a tiny smile at my reference to the event that was the height of the post-holiday social season in town. "Don't knock those pancakes, Poppy. Do you know their secret ingredient is vinegar? It's what makes them extra fluffy."

I instinctively made a face at the thought that for all these years I'd been eating vinegar pancakes. That sounded downright disgusting. "Really? I never tasted it in them. How do they do it?"

"Not sure, but that's what I've been told by none other than the Widow Dunn, and if anyone in town would know the secret ingredient in the Presbyterian pancakes, it would be her."

No point disagreeing with that. The Widow Dunn surely knew some of the town's most guarded secrets.

Suddenly, my father stood from the couch and turned toward the front door. "I think I'm going to go, honey. I want to go home and relax. You understand, don't you?"

I stood to stop him but couldn't. I knew how it felt to just want to crawl under the covers and forget the world until tomorrow. Wrapping my arms around him, I leaned my head on his shoulder. "I do, Dad. I'm sorry I couldn't take your mind off all of this."

"Oh, you didn't have to do that, honey. I'm just tired. That's all. It's been a busy morning for me. I'm just going to go home and take it easy. Are you going to be okay?"

That was who my father was. In the middle of a murder investigation and considered the main suspect, he worried about me.

"I love you, Dad. I'm going to be fine. It's you I'm worried about."

He kissed me and smiled. "Don't worry about me. I'm a tough old guy. I'll be fine."

"Okay, Dad. Call me when you get home, all right?"

After he shot me a look that said he thought I was crazy, he started to walk to the door but stopped. When he turned around, his frown had returned.

"I want you to be nice to Alex when you talk to him,

Poppy. Don't hold what he did this morning against him. He was just doing his job. I want you to remember that."

"I know. I didn't say anything to him when we were leaving because I didn't want to pick a fight and my emotions were all over the place. But don't worry. I understand he was just doing his job."

He gave me one of those wide Irish smiles I knew meant what I said made him happy. "Good. And by the way, you don't have to be so protective of me. That's my job to protect you, remember?"

"I'm not a little girl anymore, Dad. I can protect you now too, you know."

Nodding, he sighed once more. "You're so much like your mother when you're like this, Poppy."

"Well, I'll take that as a compliment," I said, proud to be compared to my mother on any part of my personality.

"It is. And with that, I'm going to go home and take it easy for the rest of the day," he said as he opened the door and walked out.

While my father recovered from his first interrogation as a suspect in a murder case, I intended on making good use of my time to make sure that would be his last time in that room at the Sunset Ridge police station. I knew I should tell Alex what I planned on doing, but I didn't and instead called the coroner on my own.

"Poppy, why are you calling me instead of your partner, the actual policeman?" Donny asked pointedly.

"I wanted to know if you found any fingerprints on the glass. It just popped into my mind, so I figured I'd call while I'm waiting for Alex so I can tell him when he gets here."

So I told a tiny white lie. In desperate times, the rules flew out the window. And it wasn't like I was trading away state secrets by asking him that question. I knew Alex would want to know about the fingerprints found on the glass too. Any good cop would.

"The health department and the coroner's office don't do that work. That's the police department's job, Poppy, as I'm sure Alex would be happy to explain to you when he gets there."

I ignored Donny's obvious jab at my fib and quickly thanked him before ending the call. If prints were exclusively the police department's job, then that's who I needed to call.

One problem, though. As the lead officer on the case, Alex would be the person I had to speak to about this. On the other hand, I could cozy up to Derek, who nearly always fell in line with what I wanted. But now that Alex and I were together as more than just work partners, I had a feeling he wouldn't appreciate me using my feminine wiles on his chief to circumvent having to approach him about this issue.

No, if I wanted to find out about the fingerprints on that glass the trace amount of antifreeze was found in, there was only one person I could speak to.

The man I loved and who I'd all but given the cold shoulder not an hour ago as I left the police station with my father.

I just hoped Alex appreciated emotional women who had the best of intentions, even if those intentions were slightly misguided.

Picking up my phone, I pressed 2 and immediately heard his phone begin to ring. Suddenly, my palms grew sweaty and I began to shake. He'd made me nervous a few times before in the beginning right after we met, but now I truly didn't know what kind of reception I'd receive when he answered the phone.

"Hello, Poppy," he said in what sounded like his usual happy tone he used when my father wasn't his prime suspect in a murder investigation.

"Hi, Alex. I wanted to talk to you about something I thought of a few minutes ago. I know this would be a police matter, so I figured I'd ask you about it. I mean, since you're a policeman and everything, it would make sense, right? Right. So I thought I'd call you. You're not busy now, are you? I could call back, but this seemed important when it popped into my head, so I wanted to call you immediately."

As usual when I was nervous, I began rambling. Not a very auspicious start. Thankfully, Alex had always been incredibly tolerant of my tangents.

"What would be a police matter? What do you mean?" he asked, confused by my near gibberish.

I took a deep breath and just blurted out my question. "I was wondering if you found any fingerprints on the glass. And if you did, whose were they?"

Strangely enough, saying I love you to Alex the first time had been less terrifying than saying those few words now. He said nothing for a long moment, which only made my fear grow exponentially, until I finally filled in the dead space with more words.

"If I'm bothering you, I could call back later. Would you rather I call back later?"

I heard the shuffling of papers and then he quietly said, "We haven't gotten the evidence yet from the health department."

"So that means you haven't had the chance to check for fingerprints yet?" I asked, barely able to contain my excitement.

"No, not yet," he reluctantly admitted.

My hopes buoyed, I said, "That's what's going to clear my father, Alex. You have to get that glass checked for fingerprints as soon as possible."

"I will, Poppy. I'll get them on it right now."

And then another long silence crept into the conversation as neither of us seemed to know what to say next. Finally, I spoke first.

"I'm sorry I didn't say anything when I left the station before. I didn't want to say anything that I'd regret, and I was too emotional. I just didn't want you to think I was angry. I know you have to do your job."

"Derek said you heard the interview with your father. I had to be thorough so when we find the killer they can't say your father's a viable suspect, Poppy. I hope you understand."

I hated hearing the conflict in his voice. Alex had never been anything but a good cop, and this case and my father's part in it made him sound like he regretted doing his job. I didn't want that for him.

"I do, Alex. I honestly do. It was just hard to watch."

"I know," he said in a low voice full of emotion.

"But my father would never do this. I know that as sure as I know you wouldn't. When you get the prints off that glass, you're going to see that."

"I'm just wondering if we're going to find his prints on that glass too since he bartended that night."

The concern in his voice struck me. "I hadn't thought of that, but if my father saw some strange liquid in a glass, he wouldn't just leave it sitting behind the bar.

He's always after me and the other bartenders to keep the bar clean."

"Okay, but I think you need to get ready for the reality that his prints might be on that glass, Poppy. I'm not saying that means he's guilty, but prepare yourself."

"I know. I just think this is an important clue in this case. Call me when you get the results, okay?"

"I'll do you one better. I'm off around dinnertime, so how about I bring over some food and what I find out? Hopefully, it's a celebration meal."

This was why I was crazy about this man. He knew exactly how to make me smile.

"I love you, you know that?" I said sweetly, truly happy for the first time that day. "I can't wait to see you and enjoy that celebration meal."

"I hope it is just that, Poppy. I'll see you in a few hours. Love you."

Pleased about how things had gone with Alex, I couldn't merely sit around my house waiting for those fingerprint results to come in. I had to do something or I'd go crazy, so I began to think about who would know Marcus Tyne in town. Although Millville was the next town over, he seemed to be almost completely unknown to people in Sunset Ridge, except for Angela Touring and Gerald Engels.

But someone else had to know something about him that could point us toward the answer to the question why anyone would want him dead.

I racked my brain for nearly fifteen minutes but came up with nothing. He didn't seem to be connected at all to this town other than through an ex-girlfriend and a fellow antique dealer.

Then I remembered a year or two after I graduated

from Sunset Ridge High School Millville shuttered their town's high school after a fire gutted the gymnasium. Since then, they'd sent their students to Sunset Ridge High. If Marcus Tyne attended school in town, then my favorite high school English teacher Eileen Matthews may know. She did spend her time with the biggest gossips in town, so perhaps she might know something else too that could be helpful with the case.

At the very least, it was worth a trip across town to the school and would get me out of the house for a little while.

SUNSET RIDGE HIGH School sat on the corner of Ashland and Hill Streets, two blocks down from Candy's Cuts hair salon and the park. A large brick building, it reportedly may have been an army barracks in the Revolutionary War. As a result, it was one of about half a million places around the country that claimed George Washington had slept there.

Few people in town believed the whole Washington slept here story, but the town happily displayed a plaque on the façade near the front doors that pronounced the tale as fact and included that interesting detail in every news article about the school, regardless of whether or not the information related to the story at all.

I arrived at the school just as classes let out, so I had to fight against a tide of teenagers eager to get out of the building to reach Eileen Matthews' room. I found her sitting behind her desk with her eyes closed looking exhausted.

"Eileen? Do you have a minute to talk?" I asked as I inched into the classroom.

Her eyes flew open and she turned her head to look my way. "Poppy, what are you doing back here in school? Missed American lit so much you had to come for a second round?"

"As much as I loved it, I don't miss high school. Once was more than enough. Do you have a minute to chat?"

As I sat down in one of the student desks and immediately felt like Gulliver in Lilliput, she chuckled. "It's different now that you're an adult, isn't it?"

The desktop pressed down uncomfortably on the tops of my thighs, and I nodded. "Yeah, it is. So how have you been? How are the preparations for the Founders' Day celebration coming?"

With a heavy sigh, she said, "Same as last year. Here's to hoping we don't have a murder in town right before the event begins, though."

I sat up as best as I could in my seat and leaned my right elbow on the desk. "That's sort of why I'm here. I'm working a case and I'm wondering if you knew the victim."

Eileen grimaced at my mention of the case. "Is this about what happened at your father's bar the other night?"

I nodded. "Yeah. I'm trying to find out all I can about Marcus Tyne, the man who died, and Gerald Engels, the other man who was poisoned."

Her eyes flashed with defiance. "I want you to know I don't believe for a second that your father had any part in that man's unfortunate death. Joe McGuire just isn't that kind of person."

Touched by her words, I swallowed hard to choke back my emotions. "Thank you. That means a lot to me.

My father has lived here all his life, but I'm worried how people will look at him now."

I didn't mention that my concern had ballooned after his interview with Alex this morning.

"The ladies considered moving their once a month meeting from McGuire's, but Mrs. Scanlon finally decreed that was unnecessary since no matter what, she was sure your father would be found to be innocent of everything involving that man's death."

That the gossips in town had decided my father deserved a chance to prove his innocence surprised me. "That's good to hear, Eileen, although I have to admit I'm a little stunned to hear them defend him. It's probably because Mrs. Scanlon liked my mother so much."

A blush colored Eileen's round cheeks, and she smiled like she'd just had a dirty thought. "They're of a completely different mind about you since you and Alex began dating, and the Widow Dunn even said just yesterday that she saw your ex, who she said came crawling back to town after that grocery store hussy dumped him, and she hoped he saw you and Alex out and about since it would serve him right after what he did."

Inside, I rejoiced at the idea of someone other than me wishing karma would visit Jared early and often. As happy as I was to hear they didn't like him either, I needed to know if Eileen knew anything about Marcus Tyne.

"Do you remember the victim, Eileen? He may have gone to school here, even though he was from Millville, because of the two districts combining after the fire at their school," I explained.

"I don't think so, Poppy, but Mrs. Scanlon said something about the other man right after it all happened about her wishing it was him instead."

Her comment shocked me. Mrs. Scanlon had a tongue like a viper all too often, but why would she want to see Gerald Engels dead?

Curious, I asked, "Are you sure about that? I've met him and he's a decent guy, as far as I can tell."

"Mrs. Scanlon said she wouldn't have had a problem if he had been the one murdered instead of just made sick. She said he was a crook from way back because he comes from crooks."

I went through what we knew of Gerald Engels. He was Marcus Tyne's friend and was willing to let him use his car. He worked with antiques, and he lived alone. Other than that, we knew nothing else, except at the moment he lay in a hospital bed recovering from being poisoned with Ethylene glycol.

"Do you know why she would say that?" I asked as I tried to imagine Mrs. Scanlon traveling in the same circles as Gerald Engels. No matter how I arranged it in my mind, I couldn't see where they would ever meet up.

"I guess his father used to have a garage in town and he was known for padding his bill, according to Mrs. Scanlon," Eileen explained. "I got the feeling she'd been his customer at one time."

"A garage? Like he worked on cars?" I asked, barely containing my excitement.

"Yeah. I think so."

Thrilled to find a connection to cars and antifreeze that didn't involve my father, I thanked Eileen as I squirmed out of the desk's hold and hurried down the empty hall out of the school to call Alex. He answered on the first ring, his voice that somber tone it had been when he spoke to my father earlier, but I knew he'd be cheered up when I told him what I'd learned.

"I found a clue that ties someone else to the antifreeze, Alex. I can't wait to see you to tell you about it!"

He didn't respond to my fantastic news, and then when he did finally say something, I knew it was bad.

"The fingerprint results came back, Poppy."

Chapter Fifteen

MY HEART SANK. Alex's voice sounded like someone had died, never a good sign, even if he was the most serious person I'd ever met. I'd hung all my hopes on hearing someone else's prints would be found on that glass.

"What is it, Alex? What came back?" I asked as I made my way down the sidewalk away from the high school.

"There were two sets of prints on the glass."

My spirits soared once again. "That's great! Now we can get to whoever's prints are on the glass in addition to my father's and find out what they know about Ethylene glycol and how it got into Marcus Tyne's drink. Why do you sound so somber? Is this your idea of a joke? If it is, it's really not working."

Alex remained silent for a long moment, so I asked, "What is it? Whose prints were on the glass?"

"Yours, Poppy. Yours and your father's."

And once again, my heart sank. "Oh, no. We can't win with this. I was at the bar the other night and that glass must have been one I washed and put away. God, I can't even get credit for doing one nice thing."

Alex began to say something but stopped.

Hesitating, he said, "I hate to have to ask this, but do you have an alibi for Monday?"

I stopped dead in the middle of the sidewalk, forcing a man and his Chihuahua to take a detour around me. "You mean other than the fact that you and I spent the day together and then the texts back and forth between us while you were at the station that night?"

Recently, I'd been worried about our texting getting him in trouble since he was supposed to be working, but now I was thankful it had been such a slow night for crime in Sunset Ridge. At least before Marcus Tyne ended up dead.

"I had to ask, Poppy. I wish there was someone other than me who could be your alibi. It's going to be hard to convince Derek to let me continue with this case now," Alex said in a defeated voice.

"That's ridiculous," I said defiantly as I crossed the street to head back to my house. "Everyone in this damn town is either related to someone or involved with them in some way. The idea that you can't do your job because you know someone in Sunset Ridge means the entire police force would never be able to work a case. I swear if Derek tries to pull that…"

"Poppy, calm down. It's not like that. He doesn't believe your father or you did anything, but he doesn't have a choice. The evidence is beginning to pile up against your father. We don't have any other suspects, except Frank Mitchell, and as long as his brother has that time card saying he was at the garage all day, it's going to be hard to say he's a better suspect than someone whose fingerprints are on the glass that held the antifreeze."

My mind raced to find something to change his

mind, but then what Eileen had said about Mrs. Scanlon saying she'd be okay with Gerald dying came back to me. "Well, how about the fact that Gerald Engels is related to someone who used to own a garage right here in town?"

"Our second victim?" Alex asked, clearly not seeing the importance.

"Yeah, that very same guy. The one you and I saved. His father owned a garage in Sunset Ridge. Gerald Engels would know all about antifreeze and would be able to get it, I bet."

"Poppy, that sounds pretty far-fetched, even to me. Is this garage still in existence? If he had a way to get his hands on antifreeze, maybe, but I don't know."

I couldn't believe my ears! He seemed to want to shoot down every theory I offered.

"Why are you acting like anyone couldn't get their hands on antifreeze any time they wanted? It's not like the stuff requires some special clearance to buy it. All anyone would have to do is walk into an auto parts store or the gas station down the road and pick up a bottle. Did you check those places in town to see if anyone bought antifreeze in the past few days? Antifreeze could probably be found in hardware stores too, I bet. Did you check into who may have purchased any recently from French's Hardware?"

"French's?" Alex asked like I'd said something silly.

The only hardware store in Sunset Ridge, French's had been around since before I was born. Chester French, who everyone affectionately referred to as Old Man French, had inherited the store from his father who had opened it back in 1935 at the height of the Depression. The story went that he gave away more product than he sold in those early years, but ever since then, anytime anyone in Sunset Ridge needed anything that might be found in a hardware store, they went to French's. Even the opening of two big box home improvement stores a few towns away in Anderson hadn't diminished French's popularity in town.

That's what sticking around and caring for your neighbors got you. I could only hope the same would happen for my father after all of this.

"Yeah, French's. I realize you're not from here, but I would have thought that you'd lived in Sunset Ridge long enough to visit French's at least once or twice."

"I'm more of a Home Depot man myself," he said with a chuckle.

"You're not taking this seriously at all, are you? This is all we have, unless you have some secret suspect you're hiding from me," I snapped.

"I wouldn't do that, Poppy," he said quietly. "I'll check out this hometown hardware store after I get off the phone with you."

"It's French's, and the man who runs it is Chester French. He's a very nice man and if he sold something in the past week, he'll know. That's what you get when you deal with a hometown hardware store."

I knew Alex wouldn't keep things about the case from me, but I was frustrated. My father was depending on me to clear his name, and now the one hope I'd hung my hat on turned out to be worse for his case, not better.

And Alex's dismissal of a perfectly good lead in French's Hardware bugged me. Sure, it wasn't Home Depot, but at French's they remembered everyone who came through the door and everything they sold. Try getting that at a big home improvement store.

"You know I wouldn't do anything to disrespect you on this case," Alex said in the most serious tone I'd ever heard from him. "I didn't mean anything when I said hometown hardware store, but I think you thought I did."

His contrition came through loud and clear, and I couldn't help but feel bad. I didn't want to pick a fight. I just wanted to clear my father's name.

"I know. Can we still have dinner? I need it more than ever right now."

"I'll be there by quarter after five."

"Thank you for still wanting to spend any time with me at all after how awful I've been, Alex. I'm just trying to do whatever it takes to show you and everyone else that there's no way my father could have committed these crimes."

I heard the smile in his voice when he said, "I don't have a choice. That's what a guy does when the woman he loves is in trouble and hungry."

As I turned onto Barn Street, I considered walking over to Simpson Street and talking to Chester French myself, but instead I kept walking toward my house. "I love you for that, Alex. See you in a little bit, and please don't forget to check out French's Hardware. You could even pick up a couple lightbulbs since the one in my upstairs hallway burned out this morning."

"Got it. Make sure to bring proof that I actually went to French's. Should I keep the receipt too?" he asked in his best snarky tone.

"Of course. I might have to return something," I joked.

"I'll see you right after five. Oh, and Poppy, don't worry. This is all going to work out. I need you to believe that."

Just like he had been forced to believe in me when he was the prime suspect in Bethany's murder, I had to believe he'd find Marcus Tyne's killer and show that my father was innocent of this crime. The only problem was even though I knew the best cop in Sunset Ridge was working the case, I wanted to be there working it with him.

A KNOCK ON my kitchen door at precisely quarter after five announced Alex's arrival, and peering out the window I saw takeout bags from Diamanti's. Excited, I flung open the door and inhaled the delicious scent of fine food.

Alex held up the bags and smiled. "Delivery for Poppy McGuire."

"Come in!" I said as I held the door and got out of his way. "That smells incredible! I'm starving."

He set the bags down on the kitchen table and began to unpack them. "I figured you would be. I bring the finest food this town has to offer for takeout."

The familiar scent of bourbon glazed pork chop floated up to my nose, and I stopped to relish it. Eyes closed, I focused all my attention on how good that food was going to taste in just a few seconds.

"You look like you're about to have an out-of-body experience over this food, Poppy," Alex said before kissing me lightly on the lips.

I opened my eyes to see him smiling at me. "Good food and a great guy. What more could a girl ask for?"

Alex twisted his expression into a scowl. "That great guy to already have his killer and this case solved by now?"

I cradled his unhappy face in my hands and shook my head at his talk of all this being on him. "We're partners, buddy. We will solve this case, so don't worry."

How long Derek would let me work on the case remained to be seen. I had alibis for both the time Marcus Tyne was killed and Gerald Engels was poisoned, but my father's fingerprints on that one glass and Tyne's showing up dead just outside McGuire's meant I was likely too involved with all of it to continue as Alex's partner.

That didn't mean I planned to sit idly by and wait for justice to happen, though. I hadn't said anything to Alex, but if the time came that I wasn't allowed to work with him officially, I'd be working the case behind the scenes, regardless of what anyone had to say about that.

Too much hung in the balance for my family for me to be forced to the sidelines in this case.

Alex nodded and smiled, but I knew he felt the weight of all this on his shoulders. "We better get to this food. Nothing like cold pork chop and garlic mashed potatoes."

We sat down and enjoyed our dinner in near silence as the two of us ate like we hadn't seen food in weeks. Diamanti's rarely disappointed, and tonight was no exception. The bourbon glaze hit the spot, and the mashed potatoes practically melted in my mouth. The restaurant cooked Alex's steak to a perfect medium well, as usual, and he couldn't get enough of the candied carrots, a Diamanti's specialty.

Once we'd gobbled down our food, Alex began talking about our trip to North Carolina, but I stopped him. "I can't even think about that right now. What if my father is in jail by then? I won't be able to leave him all alone stuck in jail."

Alex touched my hand and weaved his fingers through mine. "Poppy, he won't be in jail. I promise you we'll get the killer long before then, and we'll take our trip in July just as we planned."

I wanted to believe that—I really did—but at that moment as we sat there, each of us trying to pretend that the case against my father wasn't getting stronger as the minutes ticked by, it felt like our trip would turn out to be nothing but a pipe dream.

"I hope that's true," I said, forcing myself to smile.

With that genuinely sweet look he always got in his soulful brown eyes when he knew I needed to be cheered up, Alex said, "It will be. Have faith. So let's talk about what we're going to do once we get to that hotel we decided on."

I loved when he showed his flirty side. In public, Alex almost always appeared serious and aloof, like a typical policeman, all buttoned-up and proper, but in private, he could be downright, deliciously sexy.

"What we're going to do?" I said with a sly grin. "Well, I'm thinking that tub is going to get some good use, and after that, maybe we'll hang out in front of the fireplace before going out for a walk on the beach."

He looked at me with heavy lidded eyes, and I had a feeling he approved of my ideas. He'd been so insistent on the tub and fireplace, which sounded great, but I also looked forward to romantic walks on the beach at sunset complete with talks about the future and other topics that had nothing to do with crime or the Sunset Ridge police department.

"I like the sound of that. It will be nice to get away

for a few days. I love this place, but it gets a little claustrophobic sometimes."

"I know you mean. You think you have it bad? I've lived here all my life. I can barely walk down the street without someone noticing I'm doing it and whispering about it. But I can say I heard today that my reputation with the gossip crew is improving, thanks to you."

Alex looked surprised. Pointing at himself, he asked, "Me? What do I have to do with those old biddies and their opinion of you?"

"Well, it seems my being with you has made a decent woman out of me, in their eyes, and they're even hoping for ugly karmic justice to befall my ex now that he's back in town."

"They're not the only ones," he mumbled just under his breath as he pushed the last of his carrots around his plate.

"Good to know you and the biddies are on the same page. Maybe we can all have meetings once a week and send bad juju Jared's way," I joked.

"I'll bring the beer."

That he said those words without the hint of a smile told me how much he disliked Jared being back in Sunset Ridge. I knew it didn't hinge on jealousy so much as on his desire to defend the woman he loved against the man who did her wrong.

I scooped up the takeout boxes and paper plates, stopping next to Alex to lean down and press a tiny kiss on his cheek. "Throw the forks and knives in the sink and meet me in the living room."

"Yes, ma'am."

Alex did as I suggested and by the time I'd gotten rid of the remnants of our delicious dinner, he was already waiting for me on the couch. After the day we'd had, I looked forward to some quiet time in the arms of the man I loved. If I could have that, then maybe this wouldn't end up being the worst day of my life since my mother died.

I slipped into Alex's embrace, loving the feel of his strong arms holding me close, and when he kissed me, the horrid events of the day slipped away with every moment our lips touched. When it was just the two of us and nothing of the outside world could get in, we got to be just Alex and Poppy. He wasn't a cop and I wasn't his partner and we were just two people in love.

As we reveled in each other, his phone rang, tearing me out of the sweetest moments of my day. With a grimace, he pulled it out of his pocket and showed me the call came from the police station.

Frustrated, I leaned away and scooted onto the cushion next to him. "Can they do anything without you?"

Alex merely rolled his eyes and answered the call. "Hello?"

Someone I suspected was a fellow cop began to speak, but Alex stopped them. "Hang on. I want to put you on speaker."

He laid the phone on the coffee table in front of us and said, "Okay, start again."

I heard the voice of the man and knew I was listening to Stephen, the one person on the Sunset Ridge police force who seemed to have an unnatural dislike for me. Not only had we been interrupted by work, but we'd been interrupted by someone I could never encounter again and be perfectly happy.

In his nasally, bordering on whiny voice, Stephen

said, "I just had someone come in to give a statement about the Marcus Tyne murder. This person said he can attest to the fact that Joe McGuire was in a foul mood that day, and he saw him with some strange blue drink behind the bar on Monday. He knows Joe for years and has seen him angry before, and he believes he's fully capable of murder."

I sat stunned by his words staring at the phone like it had become some foreign object I'd never seen before. What was he saying? Who was this person who claimed these things?

"Who said this? What's their name?" I asked, my heart pounding in my chest.

True to his dislike for me, Stephen answered, "I called a fellow police officer, not some amateur sleuth."

My head began to pound like a sledgehammer sat inside my brain. Who did this guy think he was? "Excuse me, you called Alex, my partner. I don't know what your problem is, but I won't be spoken to this way. Now who is this person who gave the statement?"

"As I said, I called a fellow police officer. If you want to know official police business, you can ask him after I tell him. I'm not obligated to give the gossip writer for the local newspaper anything."

Gossip writer? Who the hell did he think he was talking to? He'd crossed the wrong woman. Now my Irish was up.

But before I could verbally slam him, Alex stepped in and asked who the person was. When Stephen answered, I could practically hear the glee in his voice.

"Jared Cooke."

I opened my mouth to speak but couldn't I sat so shocked at hearing my ex-fiancé's name come through the phone. Alex quickly ended the call and sat back against the couch, likely as stunned as I.

"That wasn't the name I expected to hear," he said quietly. "I guess I'm going to have to talk to him now."

Incensed, I barely found the strength to keep calm. "So now he's a believable person? You thought he was a stupid fool the other day, but now his word is gold?"

Alex stared straight ahead at his phone still sitting on the coffee table. "I'm not saying he's trustworthy. I'm just saying we have to check it out to make sure we can prove he's lying."

I jumped up and grabbed my cell phone. Calling my father, I said, "Of course he's lying. He's a snake, and you're dead wrong."

My father answered and I immediately put the call on speaker. "Dad, have you seen Jared since he's been back in town?"

He hesitated for a moment but finally said, "He came into the bar right after I opened on Monday like nothing had ever happened—like he'd never cheated on you with some girl from the supermarket and then ran off with her. He's lucky I didn't toss his ass right out into the street."

"Why didn't you tell me, Dad?" I said as I collapsed onto the couch, feeling completely defeated.

"I didn't want to say anything about him. He's a painful part of your past, and I didn't want to drudge up that history again because I know how much he hurt you."

"What did he say to you?"

"Just that he was back and hoped to mend fences. I told him if there was a fence nearby I'd throw him through it. Then I told him to get the hell out of my bar and never come back."

My heart suddenly felt heavy in my chest. "Oh, Dad. He told the police you were in a bad mood Monday. He told them he's seen you angry before and that he thinks you could murder someone."

"He's not wrong. I wanted to murder him when you told me what he did back then. I didn't, though."

None of this was helping. I wanted to cry. My rotten ex had lied about my father, and now my father was all but admitting he would murder someone if they hurt me.

I turned to look at Alex expecting to see the look of indictment I'd seen him give suspects before, but instead he just looked sad.

"He said he saw some strange blue drink on the bar too, Joe. Is it possible he saw anything like that?"

I knew he had to ask that question, but I still hated it.

Without hesitation, my father answered, "No. I don't know why he's trying to railroad me, but he never saw anything like that on the bar. He walked in, acting like he was some kind of returning hero, and I didn't let him get not even five feet through the door. Whatever he says he saw, he's lying."

"Dad, I'm going to get to the bottom of this. I promise. I'll call you in the morning, okay?"

I heard the sadness in his voice when he wished me goodnight and hated how helpless I felt. I wouldn't feel that way for long, though. Jumping up from the couch again, I intended on finding out exactly what Jared was up to.

Alex grabbed me by the wrist and stopped me, though. "You can't be with me on this, Poppy. You're too involved and could hurt the case."

I stared down at him in complete shock. "You mean I could hurt the case you and that ass Stephen are building against my father? Too bad."

He slowly shook his head. "You can't go, Poppy. You're going to have to trust me on this."

"No. I'm not staying here while that snake Jared is out there spreading lies about my father."

Standing, he cupped my shoulders and said, "That's exactly what I need you to do. You can't be in on this anymore."

His matter-of-fact way of telling me I'd been forced out of the investigation cut me to the quick. Hurt by his coldness, I pushed him away and turned my back to him. "Just leave. Leave me alone."

"Poppy, don't—"

I spun around and cut him off. "Don't what? Don't feel like you're betraying me when I need you most? Don't feel like I'm being forced off a case that affects me the most?"

My voice rose with each word as tears threatened to make me look like the emotional mess I truly was inside. Alex stared at me with hurt in his eyes, but all I saw was him letting me down at the moment I needed to be on this case the most.

He hung his head and quietly said, "I'm sorry, Poppy. I wish it didn't have to be this way."

"Just go. Go do what you have to do," I said as the first tears began to fall from my eyes.

As the door closed behind Alex, I broke down and cried over all that had happened that day. Everything I tried had failed and my father was in worse shape than ever in this case. Now Alex and I had fought over this, and I was standing alone in my living room sobbing.

Every ounce of my being wanted to storm out to find Jared and demand to know why he would lie like this, but what if that just made things worse for my father?

Chapter Sixteen

I KNOCKED ON the door, hoping he'd be awake and want to talk. After the day I'd had, I needed some of his wisdom, but even more, I needed the strength to go on even as it looked like I had nowhere to turn with this case.

The door opened slowly, and my father stood looking out at me with concern in his eyes. It had been a long time since I showed up to talk like this.

"Poppy, what's wrong?"

Forcing a smile, I asked, "Why do you think something has to be wrong for me to stop by and see how you're doing?"

Of all the people in this world, my father knew best when the words coming out of my mouth were lies. He drew in his eyebrows and gave me a disapproving look for my poor attempt at fooling him.

"I can see it in your expression. You're a typical Irishwoman, Elizabeth. You've never had an emotion that didn't cross your face. So again I'll ask, what's wrong?"

Just then as I stood on his porch wishing he'd let me in, I realized he probably thought my bad news meant he would be arrested at any moment. Horrified at my selfishness, I quickly said, "Oh, Dad. It's nothing about the case. I'm sorry if I made you think that."

He simply nodded and stood back so I could walk into his house. "I know. That look in your eyes wasn't worry about me. I know what that looks like. Whatever's going on is making you sad, not worried. So what's up?"

I collapsed into his dark green recliner and struggled to hold back the tears that wanted to take over again. "It's nothing. Just a long, bad day. I'm sure you know better than anyone else what I'm talking about."

My father sat down on that old brown couch of his that sagged in the middle and reminded me of a chocolate cloud. "I found out they didn't find any evidence of antifreeze here, at least. That's good news."

Sitting up in my seat, I perked up for a moment. "That is good news. Who told you that? Derek?"

A look of confusion settled into my father's face. "No, Alex. Why would Derek be the one to tell me that when it's Alex's case?"

Not wanting my father to see my sadness came from something that had to do with Alex, I looked down at my hands as I folded them in my lap. "No reason. I just thought maybe you saw Derek sometime today. You know, maybe when you went out to get something to eat at the store or something like that."

He greeted my comment with silence, but I knew if I looked at him he'd see his mention of Alex had upset me, so I continued to focus on my hands, studying my fingernails and wishing I could be the type of woman who had those long talons that made fingers like mine actually look graceful. Women like that always looked so poised and in control.

"Do you plan on staring at your hands the whole

time you're here, Poppy, or do you want to tell me what's wrong?" he said in that authoritative voice I heard a lot of as a teenager.

I didn't exactly meet his gaze, but I did stop my examination of my hands and looked around the room as I answered, "Nothing's really wrong, Dad. I just wanted to see how you were doing."

Out of the corner of my eye, I saw him smile. Leaning back on that chocolate cloud couch, he folded his arms across his chest and said, "I remember that time you snuck out of the house and I later found out you did it to take clothes to Derek. I was furious when I found out you'd climbed out your window and shimmied down the side of the house, but your mother stopped me from going after you because she said she was sure you had your reasons for doing that. She always tried to think the best of people, you know?"

Finally, I looked over at him and smiled. "Yeah, she did. I wish I was more like her. I don't know how she did it. I really don't."

"I think she trusted the people she loved. That's all it was. Trust. She knew the people she cared about were good people she could believe in, so when they did something out of character or something that went against what she thought should be done, I guess she instinctively knew they had good reasons for their actions."

"Do you know why I snuck out to help Derek that night?" I asked, curious to know if he'd gotten the whole story after all this time.

"Your mother said she heard you on the phone and Derek was in trouble."

"Do you know what kind of trouble?"

My father shook his head. "I can only imagine, but she told me to trust you, so I did. I was still angry as a hornet that you had done that, but I trusted you."

With a chuckle, I said, "He needed a set of clothes because some girl had left him naked in the woods."

At the word naked, my father's eyes opened wide in surprise. Or maybe it was horror as the thought of teenage me seeing Derek Hampton buck naked settled into his mind.

"I'm glad I didn't know. In fact, I think I don't want to know any more of this story," he said, waving his hands in front of him as if to erase the entire thing from his mind.

"Dad, nothing happened. I got his clothes from his room and gave them to him. He was hiding behind a tree the whole time."

Horror turned to curiosity, and my father tilted his head like he was trying to figure out how it had all happened. "How did you get his clothes from his room? Where were Derek's parents?

Proudly, I admitted my abilities in that night's caper. "They were home, but remember how they both loved to watch game shows all the time after work? An entire battalion could march through that house without them ever knowing a thing. The back door was unlocked, so I just crept inside and up to Derek's room, grabbed jeans and a shirt, and got out of there without either of them knowing I'd ever been there."

"I do remember their game show addiction they had for a while. I always thought that was weird, to be honest."

"Well, thank God for it because I don't think Derek wanted them to know he'd been cuckolded out in the woods near the Hotel Piermont."

My father didn't continue the conversation, likely because the image of a naked Derek and adolescent teenage me out in the dark hadn't completely left his mind yet. I may have been in my thirties and obviously a sexually active woman, but my father's open mindedness had its limits.

But then he asked a question that nearly floored me.

"Why didn't you and Derek ever date? You clearly care about him, and he's carried a torch for you since grade school. So why not?"

For a moment, my mouth hung open. My father's sudden interest in my love life surprised me, and it took me a few seconds to recover from the shock of his questions.

"Dad, Derek and I could never be more than just friends. Trust me. We're definitely not two people who should be dating one another."

He smiled and shook his head. "I was just curious. You've been close for years, and until Alex came along, I had wondered if you'd given up on men entirely after…"

His sentence trailed off, but the unspoken words hung in the air between us. What happened with Jared. After what happened with Jared, he thought I'd given up on men entirely.

I walked toward the kitchen, needing to put some space between me and that idea. "Nice to know my own father had begun to think I was hopeless like the gossips in town had. Wasn't there a soul in Sunset Ridge who still thought I might not end up alone surrounded by shelves full of creepy dolls?" I mumbled as I opened the refrigerator to search for something to drink.

"I'm not sure I thought you were as lost as the gossip

crew, Poppy. I do know one person who hadn't given up on you, though."

His comment intrigued me, so I closed the door without getting anything to drink and peeked my head around the corner into the living room. "Oh yeah? Who's that?"

"Derek."

What was with my father's preoccupation with the Sunset Ridge police chief tonight?

"Dad, what's going on? That's like the third time you've brought up Derek since I got here. In fact, it seems like he's all we've talked about tonight."

Raising his hands in front of him as if in surrender, my father smiled. "Nothing's going on, honey. You do seem very touchy about the subject of him, though."

"Of all the men in my world, Derek is the one I'm least touchy about, Dad. Trust me. Derek Hampton is a non-issue. You, Alex, and that awful ex of mine are an entirely different story."

My father stared at me intently, studying me as I stood leaning against the wall. "So do you plan on telling me what happened with Alex, or should we just argue about Derek for a little while longer?"

His ability to get right to the heart of what was bothering me didn't make me want to confess what had happened between us. If anything, it made me remember how sad watching Alex leave my house had made me feel.

Once again avoiding his gaze, I looked toward the window that overlooked his backyard and said, "Nothing happened, really. We just disagreed about something. Not a big deal."

"Not a big deal, huh? Is that why you were

practically in tears standing on my doorstep a few minutes ago?"

I snapped my head around to look at him, unhappy with his characterization of me. "I wasn't in tears. Why are you being like this with me tonight? I came over because I wanted to see if you were okay after all that went on today, and you're interrogating me like I did something wrong."

My father winced at my mention of interrogating anyone. Damnit, what was my problem? How could I be that insensitive with yet another person I cared about?

Crossing the room, I sat down across from him and reached out to take his hands in mine. His blue eyes looked at me with that fatherly gentleness that never failed to make me feel special, even after I'd been so thoughtless.

"I'm sorry, Dad. I shouldn't have said that. I didn't mean to bring up what happened this morning."

He squeezed my fingers with his rough hands and smiled. "I'm not going to fall apart just because I got hauled into the police station for some questioning, Elizabeth. I told you before. I'm tougher than you think."

I knew that. How much I wished I could be as tough as my father.

"What's your secret, Dad?" I asked, looking into those eyes for the strength I needed tonight. "How do you stay so calm? All day I've felt like I'm spinning out of control after seeing you in that interrogation room."

"There's no secret, honey. I just know I'm innocent, so it wouldn't matter if Alex had to bring me in for questioning every day for a month. The answers would still be the same because I had nothing to do with what happened to those men."

My shoulders sagged as Alex's last words replayed in my mind, and I leaned back against the chair. "I've been thrown off the case, Dad. I hate this. I feel helpless to do anything when you need me most."

The announcement didn't seem to surprise him. "I figured it would be just a matter of time before Derek put his foot down. You know, he doesn't really have a choice, Poppy, since I'm the main suspect."

So that's what all the talk about Derek was about. Now it all made sense. But my father had it all wrong. I wouldn't be so upset if he had been the one to tell me I couldn't be a part of this investigation anymore.

"He wasn't the one who threw me off the case," I admitted sadly.

That surprised him. "Really?" he asked. "Alex had to make that tough decision? I imagine you gave him hell for it too."

Hanging my head, I said, "I wish. He wouldn't fight with me, as much as I wanted him to."

"Thank God for that. You know, Alex isn't the villain here, Poppy. He doesn't deserve your anger."

I didn't want to hear a defense of Alex at that moment. I knew he didn't want to take me off the case, but that didn't change how angry I felt about being shut out of the most important investigation we'd ever had together.

"Dad, I know. I don't need you to tell me he's not a bad guy. I know that."

"And you're still mad at him for taking you off the case?" my father asked in that disapproving tone he usually reserved for when drunks started problems at the bar.

Frustrated that I seemed to be on the brink of fighting with yet another person in my life today, I tried to keep calm but my efforts failed miserably. "I don't want to talk about Alex or this case anymore. Maybe I should leave."

I stood to go, but my father grabbed my wrist to stop me. "What's going on here, Poppy? Why are you acting like this? This isn't like you."

Spinning around, I pulled my hand away and let everything that had been pressing down on me that day finally come out. "What isn't like me? Having feelings and being hurt when someone stomps all over them? Needing to know I can't be discarded like some useless piece of garbage at any time?"

"Do you mean Alex?" my father asked as I continued to let it all out.

"I'm obviously not really his partner when it comes to solving crimes. I'm just some amateur who tags along with him but doesn't have the right to be involved when things become serious. So he just pushed me aside like I was nothing and didn't deserve respect. Like I didn't have feelings he needed to worry about."

With each word, my voice grew louder and shriller as my emotions unraveled right there in my father's living room. I'd held in my feelings about Jared returning to town since I saw him at The Grounds and then again when I heard he'd accused my father of being the killer. I'd pretended to be okay after all these years, but I wasn't.

Jared's return to town brought back all those days I'd spent wondering if I hadn't been good enough to marry and all those nights I'd cried myself to sleep wishing I knew why he'd chosen Cicely over me. And now Alex just cutting me out of the investigation after rotten Stephen had treated me like some unwanted outsider made me feel the same way I'd felt back then.

"Poppy, Alex didn't discard you. He needs to do his job. You know that as well as anyone."

"Yes, he did!" I cried, wishing at least my father could understand how what he'd done made me feel. "He just discarded me. If I was really his partner, he wouldn't have been able to do that. I'm just someone he tolerates until it's not useful to him anymore."

My father stared up at me in shock. "You are not being discarded, Elizabeth. Stop saying that."

I couldn't hold back the tears anymore, and as they began to roll down over my cheeks, I shook my head. "Then why was it so easy for him to just leave me standing there in my living room? Why didn't he even try to show me that wasn't what he was doing? How could Jared leave me like that?"

The look on my father's face told me he couldn't believe what I was saying. He stood up and tried to pull me into his arms, but I pushed him away. He didn't give up on me, though, and hugged me tightly to him.

"Honey, did you hear what you said? You said Jared, not Alex. Is that what all this is about?"

His words filtered through my brain as I cried against his chest, and I realized I had said Jared's name. After all that time telling myself I'd gotten over what he did to me, he returned to town and within days there I stood falling apart.

My father held me as I cried, quietly telling me what he always told me when I got upset like this. "Let it all out, honey. Let it all out."

That's exactly what I did. I sobbed as all the

memories of how horrible I felt back then when I learned Jared had left me came rushing back. Left us and all we'd planned to wither away and die right here in Sunset Ridge.

But I hadn't withered away. I'd picked myself up and dusted myself off, and then I'd got on with life. Some days it felt like the entire world stood against me, except my father, but I held my head up high and kept living. Now, crying there as my father held me tight, I let go of all of that pain I'd held onto for so long.

With each passing minute, I accepted that my emotions about Jared's return to Sunset Ridge were going to remain raw, now more than ever after what he'd done to my father. I also accepted I'd been unfair to Alex. He didn't have a choice in taking me off the case. My only relative was his main suspect, and in truth, he probably should have told me to back away from the investigation earlier than he did.

I leaned back away from my father and wiped my tears as he looked down at me with eyes full of concern for his daughter. "I thought I had put him behind me, but I guess I was wrong."

"You put him behind you, honey, but not what he did to you," he said before kissing me on the forehead.

Sighing, I thought about that. "I'm not sure I can. I was so sure I had gotten past all that with Jared."

My father cradled my face in his hands. "Not all men are like him. Alex isn't like him, Poppy."

"See, that's the problem, though. I acted like he was the same kind of man the first time I got the sense that he was discarding me, just like Jared did. It didn't matter that it had nothing to do with another woman. I felt just like I did all those years ago."

I pressed my cheek against his chest as he wrapped his arms around me, making me feel safe and loved. I knew Alex hadn't done anything wrong. This problem belonged to me and I needed to solve it.

"Are you going to be okay, honey?"

Nodding, I slipped out of my father's hold and wiped my eyes again. "I think so. I have some stuff to work through, and I think I have someone to apologize to. Other than that, I'm the same old person I've always been, you know?"

That got me one of my father's broad smiles. "The sweetest daughter anyone could ever have, and one of the kindest and smartest women I've ever met?"

"Well, I don't know about any of that. I wasn't exactly the sweetest anything a few minutes ago, and it remains to be seen if anyone but you thinks I'm kind or smart. I have a feeling Alex might have a different opinion after our fight tonight."

"Give him a chance, honey. Something tells me he's far more understanding than you're giving him credit for. He knows you well enough to know all the good that exists in you, even when you're at your worst. I think it will just be a matter of saying those magic words and meaning them."

"Please and thank you?" I joked.

My father rolled his eyes at my silliness. "I'm sorry. Please and thank you are good too, but I think in this case I'm sorry will be better. Don't let your stubbornness get in the way of you doing the right thing."

"I won't. I promise," I said sheepishly. "I better go."

"Okay, honey. Thanks for coming by to check on me."

I chuckled at his poking fun at my lie. "Yeah, that's

what this visit was all about. You don't need me to check on you. You're tough, remember?"

He smiled and moved past me to sit down on the couch. "I remember. Someday you will too."

Kissing him goodnight, I turned to leave and then stopped to look back at him. "Did you mean it when you said you wanted to kill Jared when you found out what he did to me back then?"

His big Irish grin faded, and he nodded somberly. "I did. He hurt you, and I had to fight the urge to hurt him. Hell hath no fury like a father wanting revenge on the man who hurt his little girl."

"I think the saying is hell hath no fury like a woman scorned, Dad."

"Oh, that's definitely true, but since you couldn't give him that fury, I wanted to. He should be glad cooler heads prevailed. But then again, there's another great saying—revenge is a dish best served cold."

I liked that saying. Maybe someday I'd even get some revenge on that rotten ex of mine.

As I walked home thinking about what that revenge might look like, an idea struck me. What if Marcus Tyne's poisoning had been revenge? I still liked Frank Mitchell for that motive, but what about Gerald Engels?

Had he simply been in the wrong place at the wrong time, or had he been part of some revenge served cold too?

Chapter Seventeen

AFTER THE DAY I'd had, I barely made it to my bed before I fell asleep. So much for my plans to consider if Marcus Tyne and Gerald Engels had been on the receiving end of someone's revenge that had led to one of them dying and the other still lying in a hospital bed a few miles away.

Come morning, I opened my eyes and instantly thought to check for a text from Alex. Rolling over, I grabbed my cell and saw he hadn't messaged. Disappointed, I rolled onto my back and stared up at the ceiling. He had no real reason to text me since I'd given him such a hard time last night. I just hoped that he had found some new clue in the case and wanted to let me know my father was no longer a suspect.

And I hoped he would have messaged me to make sure I was okay.

With any other case, this wouldn't have been an issue. If he didn't text or call me, I'd get in contact with him. We didn't stand on ceremony when it came to things like that. If he had something to say, he found me. When I had something to tell him, I found him.

But this case had turned every facet of our relationship upside down. For the first time, my work partnership with Alex had been severed and my opinions on the case weren't welcome anymore. After a year of working together, I felt lost, like a huge part of my life had fallen away. I knew after the investigation ended we'd be back to solving mysteries together, but would what happened with this case forever change the dynamic we shared?

And compared to our work relationship, the romantic side of us was on downright shaky ground. As much as I knew Alex didn't have a choice when it came to the case, he did have a choice to react to my emotional outburst the way he did. I still loved him, but could I be with someone who so easily shut me out like that?

Maybe being ruled by stubbornness would hurt me in the end, but as I lay there staring up at my bedroom ceiling, I decided not to contact him. I could lie to myself and say it was because I didn't want to interfere with the investigation, but the truth of the matter was I didn't want to be the one who called first.

Even if every time I glanced at my phone that's all I wanted to do.

Better to get yourself up out of this bed and off to work, Poppy. Whatever's going to happen will happen. There's no point lying around and feeling bad about things.

Lame platitudes aside, I showered and dressed to head down to *The Eagle*. If anything could take my mind off my problems with Alex and the issues surrounding this case, some hours with my nose to the grindstone could.

Although my mind continued to be filled with worry, I couldn't deny how wonderful the morning sun shining on my face felt as I strolled down Main Street toward work. Spring in Sunset Ridge had bloomed all around me with colorful baskets of yellow, pink, and white flowers hanging from storefront awnings and standing guard beside business doorways. I loved this time of year, a true gift after months of cold, and as I passed the tiny park near the police station, I considered setting up a temporary office with my laptop right on the oh-so-inviting green grass.

But first, my stomach told me some breakfast was in order. Glancing down the street, I thought about going to The Grounds for the first time since the health department allowed them to reopen but decided to head to the Madison Diner instead. My support for Pam and Gerry remained steadfast, and of course I'd be back at their place soon to get my multiple daily coffee fixes, but today I wanted to stay away from the place I so identified with Alex and me.

Finding a booth at the back of the restaurant, I lifted the large laminated menu in front of me and did my best to hide from the rest of the patrons.

"You look like you're trying to avoid someone, sweetie," a syrupy voice said above me, and I looked up to see one of the Madison's waitresses with a nametag that said Cindy standing next to my table dressed in the usual black and white uniform they all wore. I'd never seen this woman before, and my eyes were drawn to her short platinum blond hair and the fake beauty mark drawn on her lower cheek mimicking Marilyn Monroe's famous look.

Smiling, I lied. "No, not really. It's just early. You know, some people like to talk a lot in the morning, and I'm practically catatonic before I have a few cups of coffee in me. Better to avoid people than seem incoherent."

"Coffee then, sweetie? How about some eggs and bacon to go with that too?" she asked with a twinkle in her eye like the breakfast there pleased her.

I quickly looked away from her and scanned the bottom of the menu. "How about some pancakes instead of eggs, but I'll take the bacon. Extra cream for the coffee, please."

Cindy slipped the menu from between my fingers and promised to have my breakfast to me in a jiffy. I watched her walk away and wondered how old she could be. She physically looked in her mid to late twenties, except for the Marilyn Monroe beauty mark thing, but she spoke like she was over fifty. Who said jiffy anymore?

Without my menu barrier, I suddenly felt incredibly exposed. While I knew it was likely all in my mind, I wondered if everyone in the Madison knew I'd been thrown off Alex's case by none other than the man himself, who was also the person I was dating.

In all honesty, the people sitting around me there probably either had no idea any of that had happened or didn't care. Not everyone in Sunset Ridge was a nosy gossip.

Then, just as I'd convinced myself I didn't need the menu because no one in the Madison Diner cared at all that I sat there alone, Jared walked in and zeroed in on my immediately. At first, I wanted to hide away but then the memory of those horrible accusations he'd made against my father to the police echoed in my head and I sat up straighter, ready to tell him what I thought of his despicable lying.

As I waited for him to reach me, sure he'd have the nerve to sit down across from me and turn on that charm of his, I saw the area around his right eye looked purple and swollen. Did he have a shiner?

Instantly, my mind raced as the question of if he had one was answered and I wondered who had punched Jared hard enough to give him a black eye? I definitely wanted to shake his or her hand.

He stopped at the counter and intentionally ignored me, turning his head so he didn't have to look my way. Too curious to know who had given him that black eye, I stood up and walked right up to him to ask.

Tapping him on the shoulder, I waited for him to look at me and nearly chickened out from saying anything when I saw up close how awful his eye looked. Whoever had hit him had done a number on him.

But I didn't chicken out and with a smile asked, "Run into a door or something, Jared?"

He glared down at me and winced as his eye tried to shut but couldn't from the swelling. I waited for him to answer, but he said nothing, so I took a more direct tactic.

"That looks like it hurts. Who hit you? Inquiring minds want to know."

Jared said nothing but groaned like my question hurt him. I swallowed hard as I readied myself to tell him off but good for lying about my father, but just as I opened my mouth to let him have it, he spun on his heels and stormed out of the restaurant, leaving me standing at the counter unsure what had just happened.

Oh well. Sunset Ridge was a small town, so I knew I wouldn't have to wait too long to find out who had beaten up my ex. For now, my breakfast had arrived and waited for me at my table, so I'd just create a story about how Jared got that black eye, one that included him experiencing the most acute humiliation and those lovely scorpions attacking his private parts relentlessly.

Never before had pancakes at the Madison Diner tasted so good as I sat there daydreaming about Jared getting what he deserved. It wasn't exactly revenge served cold, but revenge by proxy wasn't bad either.

I pushed my empty plate away and closed my eyes as the image of my unknown hero punching Jared straight in the face replayed over and over in my mind. Perhaps it was petty of me, but I didn't care.

"You look like an angel sitting there smiling. Was breakfast that good? Maybe we should start coming here each morning."

Slowly, I opened my eyes to see Alex standing in front of me wearing a gentle smile. He certainly was a sight for sore eyes. "Hi. What's going on?"

"Mind if I sit down?" he asked, as if I'd ever not want to sit with him.

"You know the answer to that."

He nodded and pulled the chair out to sit down. "I do."

A strange silence settled in between us. I knew it had to do with how I'd acted last night, so I said, "I'm sorry about all that last night at my house. You aren't the bad guy in all of this, and I know that."

The smile he gave me told me he was as happy as I was we weren't fighting anymore. It lit up his dark eyes, making me wish we weren't sitting in the Madison Diner.

"Good. I didn't like leaving things like that with you, Poppy. I hope you know that."

"I do. I didn't realize how much a toll this case was taking on the two of us until you left last night. Well, to be honest, I didn't realize it until I went over to see my father a little while later. He really is one of your biggest fans, you know that?"

Alex smiled at my description of how much my father liked him. "I know I shouldn't admit this since I'm the lead officer on this case, but I've never believed he had anything to do with the poisonings of Tyne or Engels. I had to do my job, but I never wanted you to think I thought he was guilty."

Reaching across the table, I touched his hand and gave it a squeeze. "I know. You don't have to explain anything to me, Alex. I was just emotional because my father's involved. I hope you didn't take anything I said to heart."

"Other than you calling Stephen an ass?" he joked.

"Well, yeah. That I meant. You heard how he talked to me. What a jackass!"

I knew I didn't have to defend myself to Alex, but I wanted him to know what I thought of Stephen's behavior on the phone the night before. If I'd had my way, Stephen would have found out how I felt too.

Alex didn't look shocked by my characterization of his fellow policeman. Nodding, he said, "I did, and when I got back to the station, I told him exactly what I thought of how he talked to you."

"Ooooh, do tell and don't skimp on the details!"

Humble as always, he simply shrugged off the suggestion. "It wasn't a big deal. Just one man letting another man know what he thought of his behavior."

Sometimes Alex could be so exasperating. "Okay, that's the exact definition of skimping on the details. Like in the dictionary next to the phrase skimp on the details, there's a picture of you sitting right there saying exactly what you just said. So how about we try that again but this time with some details, Officer Montero?"

Alex sighed, but a tiny smile cracked his serious expression. "Okay. Let's just say that I explained to him as I stood very close to him that if he ever spoke to you in any way that wasn't entirely polite and helpful that he'd have to deal with me. You could also say I reminded him that it wasn't me who allowed you to work with me but Derek, so if he stepped out of line again, he'd have to deal with me and the Chief of Police."

His chivalrous defense of my honor completely charmed me. I imagined that jerk Stephen being cocky when Alex first began talking, but by the time he finished, he probably was cowering in the corner like a scared animal.

Or at least that's how I wanted to think of it.

For the second time that day, I'd found peace by fantasizing about karma visiting someone who had it coming. Now if Alex could tell me my father had been eliminated as a suspect, I'd be walking on air.

I gazed across the table at my hero. That quiet guy who sometimes spoke not even half of what I said in a day had put Stephen in his place.

"Thank you, Alex. I appreciate you defending me. You know, I could have given him what for myself, though. If you hadn't jumped into the conversation, I would have."

He chuckled. "Oh, I know that. Stephen would still be smarting if you had told him off. I just wanted him to know that you weren't the only one who had a problem with how he acted."

"And who said chivalry is dead?" I teased him.

Alex puffed his chest out and proudly lifted his head. "Not me. I'm all about the chivalry, even if you aren't a damsel in distress."

"You underestimate how bad these last few days have been, between seeing my father interrogated as a murder suspect and my ex coming back to town and promptly accusing him of that very crime," I joked.

My comment made Alex's eyes open wide in excitement. "Speaking of that, I can say without hesitation that Jared Cooke's statement has been shown to be entirely false."

This morning was turning out to be pretty good. Eager to hear the details of how he had found out my ex's claims were complete lies, I asked, "How do you know? And by the way, if you skimp on these details, I might have to come over the table."

He winked at me. "Promise?"

"Flirting later. Details now, please. I'm dying here. And can you tell me if you know anything about how he got that black eye?"

A self-satisfied smugness settled into Alex's expression. "He's sporting a black eye today? I had a feeling he might be."

He stopped talking as I sat on the edge of my seat waiting to hear what happened to make him know Jared had lied. After a pregnant pause I had a feeling was for effect, Alex began his story.

"Last night after I left your house, I stopped in at Diamanti's for a quick drink before going home. I saw him at the end of the bar regaling some people with his story of how he was back in town and planned to win back the woman he'd left years before. One of his fellow drunks reminded him that he hadn't just left you but broke off your engagement, so it probably wouldn't be as easy as he thought to get you back."

I interrupted Alex, grumbling, "Like that could ever happen."

"Do you want me to tell this story or should I stop?" Alex jokingly chastised me.

"Tell the story, of course. I just felt the need to make sure the record reflected there is not even a snowball's chance in Hell of him ever getting me back."

Alex smiled. "Duly noted. Where was I before you interrupted me?"

"Drunk guy telling my ex it wouldn't be a cakewalk getting me back because he dumped me for the local grocery store tart."

I saw in Alex's eyes his amusement at my vivid description of Cicely. That was the nicest way I'd ever thought of her. If he only knew what I said about her to myself.

"Well, brace yourself. This gets a little rough. He went on to explain to his drunk friend he left you because you weren't woman enough for him back then but now that he's older and willing to settle, you're just what the doctor ordered. By that time, I'd downed a glass of scotch and figured it might be time for Jared and me to get better acquainted. So I tapped him on the shoulder and told him he needed to watch his mouth. Your ex was too drunk to listen to good advice, unfortunately."

Thrilled by this story, even if I didn't like the part about me not being enough woman years ago, I inched forward on my chair as I waited to hear more. "So that's when you slugged him straight in the eye?" I excitedly asked.

Shaking his head, Alex held up his hand. "No, not yet. Patience. There's more."

"Okay. Keep going. Sorry I stopped you."

"So he began to brag that he had told your father the same thing, and like me, he'd told him to shut his mouth before he got it shut for him."

I sat there fuming at the thought that my father had been forced to hold back from leveling that rotten bastard.

"I asked him if whole blue drink thing was a lie, and he laughed it off, saying it might be," Alex said with a frown. "He's really a piece of work."

"Is that why you hit him?"

"The official record is that he took a swing at me and I defended myself. At least that's what Derek and his new girlfriend saw, along with dozens of other people enjoying themselves at the bar. I think he just posted bail after a long night in jail."

I couldn't believe it! Alex had defended my honor and put Jared in jail. I could barely contain my glee.

"My hero! And he spent a night in jail too? And who is Derek's new girlfriend?" I asked, dying to know the details.

"So much for focusing on the important stuff, Poppy," Alex said, rolling his eyes.

For a moment, I didn't think about my father still under investigation for the murder of one man and the attempted murder of another, but my happiness didn't last for long and my dread of what would happen to him came rushing back seconds later.

"Any chance after all that you found some clue and my father's off the hook?" I asked, hoping against hope he had.

He hesitated in answering, so I added, "I know you

probably can't tell me anything now that I'm not allowed on the case because I'm too close and my father's still a suspect, but if you blink once for yes and twice for no, that would be good enough. At least I'd know."

"Poppy, I'm going to do everything I can to show that your father had no part in this crime. I promise. But until I can…"

He didn't finish his sentence, but he didn't have to. I knew what the answer was. As long as my father was a suspect, I would have to keep my nose out of the case. I tried to pretend like it didn't bother me, but my Irish face couldn't hide my true feelings.

"Oh, forget the damn rules. You're my partner, and that means you should be working this case with me, no matter what. We have work to do, so if you're finished with breakfast, let's get going," Alex said, instantly cheering me up.

"Are you sure? I don't want you to get in trouble or for my being with you to affect the case against my father."

"Don't worry about that. I'll handle any questions that come up. For now, we have work to do. After my little field trip to Diamanti's last night, I did some investigating on our second victim. I want to go speak to him again, so finish your breakfast and we'll go back to the hospital."

Quickly downing the rest of my coffee, I asked, "Investigating on Gerald Engels? So you don't think I'm crazy about him being a possible suspect in all of this?"

Alex smiled in that sexy way that always made me want to take him in my arms and kiss him. "I never think you're crazy, Poppy. When are you going to realize that?"

Chapter Eighteen

"SO IT SEEMS Marcus Tyne and Gerald Engels weren't as close as we originally thought," Alex said as we drove toward Sunset Ridge Regional.

Surprised to hear the two friends hadn't been just that, I said, "Really? How is it we didn't know this before?"

My question got a smirk from my partner. "Because someone got sidetracked with antifreeze and other scientific nonsense."

"Scientific nonsense?" I asked with a chuckle. "Be careful there. I'm a big fan of that kind of evidence. Science never lies."

I knew the irony of my saying that and still completely believing my father had nothing to do with Tyne's death or Engels' poisoning sounded strange, but there it was. I trusted science, even though it currently pointed to antifreeze being at McGuire's and therefore made my father the prime suspect.

"They had a falling out a while back and hadn't talked for months," Alex explained. "Then all of a sudden on Monday afternoon, Gerald called Marcus about meeting up that night for a drink. He said he wanted to talk things over and clear the air."

"How did you find all this out?"

Smiling like he was pleased with himself, he looked over at me as he shifted the police cruiser into park. "I got the phone records for Marcus Tyne's house and cell this morning. Gerald called him on Monday around noon and left a message on his voicemail about meeting up and burying the hatchet. Then Marcus called him back, ostensibly to say yes to meeting that night and likely to suggest going to McGuire's since that's where they ended up a few hours later."

"Interesting that Gerald never mentioned any of this, but then again, we did talk to him that first time when he'd been under the influence of the antifreeze in his system making him loopy."

Alex grimaced. "Under the influence of antifreeze. That's something you don't hear every day. Well, regardless of how he was feeling that day, he wasn't under any influence when we talked to him in the hospital. He could have mentioned something about this disagreement that lasted for months then."

As we closed the car doors behind us, I wondered what had caused the falling out between the two men. Business deal gone bad? They did work in the same profession. Maybe antique dealing was more cutthroat than at first glance. I could see my boss practically jumping for joy already at the juicy article I'd write detailing the ruthless world of antiques.

Then an idea struck me. "I bet it was a woman!"

Alex stopped dead just before reaching for the hospital glass front doors and spun around to face me. "What?"

"I bet they fought over a woman."

He thought about my theory for a moment but

quickly dismissed it. "I don't know, Poppy. We have no indication they dated anyone in common. It's not like these two guys were exactly studs."

I walked through the door as he opened it, undeterred by my partner's unwillingness to jump to the same conclusion. Two men fighting meant a woman or money. I placed my bet on a woman.

The question was, though, who was this woman?

We got into the elevator, both of us staring straight ahead, and Alex said almost under his breath, "I'm not convinced there's a third person involved in this case."

"So are you saying you think Gerald Engels killed his friend and then drank antifreeze to throw the police off his trail? That doesn't seem like a very smart move since he could have died."

He turned to look at me and shook his head. "Did I say anything like that?"

"Well, if you don't think anyone else was involved, that means you think Gerald put the antifreeze in his friend's drink to kill him and then drank some of it on his own to make it look like he was another victim."

Alex thought about that for a long moment before his face lit up like a lightbulb had just been turned on inside his head. Pointing at me excitedly, he said, "But he didn't. In fact, remember the doctor explaining that there wasn't enough in his system to kill him? Maybe he knew exactly how much to ingest and did that."

As the elevator doors opened, I tried to imagine Gerald Engels being the type of man who would risk death that way. Granted, I'd only seen him loopy from being poisoned and then recovering in the hospital, but he hadn't struck me as a daring soul willing to leave his fate to the exact measurement of a poison that might kill him if he ingested merely an ounce too much.

"I don't know. I didn't get a devil-may-care vibe from him. He's more of a measure-twice-cut-once kind of guy," I said to Alex as he followed me into the third floor hallway toward Gerald's room.

"Well, we'll soon find out."

We reached Room 319 and both of us stopped dead in the doorway. The bed where Gerald had been in for the past week sat empty, its white sheets neatly made and the white blanket carefully folded at the foot of the bed. Stunned, Alex and I stared into the room and then at each other like we didn't know what to say.

He turned on his heels and stormed over to the nurses' desk on the middle of the floor to angrily demand to know where Mr. Engels had been moved to and why the police hadn't been informed. As he barked at the woman standing behind the desk, a horrible thought tore through my mind.

What if Gerald Engels had died?

Quickly, I hurried over to stop Alex before he went any further with his impromptu interrogation of the staff. Grabbing him by the arm, I whispered in his ear, "Alex, did he pass away and that's why he's not in there?"

A look of horror crossed my partner's face. Looking back at the nurse, he asked in a much lower voice, "Did Mr. Engels die? Is that why he's not in his room?"

The nurse shook her head quickly back and forth, making her long ponytail swing left and right as she indicated he hadn't passed away. "Oh, no. Mr. Engels left the hospital this morning against his doctor's advice."

I'd never seen Alex move so fast to call anyone in all the time I'd known him. His phone came out of his pocket like a cowboy's six-shooter from a holster in one of those old western films my father loved to watch.

As he called the station, he pointed down the hall. "Poppy, we need to talk to Dr. Carter now! I need you to find him."

The nurse understood the urgency by the frantic tone of Alex's voice and hurried out from behind the station. Looking to her left, she said, "Dr. Carter should be in the lounge at the end of the hall. I saw him walking that way about fifteen minutes ago. I'll page him too, if you want."

"That would be great! Thanks!" I yelled as I took off down the hall to find him.

Dr. Carter sat alone reading a magazine at a large round table in the lounge. As I approached him, catching my breath, I heard the woman's voice come over the loudspeaker telling him he was needed at the desk. He rose to leave and nearly ran into me.

"I'm sorry, Dr. Carter. Officer Montero needs to speak to you about your patient, Gerald Engels," I said while I hurried him out into the hallway. "We need to know what happened to him."

Halfway to the nurses' station, Alex reached us, and before the doctor could get a word out, he said, "I want to know how this man could have walked out of this hospital when he nearly died just a few days ago. What's going on here?"

Dr. Carter took a step back and looked startled, likely because he hadn't expected to have to endure the inquisition simply because one of his patients decided to leave the hospital against his advice. "I couldn't stop him, Officer Montero. He wanted to leave, and no matter what I told him about how imperative it was to stay in bed longer, he wouldn't hear of it."

Placated by that answer, at least for the moment, Alex sighed. "Let's leave the fact that I should have been contacted immediately to the side for a moment. I need to know what kind of shape he's in. Just the other day he was at death's doorstep, so what's he like now?"

Moving to walk toward the nurses' station, the doctor said, "Let me check his chart."

But Alex's patience had come to an end. He stepped in front of him and shook his head. "We don't have time for that. I don't need specific stats. I just need to know if he's going to be on certain medicines or if he'll need to rest often. Things like that."

"Well, I don't usually do things like that. I prefer to see the chart, to be honest, officer," Dr. Carter hedged, taking a step to his left to get around Alex.

He didn't get far, though. "We don't have time for that now. Mr. Engels is part of a murder investigation, and at the moment, you're impeding that very investigation by not giving me the answers I need. Now for the last time, doctor, tell me what I need to know!"

The demanding tone of Alex's voice shocked the doctor, who looked like he wanted to protest even further for a moment before accepting the urgency of the situation. Finally, he gave in to Alex's strongly worded request and answered, "He won't be able to go very far without resting since he's still recuperating from cardiac arrest. He'll need more fluids than a normal person would, so I expect he'll be consuming a lot of liquids. He didn't take any prescriptions with him, that I remember, but overall, I wouldn't expect him to be feeling anywhere near one hundred percent yet."

"Thank you. Oh, by the way, why did Mr. Engels

want to leave the hospital all of a sudden today?"

The doctor's shoulders sagged in relief that this question didn't force him to go against any of his usual methods. Nodding, he said, "I think it was the woman who came to visit him yesterday. Ever since he talked to her, he wanted to leave."

"A woman?" I asked before Alex could get the words out of this mouth. "Who? What did she look like?"

Dr. Carter shrugged. "I don't know. I didn't see her. All I know is after he got that visit, he couldn't wait to leave here."

Turning to face me, Alex said, "We need to get to Gerald Engel's house right now."

As we raced to the elevator, I wondered aloud, "I hope he made it that far. From what the doctor said, he doesn't sound like he's going to be standing for long. And who's the woman who came to see him?"

Tapping his fingertip on the down button, Alex said, "I don't know, but I fully intend on asking Gerald. And if he's unable to stand, then he can answer my questions lying down."

I elbowed Alex in the arm. "See? I told you a woman was involved."

ALEX STARED STRAIGHT ahead as the kindergarten class from Sunset Ridge Elementary School waddled across the intersection like a bunch of ducklings behind a mama duck. Each child held hands with the child in front of them and the one behind, and at the rear of the line followed a tall older woman wearing a stern look like this outing didn't please her at all.

"I know Derek told us to go easy on using the sirens

and lights because the town council had received complaints from some people in town, but we're wasting time sitting here. We've got to get to Engels' house before he skips town."

Reaching over, I gently touched Alex's forearm. "He's not going to go anywhere in the five minutes we're sitting here. Relax. They're just kids out for a stroll on a beautiful spring day. Look at how cute they are! That last kid in front of the cranky woman is having the time of his life because he only has to hold hands with that one little girl. He's feeling like the king of the world."

As Alex groaned and grew increasingly impatient, I watched that little boy at the back of the line with his giddy smile and cute little blue windbreaker with the zipper he kept pulling up and down as he walked. How great it must be to feel that good about something so simple.

I nudged his arm and pointed toward the woman in charge of the end of the line of kids. Only halfway across the street, she looked about as irritated as Alex. "That's what you look like, except you don't have the excuse of having to deal with twenty kindergarteners."

He turned his head and glared at me. "I have you, though."

"Funny. Are you comparing me to a class full of little kids?"

Sighing, he shook his head. "No, I'm sorry. I'm just on edge about this because every minute we sit here, Gerald Engels could be getting away."

I gave him my best sympathetic smile. "I know. Trust me. My father's reputation and freedom depends on us solving this case, but I don't think Engels is getting anywhere too far."

At least I hoped he wouldn't.

The line of children stepped up on the curb, and the irritated older woman followed them, leaving the road open for us to continue toward Gerald Engels' house. Just as Alex pressed his foot on the gas, that last little boy with the blue windbreaker waved his tiny hand at us and smiled, like his day had been made seeing the police car.

We took off down the road as Alex huffed, "Finally. I really need to say something to Derek about us getting to use the sirens and lights more."

"I think he's the reason why people started complaining in the first place. Nobody loves the sirens and lights more than Derek. It's been a running joke for a while that he's a little too liberal with all that for people around here. Even with simple parking tickets he's been known to use them."

Alex didn't seem impressed by my opinion on the chief's overuse of the sirens and lights and instead remained focused on simply driving as fast as he could up Gerald Engel's street. I wanted to ask why he seemed particularly out of sorts about this case, but his mood appeared to have gotten even worse after sitting at that crosswalk, and I didn't want to risk us fighting again.

We'd had enough spats on this case already.

A few minutes later, the car skidded to a stop in front of the house we'd visited earlier this week when we saved Gerald's life. Now, just days later, we were there for an entirely different reason, one I still wasn't sure about.

Alex didn't say a word as he headed up the sidewalk to the house. I followed quickly behind praying we'd find Gerald sitting in that same recliner and hopefully in good enough shape to answer Alex's questions.

He knocked on the door, yelling into the house,

"Gerald Engels, open the door! It's the Sunset Ridge police! We need to talk to you."

His words were answered with silence. Banging on the door this time, he repeated his demand for Gerald to open the door, but it was no use. I peered in through the window I'd looked through last time and saw no evidence anyone was inside.

"He's not home," I said as I rejoined Alex at the door. "So he leaves the hospital for some unknown reason and doesn't go back to his house?"

Alex let out a sigh of frustration. "Or he was here and is already long gone. Damnit!"

I gently touched his shoulder in the hopes that I could make him see we weren't finished by any stretch of the imagination. "Hey, we'll find him. Don't let this get you down. But you seem to be really stressed out about this case, and that's not your style. What's going on?"

Looking off in the distance, he quietly said, "I feel like I've let you down on this case, Poppy. Your father is still our only reliable suspect because of that science you love so much, and I haven't been able to find anyone I can honestly tell Derek would be a better suspect."

"Oh, don't say that, Alex. You haven't let me down at all," I said before kissing him softly on the cheek.

"I had been so sure we'd find something out when we spoke to Gerald, and now that he's gone, I'm sure he knows something about Marcus Tyne's murder, but now he's in the wind and we may never find him."

I slipped my arm around Alex and hugged him. "He's not going to get far. We'll find him."

Shaking his head, he said, "Not if that woman who visited him yesterday is helping him. They could be halfway to Canada by now."

His mention of that woman made me wonder why we hadn't heard of any female associated with Gerald Engels before today. Had it really been because the police had been exclusively focused on my father as the main witness, or had it been because we were meant to see Gerald as single?

"About her. Why didn't he say anything about a girlfriend or wife when we spoke to him? Nobody lives in this house with him. We know that. I mean, just look at it. No woman would live amongst so much stuff. I can't imagine any woman being able to deal with all those piles of knickknacks and things he has in there. Just the thought gives me the chills. I'd go crazy if I had to come here very often."

Alex stared at me like I'd grown a second head. "What did you just say?"

"I'd go crazy if I had to come here often? I would. All that stuff would give me a headache."

He waved his hands at me and shook his head. "No, before that. You can't imagine anyone dealing with piles of stuff?"

"Yeah," I said as I thought about the narrow path lined with stacks of old records and other people's garbage in his dining room. "I'd have to take a shovel to this place if Gerald and I got together, I swear."

"Poppy, where else have we seen piles of stuff we had to walk around recently?"

I thought about his question and immediately remembered the garage at Millville Motors. "The place Frank Mitchell works!"

Running over to the window, I looked into the dining room again and saw that the piles and pathway looked almost identical to how the boxes of auto parts had been arranged at the garage. "Birds of a feather?"

"I don't know. It might be just a coincidence, but both these guys knew Marcus Tyne."

"And Angela Touring!" I said excitedly, now genuinely frightened she might be the next victim.

Quickly, I called the Hotel Piermont to make sure she was safe. The front desk person answered on the second ring.

"I need you to connect me to Angela Touring's room. She's on the second floor," I said, forgetting her room number.

"Miss Touring checked out this morning, miss," the woman's voice said sweetly.

I pressed END and looked over at Alex. "Angela Touring must be feeling much braver now. She checked out of the Hotel Piermont this morning. What are the chances she and Gerald knew each other and she was the woman who visited him yesterday in the hospital?"

"No idea, but we need to get over to her house right now because either she's in danger because Frank Mitchell wants to kill her, as she claimed, or she's involved in the murder of Marcus Tyne. Either way, we need to find her."

We ran to the car as I thought about how convincing her scared little victim act had been that day. I'd been so sure Frank Mitchell would try to do something to hurt her that I paid for her stay at the Hotel Piermont.

Damn, I was such a fool!

Alex started the car and it lurched forward down the street, picking up speed as we raced to Angela's house a few minutes away. After he radioed into the station to tell Stephen we needed backup, he turned to look at me and said, "I know what you're thinking. Don't."

"That I was a complete fool for falling for her act?" I asked, smarting from how stupid I could be.

"You weren't a fool, Poppy. You're just good-hearted with small town beliefs. Unscrupulous people take advantage of that."

"But she's from Sunset Ridge too," I protested, knowing exactly what he meant even as I tried to find another excuse for my idiocy.

"Then you're just good-hearted. I don't want you to beat yourself up over this, though. Clearly, this big city detective didn't see through her act either."

He cut the wheel, turning the car sharply onto Angela's street. Hanging onto the door handle, I said, "But you didn't foot the bill at the hotel to keep her safe. At least you were sort of skeptical. I bought that story of hers hook, line, and sinker. I'm so stupid."

My bemoaning my trusting nature made him smile, and as he jammed the car into park a little ways down the street from Angela's house, he turned toward me and cupped my chin. "You aren't stupid. You're sweet and kind, and I suspect Angela is anything but. For now, I want you to stay here until backup comes. Don't fight me on this, okay? I'm not sure what we're walking into here, so stay put until I come back."

I opened my mouth to explain that I wanted to go with him, but he kissed me, effectively stopping me from saying anything. Leaning away, he said, "I mean it, Poppy. Don't fight me on this and don't move from this car until Stephen gets here."

Frustrated from being cut out of the action but understanding his reasons, I sulked but accepted his rules. "Fine, but if Stephen is an ass to me, he's getting it both barrels this time."

"Agreed. Now wait for him and I'll be right back, okay?" he said sweetly with that look in his brown eyes that never failed to make me want to do just what he wanted.

I forced a smile before he left the car to walk up to Angela Touring's house, but every cell in my body wished I could be right there with him when he questioned her about all the lies she'd told.

Chapter Nineteen

I WATCHED ALEX walk up the sidewalk to Angela Touring's front door while a knot formed in the pit of my stomach. He insisted I wait there in the car because he worried there might be a problem and he didn't want me to get hurt, but what if he got hurt? Just the thought of him in danger made my chest tighten until I could hardly breathe.

Silently, I begged him to be careful even though I knew he wouldn't take any unnecessary risks. At least I could count on that.

But I wanted to be standing on that front porch with him. That's where his partner would be, if I was a real partner and not just some silly woman who tagged along giving her half-baked opinions and making him worry instead of focusing one hundred percent on his job. Maybe Stephen was right. Maybe I didn't deserve the respect I thought I did.

As his nasty words from the night before replayed in my mind, he walked up to the police cruiser and tapped on the driver's side window, jarring me out of my thoughts. I looked over at him, and even now after Alex had told him what would happen if he insisted on being rude again, he glared at me through the glass like some petulant child staring into an exhibit at the zoo and unhappy because the animals weren't acting like he thought they should.

Despite wanting to tell him to go away, I forced myself to smile and waved at him. He opened the door and barely poked his head in.

"Where is Alex?" he asked in a voice to match that petulant child expression he still wore.

This guy wasn't very bright. A quick look around would have given him his answer without having to sully his time there by talking to me.

I pointed toward Angela's house where Alex still stood on the front porch. "He's at Angela Touring's house."

For any other cop, I would have added more information just in case they didn't remember every detail like Alex and I did simply because we'd worked the case from the beginning. For this guy, though, I offered just the facts and no more. The less I had to speak to him the better.

Without moving his head, he averted his gaze to look out the back window at where Alex stood and mumbled something I thought sounded like the word, "Fine."

It sounded odd, like some kind of unneeded opinion on a co-worker's actions. I wanted to tell him that, in fact, Alex was fine and likely didn't need his help, but I knew that would be unprofessional. Alex didn't need any grief from Derek, so I kept my mouth shut and silently critiqued Stephen's uselessness.

Finally, I turned to look at the porch and saw the front door open. Angela Touring stood looking out at Alex as he spoke to her, but a quick assessment of her body language told me this visit wasn't anywhere as pleasant as the last time he'd been there to see her. He stood ramrod straight, appearing official the entire time, but after a few seconds, she put her hand on her right hip and shook her head. Then she slammed the door in his face.

From behind me, I heard Stephen mumble, "Damn. Someone doesn't want the police around."

He really had a grip on the obvious, this one.

Alex hurried down the sidewalk and came up alongside the car to where I sat. Opening the door, he leaned down and shook his head. "I couldn't see inside because she kept the door closed, but she's not going to let me in there without a search warrant. I'm going to have to bring Derek in on this."

"I'm sure you'll be able to get a warrant," I said. Magistrates in town signed warrants for far less than we had on this case, so I didn't doubt he'd have one in just a few minutes.

I just hoped it would be in time before Angela jumped in her car and sped away for points unknown. Now that she'd be on guard after seeing Alex at the door, she'd be eager to flee at any moment.

Without even a cursory glance at Stephen, Alex took out his phone and called Derek, who by the way the conversation sounded on our end seemed happy to finally have a break in the case after making my father a suspect.

Alex, on the other hand, appeared unhappy with what he heard. "Judge Harlow? I thought he announced he was going on an extended vacation," he said with a groan. Looking down at his watch, he sighed. "Maybe you can catch him before he gets his first drink in him. I hope so."

I heard Derek say something about eleven in the morning being pretty early to be in the bag, but Alex didn't look convinced. We'd had to deal with the judge before, and I'd known him for years. My father had told me many times that the judge was often his first customer of the day, and usually that was even before noon.

Derek asked, "What's your theory of the case involving Angela Touring? I need to know just in case Harlow is feeling particularly curious today. Sometimes he likes to know what he's signing."

For a moment, Alex didn't speak. I knew why. We had a sense that Angela was involved in Marcus Tyne's murder, but how exactly she played a part still hadn't been something we'd teased out of this mystery yet. For my part, I felt pretty secure in my assumption that it had something to do with romance. The problem was with who.

Alex, on the other hand, hadn't bought into the romance facet of this case yet, but he agreed she definitely played a part in Tyne's death. Now that Derek had asked for his theory, he'd have to give him something more to go on other than he thought it suspicious that she'd suddenly checked out of the Hotel Piermont this morning after doing or saying something when she possibly visited Gerald Engels to make him leave the hospital and risk his life a few hours ago.

"Well, to be honest, I'm not entirely sure what she's done, but she was Tyne's girlfriend until a few months ago. They have a history that includes domestic violence, at least officially, which she very likely might have wanted to get revenge for. And we know Frank Mitchell, the guy she cheated on with Marcus Tyne, could easily get his hands on antifreeze since he works at a garage, and he's been telling his boss that they're back together and engaged to be married."

He stopped for a moment and then said in a low voice, "As for Gerald Engels, we aren't really sure what part he played in all of this, if any."

I had to admit as I sat there and listened to him describe it like that, the case sounded pretty convoluted. Leaning toward Alex, I listened to hear if Derek thought that too.

"It sounds like she's less a suspect than Frank Mitchell, Alex. It also sounds like you have a lot of loose ends."

Leave it to Derek to miss the obvious.

Positioning my mouth close to Alex's cell phone, I said, "She's involved with at least one of these guys, if not both of them, Derek. The romantic angle is there. I know it. I think she's been playing Frank or Gerald to get her revenge."

Derek's surprise at hearing my voice came through loud and clear. "What the hell is Poppy doing there? Her father's still the only real suspect we have."

I knew I shouldn't say anything more, but his silliness was wasting precious time. "Derek, worry about reprimanding Alex later, please," I yelled as Alex backed away from the car. "We need that search warrant right now before Angela Touring takes off."

The horror on Alex's face telegraphed I probably had irritated yet another person on the Sunset Ridge police force. Derek I could get around. He'd chastise me and I'd pretend to listen before turning on the charm and reminding him that we'd been friends forever so he couldn't be mad at me.

Alex was a different story. I had a feeling that the angry look he wore wasn't going to go away any time soon if I ruined his chances at getting a search warrant by being there at the scene.

He paced back and forth outside the car, and with each pass looked unhappier by the second. Finally, he stuffed his phone back into his pocket and returned to stand next to the car.

Talking over the roof, I heard him tell Stephen to head out to Frank Mitchell's place in Millville. As he began to walk to his car, Alex yelled, "And if he's not there, check Millville Motors. That's where he works supposedly long hours."

When he didn't come back to the car, I tentatively inched out toward the front of the car until he said in a low voice without even looking at me, "Poppy, you should get back into the car. I don't want you to get hurt."

But nothing in his tone told me concern was at the bottom of why he didn't want to deal with me at that moment. I knew he wished I would listen to his suggestion this time, but I couldn't. I felt too bad about what I'd done.

I walked over to where he stood at the edge of the bumper and stopped in front of him. He intentionally looked over my head down the street, so I stepped back away from him in the hopes of forcing him to look at me.

"Please don't move far away from me. I don't want to see you get hurt," he said in a low voice, finally looking me in the eyes.

"Why do you keep saying that? Do you think Angela is going to suddenly turn all sharpshooter and gun me down out here?" I asked, looking around for a shred of evidence anything I'd said could happen.

With a heavy sigh, he hung his head. "I have no idea what she's going to do, but no, I don't think she intends on gunning anyone down today. But I really don't know what she's thinking at the moment."

I stepped forward closer to him and wished I could take him into my arms for a big bear hug. Tilting my head up, I saw worry in his eyes as he looked at me.

"What's wrong? Are you angry at me for what I did with Derek? Because if you are, don't worry. I promise I'll make sure I say all the right things to him and smooth things over like they've never been smoothed over before. Things between you guys will be so smooth you'll be like glass."

"I'm not worried about that, although I wish you hadn't done it. No, I'm just worried that Harlow won't give us a search warrant and I'll have no leg to stand on to even bring Angela in for questioning."

I brushed my hand against his as it hung at his side and gave it a quick squeeze. "Judge Harlow signs everything, Alex. Don't worry. Derek is very persuasive. Who knows? He might slyly suggest the judge should join him at the bar later as they're talking to convince him to sign the request for the warrant. I hate seeing you worried like this."

He looked back at Angela Touring's house, and then turned to face me as his shoulders sagged. "I hope you're right. I just wish we knew what her story was."

"What did she say when she answered the door? I read her body language and all I can say is that woman was giving off some seriously negative vibes."

"She wasn't as nice as the last time we were here. I

can tell you that," he explained with a frown. "I told her I wanted to come in and talk to her about the Marcus Tyne case, and she said she knew I couldn't come in without a warrant. Of course, that's true, so I suggested we talk outside on the porch, but she wasn't having any of it. She said she had nothing else to say about Tyne's death and slammed the door before I could even ask her if she visited Gerald Engels yesterday."

"Well, once Derek gets here with the warrant, maybe she'll change her tune. In the meantime, we're here, so it's going to be okay."

Alex shook his head slowly. "Not if she drives away, which we can't do a damn thing about since I don't even have cause to question her right now. That's why I'm worried Judge Harlow is going to deny me the search warrant."

As he spoke, out of the corner of my eye I saw something move in Angela Touring's yard. I turned my head quickly in fear Alex had been wrong and she actually had decided to begin shooting and I saw an amazing sight.

Angela and Frank Mitchell running full speed down the steps on the side of her house into the backyard. I grabbed Alex's arm and pointed at them. "She and Frank! They're running!"

I don't think all the words were out of my mouth before Alex took off sprinting after them. I followed as well as I could in my new strappy spring sandals I instantly regretted wearing that day, but it was no use. Even in sneakers, I couldn't run as fast as Alex. I only made it to the side steps before he was running back toward me looking panicked.

"Get back to the car! They got into a car in the

alleyway behind her house! Come on, Poppy! We need to catch them!"

A rush of adrenaline pumped through me, making me run faster than I'd ever run in my life, especially in sandals. I reached the car right after Alex did, so by the time I slid into the passenger seat, he was jamming the car into drive and taking off down Angela's street.

All the pain from running in my new sandals came rushing back as Alex talked into his radio to the station. "Officer in pursuit of suspect going west on Crimson Drive. Suspect is with another man in a black sedan. Request backup."

Alex took a corner off Crimson onto Terrace Road nearly on two wheels while I rubbed the soles of my feet and hoped I didn't die on this case. I'd never seen him so focused and driving so fast. Every instinct inside me said I was in danger, but I trusted him, even if I didn't like racing through the residential areas of Sunset Ridge at seventy miles an hour.

"Where are they going?" he asked like he couldn't understand their desire to run from the police.

As the black car crested a hill and disappeared, I said, "I'm guessing anywhere we aren't so they don't get caught killing one man and trying to kill a second. What I don't understand is why try to kill Gerald Engels?"

We nearly soared over the hill a few seconds later, so fast that I held on afraid we might go airborne. Alex's hands tightened their grip on the steering wheel as the car hit eighty, making me think I might have to say something about how safe all this was.

I focused on the stretch of road ahead and saw no sight of a car anywhere in front of us. Confused, I squinted, thinking I was seeing things. Or not, for that matter. But there was no one in front of us now.

"Where did they go?" I asked as Alex kept his focus straight ahead.

We sailed past a thicket of trees and continued racing toward the northern side of town, but then Alex looked up for a moment to check his rearview mirror and that's when he saw them.

"They're behind us turning onto that side street!" he yelled just as he jammed his foot on the brake and spun the car around one hundred and eighty degrees so we were facing the opposite way we'd been going just a second earlier.

My heart slammed against my chest as my life passed before my eyes. Never in all the time we'd worked on cases together had I experienced a high speed chase like this. Sunset Ridge was a sleep little hamlet. I wasn't even sure high speed chases had ever happened before in town.

As Alex floored the gas again after turning onto the side street, I grabbed hold of the door and said, "Hey, maybe we don't need to go Mach two, okay? We'll catch up to them, but people live around here, Alex. We don't want anyone to get hurt, especially us, right?"

My words seemed to reach him even as he looked almost lost in the pursuit he'd described on the radio a few minutes earlier. Easing his foot off the gas, he looked over at me for a split second and nodded.

"Right. I forgot where I was there for a second or two. I think I know where they're going, though."

I saw a street sign on the corner ahead and understood too. Sycamore Street. But why were they going to Gerald Engels' house?

Chapter Twenty

ANGELA TOURING AND Frank Mitchell practically leaped out of the car in front of Gerald Engels' house and tore up the sidewalk to the front door. Alex stopped the car a moment later and jumped out to flash his badge.

As I followed him, he yelled, "Stop! Sunset Ridge police! Stop!"

Neither of them paid attention to his order, so Alex ran after Frank to keep him from entering the house. Catching up to him on the front lawn, he tackled him to the ground. The two men hit the grass hard, and when Frank had the chance, he took a shot at Alex, landing a punch square on his jaw.

Alex answered with a punch that knocked Frank out cold and yelled to me, "Don't let her get inside!"

I looked up at the porch and saw Angela opening the front door, so I ran toward her as the adrenaline once again tore through me and caught her just as she got inside the house. Angela may have been skilled in fist fighting, but the last time I'd hit anyone had been in grade school when Derek's brother Dominick teased me too much one day.

So I did the next best thing. I grabbed her purse

strap and yanked hard, taking her down to the floor in one fell swoop. My attack stunned her, or maybe it was how hard she hit her head on the hardwood floor when she fell, but she didn't move when she landed flat on her back.

Staring down in shock at how I'd actually stopped her, I panicked when she began to try to sit up. "Alex! I need you in here!"

I had no idea what to do. I couldn't leave or she might get up and run away, but I needed something to keep her there. My mind raced with what I could use for handcuffs until Alex arrived. Was it even legal for me to restrain her?

There was no time for that now. Quickly, I scanned the room for something to use and saw the plastic rings from a six-pack sitting on top of a table in the corner of the dining room. They wouldn't hold her for long, but hopefully they didn't need to.

I ran over and grabbed it before returning to her just as she sat up. Still dazed, she didn't put up much of a fight as I slid her hands through the rings and then doubled up on each wrist.

"What the…?" she asked as she tried to extract her hands from the plastic rings, clearly confused about my unique method of keeping her put.

"Alex! Now would be a great time to help!" I yelled, afraid she'd rip them off her at any second.

I turned to see him escorting Frank in handcuffs through the front door and smiled in relief. His eyes immediately settled on my solution holding Angela's hands in place, and his mouth dropped open in amazement.

"Don't say a thing. You weren't here and I had to do

something," I said in my defense as he sat Frank down in a chair in the next room.

He returned to where I stood over Angela and chuckled. "I wasn't going to say a word, Poppy. Thank God you suggested this so I could use them since I didn't have a second pair of handcuffs on me. Good thinking."

I stared in disbelief as he took credit for my fantastic idea. "Huh? What do you mean thank God I suggested this so you could use them?"

Alex said nothing but gave me the furrowed brow look that said I needed to drop my protest immediately. In the flush of success, I didn't understand at first, but then it dawned on me. He was trying to protect me by taking the responsibility for those plastic makeshift cuffs.

He lifted her up off the floor and sat her down in a chair next to Frank in the living room. She cursed at him as she tugged at those plastic rings but couldn't get out of them.

"Enough!" he barked. "I want some answers and I want them now."

Both Angela and Frank sat stony-faced refusing to speak. I'd expected that from him, but from her it surprised me. I really had been duped by her whole poor me act.

"I know what's been going on with you. I need to know where Gerald is. He's sick and needs medical assistance," Alex said, glaring at the two of them.

In turn, they both denied knowing anything about Gerald Engels or where he might be. Frustrated with their lying, I asked, "Then why did you come to this house then?"

When they didn't answer, I continued. "Were you just making sure you finished him off this time?"

They just shook their heads, but from behind them a pile of knickknacks fell over and there stood Gerald Engels with a gun pointed at us, sweat pouring down his face and his hands trembling. He looked even worse than Dr. Carter said he would, and I doubted he would last much longer without medical care.

"Mr. Engels, we've been looking for you," Alex said calmly. "You look ill. Maybe you should sit down."

He inhaled a deep breath and shook his head. "No. I want you to hear the truth before I go," he said, panting as he spoke.

"Okay, okay. Maybe if you just sat down, though, you might feel better."

Gerald shook his head sadly. "It doesn't matter. It doesn't matter anymore."

Angela and Frank looked almost giddy at the possibility that Gerald might die at any moment. I knew Alex saw it too when he turned to them and said, "You two will be up for murder when he dies. Right now, it's just attempted murder, unless one of you tells me the other one did it."

The two of them stared straight ahead, their faces emotionless after what Alex said. I knew what they intended on doing. They planned to wait it out until Gerald died and then they'd stick together and likely make it next to impossible to convict either of them.

But I wasn't going to let poor Gerald die over this twisted Romeo and Juliet act these two had going. Alex and I had saved his life, and I wasn't going to let them ruin that.

I looked over at Gerald as he leaned heavily against the table, barely strong enough to hang on. "Gerald, let us call an ambulance. We can get you to the hospital so

Dr. Carter can take care of you. Remember the last time we helped you? We got you to the ER in time and you were getting better. What happened to make you want to leave the hospital? Who was the woman who came to visit you yesterday?"

He looked over at Angela and then Frank before he let out a rush of air from his lungs and fell to the floor. Alex raced over to help him and tossed me his cell phone. "Call 911! He needs to get to the hospital now!"

I called and gave the operator the address as Alex tried unsuccessfully to keep him alert. He stood from Gerald's side and waved me over to him. "Keep him comfortable. The paramedics will be here in a few minutes."

Looking over toward Angela and Frank, he said, "As for you two, this is your last chance. Whoever wants to save their skin should start talking right now."

Angela set her jaw defiantly and stared straight ahead. Whatever her part in all of this, she intended on seeing it through to the end.

But for the first time since I'd met him that day in the Millville Motors garage, Frank Mitchell looked scared. His eyes darted back and forth between a nearly dead Gerald and Alex, and more than once he opened his mouth to speak but then immediately pressed his lips closed like he couldn't bring himself to say the words.

Alex pointed to where I sat comforting Gerald and barked, "He's dying! Are neither one of you going to tell the truth? Not even now?"

His eyes flashed the anger I knew he harbored for this case and all we'd gone through because of these people, and now when they had the chance to finally do something good, even if it was to save themselves, they still chose to stay quiet. I knew how he felt. I wanted to hit someone for what they'd done to my father, to us, to Marcus and Gerald.

And for what? Why had they committed this horrible crime that by the end of that day might leave two men dead?

Frank once again opened his mouth to say something, but Angela quickly snapped at him. "Just keep your mouth shut and they won't be able to do a thing to us, baby. Not a thing."

Alex got in his face and shook his head. "She's wrong there, Frankie boy. You keeping quiet doesn't help you as much as it helps her, I suspect, so if you have something to say, now's the time."

He pointed at Gerald lying on the floor and continued "As I said, right now, this is attempted murder, and maybe not even that for you, depending on your part in all of this. If he dies, it's murder and premeditated at that. Now we may not have the death penalty here in Maryland anymore, but that doesn't mean you aren't going to pay and pay dearly, like to the tune of the rest of your life if you're found guilty of first degree murder."

That was enough to loosen Frank's tongue. With one last glance over at his partner in crime, he began talking. "Gerald and I were just shooting the breeze. That's all. We were at the Sunset Lounge last month and we got to talking about things and one thing led to another and we both realized we hated Marcus for different reasons. But we never would have killed him if it wasn't for Angela. She's the one who wanted him dead. We just wanted revenge."

"For what?" Alex asked, listening intently.

Before partner in crime could answer, Angela ordered him to stop talking. "Frank, don't say another word. They have nothing on us, baby."

Her thin lips all but disappeared as she put on a fake smile for him, and even a giant clown like Frank knew she had it all wrong.

Alex repeated his question. "What did you two want revenge for?"

"I wanted revenge on Marcus for stealing Angela away, and I think Gerald wanted to get his revenge for some antiquing thing that Marcus did to him. It was all just talk, I tell you. We were just two guys getting drunk and blowing off steam."

"Why now?" I asked, directing his attention to me and Gerald. "It had been months since Angela cheated on you. Why do this now?"

Frank pointed at her and nodded his head. "That was all her! I swear. I hated the guy, but I would have gotten over what he did after a while. But Angela couldn't. She stewed and stewed about how he insulted her by dumping her, and after a few months, it's all she could talk about. That was one reason why I was at the Lounge drinking that night when I first started talking to Gerald. I couldn't take her bitching about Marcus anymore."

"I find it hard to believe she and you didn't know Gerald. He and Marcus had been friends for a while, so she would have known him from when she dated him," Alex said, apparently poking a hole in Frank's story.

"I don't know what she knew, but I didn't know the guy until last month. I came home and told her I met some guy who hated Marcus like we did, and that's when she told me we could kill him and she knew of some treasure he had that we could all share if he was gone."

As the sound of the ambulance siren coming closer filtered into the house, I quickly asked, "What was this treasure?"

Frank looked over at Angela, who turned away and shook her head. "I never did find out exactly what it was, but these guys have tons of junk between them. She said he told her about it when they were dating."

"Probably the reason why she was so upset when he dumped her," Alex said as he walked to the front door to direct the paramedics inside to where Gerald and I sat.

The man and woman hurried inside and began working on him, but he needed more help than they could give him, so they quickly loaded him onto a stretcher and took him out to the ambulance. Alex returned with Derek in tow and his handcuffs, just in case Angela wriggled out of the plastic soda holder ones I'd used to improvise.

Looking down at the two suspects, he asked, "So these are the two responsible for Marcus Tyne's murder?"

Alex looked at both of them and nodded. "That's what it sounds like."

"No!" Frank exclaimed, looking like he would begin to cry at any moment. "It was her and Gerald more than me! I only got the antifreeze. Gerald made sure it ended up in his drink, and Angela was supposed to make sure we all split the treasure."

"Then how did Gerald Engels get poisoned by the antifreeze?" Alex asked, clearly not believing Frank's version of the story.

For his part, Frank seemed a bit hazy on that. "I

don't know. He knew he had to put the stuff in Tyne's drink. The antifreeze was in a flask that Gerald had in his coat pocket Monday night. He'd arranged to meet Marcus that night at McGuire's for a drink to patch things up over some fight he said they'd had."

"Why did you two go to McGuire's instead of the Sunset Lounge?" I asked, desperate to know if revenge on my father had played any part in their grand plan.

"Because we didn't want to go back to the Lounge where people had seen us together. Gerald suggested the other bar because he'd been there a few times and said the guy who runs it leaves the bar unmanned a lot if he's alone."

So much for small town values and kindness. At least my father hadn't been an intentional target of theirs. For that, I breathed a sigh of relief.

Derek looked over toward Angela, but she simply stared straight ahead like she was looking right through him. "Let me guess. If Gerald lives, he's going to tell us this one promised him it would be just the two of them sharing that treasure if he put the antifreeze in Marcus Tyne's drink. Am I close, Miss Touring?"

His accusation received no response from her, except for a glare she shot him before looking away.

Frank appeared stunned by it, though, and turned to look at her like he couldn't believe she'd betray him like that. "Is that true? Did you tell him it would be just you two sharing the booty? What were you planning to do about me? Was I the next one to get the antifreeze treatment?"

When she didn't answer him, he looked over at Alex and said, "Check her computer. That's where she found out about the antifreeze being a good poison because you could put it in someone's drink and they'd never know. She told me about it. Check her computer and you'll see this was all her idea."

"Oh, I plan on it, but we still don't have an explanation how Gerald Engels got poisoned, and even though you looked surprised when you heard what my chief had to say, you're still the prime suspect in his poisoning. You better hope he lives to prove us wrong."

"I never gave him anything! I swear! I couldn't have. I worked all day that day. You saw my time card."

Alex shook his head and grimaced at Frank's lame alibi. "Yeah, we know all about you working for your brother. Something tells me he isn't exactly going to hold up under cross examination at trial."

Frank sputtered for a moment, clearly grasping at whatever could prove he wasn't the one who poisoned Gerald, and then his eyes opened wide. Eagerly, he offered another alibi option. "The camera! My brother had a security camera installed three weeks ago after someone spray painted one of the cars out back. I had to go out into the lot at least a dozen times that day, so check the security tape. You'll see I'm on it all day."

Then I remembered Gerald hadn't poisoned on Monday. "It doesn't matter what the tape says about that day because Gerald Engels ingested the antifreeze on Tuesday. Looks like your alibi just went up in smoke."

For a moment, I thought Frank Mitchell might break down in tears, but then he shook his head wildly. "No, no! What time on Tuesday?"

I looked over at Alex for when Gerald may have been poisoned, and he said, "Early morning, according to what we've found out about how the poison works, according to his doctor."

"Even better!" Frank said with a smile. "My brother had a toilet back up on him in the garage, and when we got there at six that morning, we had sewage all over the floor in the back room. We had to get a plumber out there, and he spent until early afternoon working on that pipe. He can tell you I never left the garage the whole time he was there because I was helping him. I didn't poison Gerald. I swear!"

Derek, Alex, and I looked at each other, confused about how Gerald Engels had gotten the antifreeze in his system. Finally, tired of this whole case, Alex said, "That's something we'll leave for the district attorney to figure out. For now, we have enough to arrest both of them on murder and attempted murder charges, which is good enough for me. You okay with that, Chief?"

Shrugging, Derek nodded. "I'm fine with how this all shook out. I'm just happy that Joe is in the clear. I'll let you tell him, Poppy. In the meantime, Alex and I have work to do back at the station getting these two booked."

Thrilled to hear my father had been completely exonerated, I smiled. "I will. I can't wait to tell him!"

They pulled Angela and Frank up out of their seats and read them their rights before leading them out to the squad car. As I followed behind to join Alex in his car, I heard Derek say, "What the hell? Why are her hands cuffed with a six-pack ring?"

I wanted to brag about how ingenious I'd been at that moment, but Alex quickly answered that he'd had to think on his feet since he had one suspect in handcuffs and another trying to get away, so the plastic ring was all he could find in a pinch.

Derek didn't seem to put much thought into the explanation, but as he closed the car door after putting Frank into the back seat, he flashed me a suspicious look that said he questioned Alex's version of the story.

For my part, I still thought it had been one of my more clever moments.

*

Chapter Twenty-One

D EREK'S BLAND OFFICE walls surrounded me, threatening to close in around me if I had to sit there much longer waiting for him. He'd ordered me to stay right there while he discussed some issue with another officer, so I had more than enough time to examine the bare beige walls while my mind raced with what he wanted to discuss with me.

Was it my problem with Stephen? My having a feud with one of his cops likely didn't exactly sit well with him. Or was it my rudeness to his friend Jared, who I personally didn't think should still be deserving of the title of friend by anyone who claimed to care for me in the slightest.

Or was it that I had continued to investigate with Alex on a case that my father was a prime suspect in when I should have quietly backed away?

As I thought about it, that was probably the reason he had me sitting there like some disobedient child sent to the principal's office. He intended on reading me the riot act for not knowing my place and endangering Alex's case unnecessarily.

And I had no excuse. I truly didn't. Well, other than being stubborn and wanting to protect my father, but that likely wouldn't work on Derek this time.

That only left charm, which had always worked on him, and I wasn't above using that to get out of being barked at for upwards of an hour or more. Well, I had one other weapon I could use, but I generally reserved crying for true emotional moments. However, being on Derek's bad side did make me strangely emotional, so who knew? Maybe the crying would come out. This had been an incredibly taxing case for me.

I heard the door click closed and turned around to see Derek enter his office. Taking a deep breath, I steeled myself for what was to come.

He sat down behind his desk and stared at me with a look I knew was intended to make me understand how upset he was but only made him seem like he was checking me out. Derek had never been very good with pretending to be something he wasn't. It was one of the things I liked best about him.

"Poppy, we need to talk."

Uh oh. Those words never preceded anything good. Ever.

"I know what you're going to say, Derek, and you're right. I know that."

My statement surprised him, if how far his eyebrows traveled north into his forehead was any indication. "You do?"

"Of course. I know what this is all about. You're going to reprimand me for not stepping away from the case. You're right. I should have. I couldn't, though. If my father hadn't been involved, I might have been able to, but I had to do everything in my power to help Alex prove he was innocent. I know you understand that, Derek. Of all the people in this town, you can understand why I did what I did."

My explanation only made Derek's job harder. He sighed and closed his eyes, pinching the bridge of his nose to relieve the stress. "If your father wasn't involved, Poppy, there wouldn't have been a reason for you to step away."

"If I promise to not do it again, will that help?" I asked, genuinely wishing I could make him feel better. Derek was a lot of things, some of them irritating, but he was my friend, first and foremost, and making him unhappy wasn't something I enjoyed.

He looked up at me and shook his head. "I'd prefer if you didn't lie to me. I think after all these years of being friends and good friends at that, I think I deserve at least the truth."

This conversation wasn't going like our talks usually did. Most of the time, if I promised not to do something again, that was enough to make him happy. Or at least placate him.

But this time something strange had crept in between us as we sat there. What was going on?

"Derek, I don't lie to you. I know you're upset with me, and I'm sorry. I wish I wasn't like I am and could just let someone I care for twist in the wind, but that's not who I am. You know that. I apologize for how I acted on this case because it's something that obviously is giving you trouble, but I can't honestly apologize for trying to show my father isn't a murderer. He's my father, Derek. What was I supposed to do?"

He opened his mouth to say something and then simply sighed heavily. "I understand, Poppy. I know this is partly my fault. Maybe I should have never let you get involved in cases in the first place. I spend most of my time worried you're going to get hurt anyway, so don't think I haven't considered that was a mistake."

I leaned forward toward him and rested my hands on the edge of his desk. "Alex would never let me get hurt, Derek. You know that."

"I do. I also know that means he has to worry about you in addition to what's going on with cases, which can't be good for anyone involved."

Suddenly, my heart sank. Was Derek stumbling through our conversation because he was trying to find a way to tell me I couldn't work with Alex anymore?

"Are you about to say I'm not allowed to be Alex's partner? Is that what this is? If so, I promise I'll obey your rules from now on. I promise, Derek. Just don't do this, okay?"

His eyes narrowed to squints, and he looked at me with complete confusion written all over his face. "What are you talking about, Poppy? Did I say anything about you not being able to work cases with Alex anymore? No. So why are you jumping to conclusions?"

"I don't know. It's what I do. It's part of my charm, or so I hear."

Derek rolled his eyes. "That's because the person who has to deal with you jumping to conclusions the most is in love with you. For the rest of us, it's not as charming as you think."

I sat back in my seat, unsure what we were talking about now. "So are you reprimanding me for my behavior on this case and telling me I can or cannot work with Alex from now on?"

"I'm officially reprimanding you and putting you on notice that if you ever disobey your partner like that again, you won't be allowed to work with him."

His pronouncement sounded like something a principal would say right before they sentenced a student to detention. I waited for the other shoe to drop, but oddly enough, nothing more came.

But the uncomfortable look that remained on Derek's face told me we weren't done talking.

"Okay. I promise I won't do it again. Did you want to discuss anything else?" I asked, uncertain what else he could want to talk about.

He hesitated for a moment and then finally said, "I'm sorry about what Jared did."

Relief washed over me. So Derek wanted to talk about my ex. I could do that. A few minutes of bitching about Jared might even feel good this morning.

"Well, it doesn't surprise me, although I guess I never thought he'd be so nasty to my father. I thought his mistreatment of the McGuire family began and ended with me. I certainly hope he gets into some kind of trouble for giving a false statement."

I knew how unlikely that would be, especially since he and Derek were still close friends. With his return to town, they'd picked up right where they left off when Jared fled with that grocery store tart.

"Poppy, I'm not talking about what Jared did now. I'm talking about what happened when he left you for Cicely right before your wedding."

His words struck me right in my heart. Derek had never said anything about what his friend did. We'd never talked about it until this very moment, even though I suspected he likely knew about Jared cheating on me even before I did. In some way, not knowing that for sure had helped me stay friends with Derek.

Now it made me wonder just how close we were.

"Oh that. Well, it's water under the bridge. All in the past. You know, that kind of thing. Forgive and forget. Well, not forgive. I won't be forgiving. But the forget part is still worth something, don't you think?"

I'd officially begun rambling. It happened a lot in my mind when I thought of Jared and all the things I wanted to say to him, but usually when I opened my mouth, I kept some kind of control over myself. Clearly, that wasn't the case now, though.

Derek's eyes filled with sadness. "I'm sorry, Poppy."

With as much bravado as I could muster, I forced a smile and waved away his concerns. "No need to be. That was then, and this is now. I'm fine, so no need to worry."

But the sad look remained.

"I'm sorry that I didn't do what a friend should have back then. I wasn't a champion for you against him when you needed me to be, and I'm sorry for that. I never meant to hurt you by trying to stay neutral. I thought that's what I had to do because I was friends with both of you, but now I see that was wrong."

Derek's confession surprised me, and I quietly said, "It did hurt, but I understand loyalty."

Frowning, he shook his head. "I'm sorry for being loyal to someone who never grew up out of high school. You were too good for him back then, and the idea that he thought he could come back and just convince you to go back to him now is ridiculous. I told him that when he started bragging about giving you a second chance to have him. I think that's when I realized I'd been wrong all these years."

Although I appreciated the sentiment, I desperately wanted to change the subject, so I smiled and asked, "So who is this new girlfriend I've been hearing about all over town?"

"All over town? If the people around here spent time talking about my private life, I'd be stunned," he said with a chuckle.

"If they spent time talking about your private life, they'd never have time to talk about anything else, Derek. You go through women like I go through coffee. So who's the flavor of the week?"

A sheepish look settled into his face. "I don't know if I should tell you. We just had a nice moment there. I don't want to ruin it."

Confused, I stared at him trying to figure out what he meant. "Why? What could you say that would ruin anything?"

And then it dawned on me. "Oh my God! You hooked up with the grocery store tart who ran off with my ex! Is that it?"

Derek shook his head. "No, no! Cicely ran off with some guy she met when Jared took her skiing one day over the winter."

Even though this conversation had definitely taken a turn into total confusion, I liked hearing that. "Good. It couldn't happen to a nicer person. But if you aren't dating the Savings King tart who stole my fiancé, then why won't you tell me?"

After a pregnant pause, he finally said her name. "Solange. Her sister."

"Oh," I said, sort of stunned by the news. "I didn't know she had a sister."

All I knew about Cicely was she had been a grocery store clerk and had run off with my fiancé knowing full well he was engaged to be married to me when they met.

I hadn't bothered to get the details on her family tree when I found out about her.

"I know you're probably still holding a grudge, and I can see why, but Solange isn't like her sister."

"I still hate Cicely, but I can't rightfully hold that grudge against her relatives, and if you're happy, that's all that counts, Derek."

My answer clearly relieved him, and he smiled broadly. "Good. I'm happy to hear that."

Happiness looked good on him. He tended to date women for such a short time that the gossips barely had time to learn the current girlfriend's name before he moved on to the next, but something in the way he looked at me now said maybe this time was different.

"So, is it serious? I know for you that means something completely opposite from what it does for most of us in this world, but you look like this could be serious."

For what may have been the first time in all the years I'd known Derek, he blushed. With a smile, he shook his head. "I don't know about serious. Let's not get ahead of ourselves. I have a reputation to uphold in this town."

I threw my head back and laughed. He certainly did. "Well, if you're happy, I'm happy. I hope whatever this is, it's exactly what you deserve, which is the best, Derek. I hope you know that."

"Okay, okay. We don't have to make this all touchy-feely. I'm guessing your partner is waiting for you out there, so promise me you're going to follow the rules and we can be done here."

Convinced I'd hit a nerve, I relented on the touchy-feely talk and promised I'd do what I was told from now on. That I likely wouldn't was sort of an unspoken truth between us.

I stood to leave and stopped just as I reached for the doorknob. "Thanks for being my friend above everything else, Derek. I know my father would say the same thing. You're a good egg."

Rolling his eyes again, he pointed toward the door. "There goes my reputation again. How about we keep this good egg business to ourselves, okay?"

"Got it, Chief. Talk to you later!"

I hurried to Alex's office where he sat waiting for me dressed in his street clothes. Even though he had the day off, he insisted on being at the station while I went to my meeting with Derek. I had a feeling he had plans to come riding in on his white horse if his boss even hinted at putting an end to our working together.

That's why I loved Alex. Well, one reason among a thousand more.

Stepping into his office, I cleared my throat and he looked up from his laptop with knitted eyebrows and concern in his eyes. Since my meeting had gone so well, I felt like teasing him a little.

I sighed heavily and slumped down into the chair in front of his desk as I avoided meeting his gaze. "Well, that wasn't horrible, I guess."

"What happened? I can't believe Derek would come down hard on you, Poppy. You're like the little sister he never had and isn't sure he ever wanted."

"What's that supposed to mean?" I asked defensively, forgetting all about playing my trick on him.

Alex leaned back in his chair and grinned. "I hear the meeting went well. Did you think you were going to fool me into thinking he said we can't work together anymore?"

Deflated, I admitted the truth. "Yeah, but how did you know? Do you have your chief's office bugged?"

He held up his cell to show me a text Derek had sent that said *All good*. "He messaged you that quickly? Why?"

"I assume because he knew if he didn't and I thought you had been told you couldn't be my partner anymore that I'd come into his office guns blazing and you know how much he hates that," Alex explained with a little too much smugness for my liking.

"Well, thank you to him and you for ruining my fun," I said, pretending to be glum about his one-upping me.

"Well, here's something that might cheer you up. The DA called and said he got a full confession from Angela Touring. I guess they made a deal and she sang like a canary about poisoning Gerald. And how about this? She poisoned him not once but twice."

"In the hospital too? Oh, she's the devil behind all of this. But why did she do it? That's what I want to know."

Alex shrugged. "I think she wanted to be with Frank after all."

"I told you those two were in this together. Oh, my prophetic soul!" I said with a grin.

"Yes, you did," Alex admitted, although I sensed a touch of reluctance in his tone. "She didn't get what she wanted, but maybe when they both get out in twenty-five years they can pick up where they left off."

The thought of those two together at any time made my skin crawl. "Yuck. Well, at least Gerald should recover, right?"

"Yeah, and then he'll go on trial for his part in Marcus Tyne's murder. Part of me wonders if he doesn't wish that antifreeze hadn't done what Angela intended."

I shook my head, refusing to believe that. "No way. We were part of saving his life, and I say life is always worth it, even if it's life behind bars."

He came around the desk and held out his hand. "Let's get out of here. I have the day off, and I think we deserve to kick back and relax."

"Are we hanging out at your house or mine tonight? Do you work tomorrow?" I asked as I took his hand and stood to leave.

With a smile and a wink, he said, "Your choice, and no, I'm not scheduled tomorrow, so we can sleep in, assuming your boss doesn't get angry about you working from home."

Howard likely would be upset that I'd be out of the office once again, but I fully intended on talking up the case and convincing him I'd be spending my time working on beefing up next week's police blotter. What I planned to be doing with Alex wasn't anything close to that, but Howard didn't need to know that.

"I like how you think, Officer Montero. I think a nice night out at your house might be good. Any chance I can get you to cook for me, or is that asking too much? You know how much I love your cooking."

Alex raised his eyebrows and looked down at me. "You don't have to charm the man who loves you, Poppy. You can save that for people like Derek."

Before I could answer, he turned and walked away. As I hurried to catch up to him, I said, "You think that was charm? Oh, that was just me being honest. I can turn on the charm, though. Just say the word."

He held the front door to the police station open for me and grinned as I passed. "Later, Miss McGuire. For now, we have somewhere we need to go."

*   *   *

WE WALKED INTO McGuire's to find the bar empty except for one older man sitting at the end of the bar nursing a glass of ginger ale and regaling my father with his tales of how he'd been part of the town council when some streaker made his appearance at one of their monthly meetings back in the late seventies to protest the town's decision to not allow a famous fast food restaurant in Sunset Ridge. Instantly my heart sank. What I had feared all along with this case had come true.

My father's business had been ruined.

"Poppy! Alex! I'm so happy to see you two!" my father said as he came toward me with his arms open ready to take me into them for a hug.

"Dad, I'm so sorry. It's happy hour and nobody's here. This is so unfair."

He kissed me on the cheek, ignoring my comments, and then turned to shake Alex's hand. "How are you, Alex? What can I get you two? We need to make a toast to you solving the case."

"I'll take a scotch on the rocks, Joe," Alex said as he sat down on a barstool near the door.

"Make that two, Dad. Do you want me to get them?" I asked as I inched my way toward behind the bar.

My father put his hand up to stop me. "No. Get back out there and sit down. You two are the honored guests tonight. I'm even going to have a drink to celebrate."

He poured our drinks and placed them in front of us. Lifting his own glass of scotch, he smiled. "To Alex and Poppy for solving the case and clearing my name."

The three of us took sips of our drinks, but I couldn't help think that we hadn't done enough or done it soon enough. Looking around at the empty bar, I said, "But Dad, there's no one here. It's dead."

"Don't worry, honey. The people of Sunset Ridge will return and this place will once again be bustling in no time."

Alex raised his glass to make a toast. "To that happening just as soon as possible."

We drank to my father's bar becoming a success again, and then my father had to answer the phone so he left us sitting alone. Alex turned to me and shook his head.

"I can't help but admire how much Joe still believes in the goodness of small town people. You have to give him that. He's a true believer."

"That's all my father can do, but he does believe with all his heart that the people of Sunset Ridge are good. He always has."

The big city past in Alex made it hard for him to understand how my father could think that way. "No matter how many of them I can point to who aren't."

I gently elbowed him in the side and joked, "What is it they say about a few bad apples? So Sunset Ridge has a couple rotten ones."

His face serious, he said, "Poppy, a few bad apples can rot an entire barrel."

"You and the other cops on the Sunset Ridge police are what stops the town from becoming a rotting barrel of apples."

He leaned in and kissed me sweetly on the lips. "You too. You're part of that effort."

I smiled and kissed him back. "So now that the case is over, let's talk about our vacation that's less than two months away."

With a look that was entirely too sexy, he said, "I think we might need to practice that whole tub thing before then. What do you say to going home and doing that tonight?"

I loved how serious Alex could be and then how sexy he became when it was just the two of us like this. "A practice makes perfect kind of thing?" I asked with a smile as I thought about how delightful it was going to be to practice that.

"In a way, although I think what we have going on right now is perfect. I just don't want to see you end up having to go to the ER on our vacation."

I couldn't help but laugh at his teasing me about my almost complete lack of physical fitness. He worked out every day, but it had been since sometime last year when pumpkins were all the decorating rage in the fall since I'd stepped on my treadmill, which had unofficially become an extension of my closet in that time.

Cradling his face, I kissed him and whispered, "I'm amazingly limber for someone who doesn't work out much. I think you know that."

"That I do. I'm always impressed at how flexible you are, Poppy. So maybe we don't need to practice?"

"Well, I don't want to be hasty about things. A little practice never hurt anyone," I teased back.

Tipping his glass to his mouth, Alex downed what remained of his drink and pushed the glass away. With that look in his eyes that never failed to make me melt, he said, "Then I think it's time we took this celebration home. Are you with me?"

As he took hold of my hand, I smiled at how sure my answer to that question was.

"Always."

Poppy and Alex return in The Witching Hour: A Poppy McGuire Mystery (Poppy McGuire Mysteries #6)

About The Author

Anina Collins has always loved a good mystery. From Agatha Christie's Hercule Poirot to Sir Arthur Conan Doyle's famous detective Sherlock Holmes to Dan Brown's intrepid Professor Robert Langdon, she's spent some of her favorite reading times with mystery novels. When she's not writing her favorite mystery couple, she can be found watching entirely too much Supernatural and dreaming about the beach.

Visit Anina's Facebook page for news about her books, along with giveaways and other fun stuff!

And sign up for her newsletter today for exclusive news first! Visit her website at aninacollins.com for more details.

Books by Anina Collins:
The Eleventh Hour (Poppy McGuire Mysteries #1)
After Hours (Poppy McGuire Mysteries #2)
Top of the Hour (Poppy McGuire Mysteries #3)
The Darkest Hour (Poppy McGuire Mysteries #4)
Happy Hour (Poppy McGuire Mysteries #5)

Look for The Witching Hour (Poppy McGuire Mysteries #6) coming soon!